An
UNEXPECTED
REDEMPTION

a novel

FRONT RANGE BRIDES
BOOK 2

DAVALYNN SPENCER

Books by Davalynn Spencer

Historical

THE FRONT RANGE BRIDES SERIES

Mail-Order Misfire - Series Prequel
An Improper Proposal - Book 1
An Unexpected Redemption - Book 2
An Impossible Price – Book 3

THE CAÑON CITY CHRONICLES SERIES

Loving the Horseman - Book 1
Straight to My Heart - Book 2
Romancing the Widow - Book 3
The Cañon City Chronicles - complete collection

Novella Collections

"The Wrangler's Woman" - *The Cowboy's Bride Collection*
"The Columbine Bride" - *The 12 Brides of Summer*
"The Snowbound Bride" - *The 12 Brides of Christmas*

Contemporary

The Miracle Tree

Novellas

Snow Angel
Just in Time for Christmas
A High-Country Christmas – complete collection

Sign up for my Quarterly Author Update
and receive a free historical novella!
http://eepurl.com/xa81D

To the One

who redeemed me.

*"Therefore, turn thou to thy God:
Keep mercy and judgment,
and wait on thy God continually."*

Hosea 12:6

Come, Thou Fount

Come, Thou Fount of every blessing,
Tune my heart to sing Thy grace;
Streams of mercy, never ceasing,
Call for songs of loudest praise.
Teach me some melodious sonnet,
Sung by flaming tongues above;
Praise the mount! I'm fixed upon it,
Mount of Thy redeeming love.

Here I raise my Ebenezer;
Hither by Thy help I'm come;
And I hope, by Thy good pleasure,
Safely to arrive at home.
Jesus sought me when a stranger,
Wand'ring from the fold of God;
He, to rescue me from danger,
Interposed His precious blood.

Oh, to grace how great a debtor
Daily I'm constrained to be!
Let Thy goodness, like a fetter,
Bind my feeble heart to Thee.
"Prone to wander, Lord, I feel it,"
Prone to leave the God I love;
"Here's my heart, O take and seal it,
Seal it for Thy courts above."

~~~

CHAPTER 1

Olin Springs, Colorado
Late August 1881

Elizabeth Beaumont had been thrown off green-broke horses and out of rooming houses, but never from a train.

That's what it felt like as brakes squealed, the car jerked against its couplings, and the conductor opened the door into darkness. He jumped to the platform, set down his step, and glanced at the depot. "Hope someone's meetin' you, miss."

He offered his hand. "Looks like there's trouble aplenty in town."

Thin light haloed the train station, wavering behind it like an uncertain sunrise. Like Elizabeth's confidence. "But my trunk and crate?"

"Yes, ma'am." He pointed back down the platform. "There. You hurry now."

She descended into moonless night, and he snatched up the step, pulled himself inside, and closed the door.

Not exactly *thrown* off, but close enough to it.

The passenger car eased ahead. Another slid by and the mail bag hit the platform with a thud. She assumed it was the mail bag and not a body.

Startled by the thought, she squinted at the shapeless lump until assured it was made up of letters and not limbs.

Touching the back of her hair, she adjusted her modestly plumed hat, then tugged at her gloves and reticule, both the same deep navy as her plaid traveling suit. It mattered little now since all was a colorless black and no one was meeting her. Still, little was more than not at all.

Some might consider arriving under cover of night weak-hearted, but why suffer scorn when it could be avoided? Six years ago, she had disappeared without warning. An impetuous seventeen-year-old. Now she returned in a similar manner, much preferred to stepping off a morning train to the judgmental whispers and shaking heads of local gossips.

Click-clacking out of town, the train chased its feeble lantern along the tracks, the whistle wailing around the bend for the mountains. In the quieting aftermath, more urgent sounds arose. Men shouted. Horses scrambled.

Coal smoke and steam gave way to the pungent scent of burning wood, nothing like a comforting hearth or campfire. The eerie flicker beyond the depot drew her with morbid interest.

Gathering her skirts, she hurried around the end of the depot and stopped at the next corner. Terror clutched her throat. Two blocks south, bright flames blazed from the second-floor windows of the Olin Springs Hotel.

Men ran past, one snagging her skirt on the bucket he carried. She stumbled forward, but the fabric gave and the bucket ripped away, leaving her petticoat exposed.

Someone shouldered her from behind. "Get out of the way. This is no place for a woman!"

At a trough in the next block, a man worked the pump. Those running with buckets handed them over and rushed ahead to take their place in a growing line.

Elizabeth ran toward the far end, elbowing her way between an older man and a boy. She grabbed the bucket shoved toward her, then handed it off to the youngster and turned for the next one coming down the line.

Time slowed in the wavering glow of yellow flames, and at a lull in the passing, she pulled off her gloves and glanced up at the hotel. Wood groaned and snapped, and debris and sparks spewed skyward as the second floor roared down onto the first. Horses tethered at hitch rails across the street reared and broke loose, then thundered away with heads high and reins flailing.

Had the town no fire brigade? No hose team? If the flames weren't stopped, they'd consume the entire block.

With her senses numbed by the endless lifting and passing of leather, wooden, and metal buckets, Elizabeth missed the moment that dawn blinked upon the scene. She was weary, filthy, and soaked to the bone. Only her mouth was dry, her throat raw from smoke and ash.

The buckets slowed, and she stepped back from the line. Others did the same, eyes white and ghostlike in their soot-covered faces. Shoulders drooping in fatigue and failure.

Little had been saved.

Only then did she notice the young couple watching from the street, one quilt wrapped around both of them. Feet bare and hair disheveled, they clung to each other. Horror marred their faces as if they'd just watched all their worldly possessions go up in flames.

Likely, they had.

Elizabeth dragged herself closer to the hotel's black skeleton. Brass and iron beds had fallen through from the upper floor, landing in distorted heaps below. Wash basins, chairs, and trunks lay broken or scorched. Ashes formed rectangular patterns where once-fine furniture had stood.

One corner of the hotel remained oddly intact, a reminder of its former glory.

Turning away, she again faced the desperate-looking couple, clinging to each other and their quilt, unmoving as others milled around them. She had a room reserved at Margaret Snowfield's boarding house. Where would *they* go?

"Excuse me." With the back of her hand, she pushed grimy hair from her face. "I'm Elizabeth Beaumont, and I couldn't help noticing you standing here. Were you staying at the hotel?"

The woman's face crumpled into tears, and she hid against the man's shoulder.

"Yes." He tightened one arm around her. "We arrived three days ago to set up shop. I'm Hiram Eisner, a tailor, and this is my wife, Abigail."

Abigail peeked out and started weeping anew.

"Do you have a place to stay?" A pointless question, since Elizabeth had nothing to offer but her own room, if she still had a room.

"We will stay in our shop," Hiram said as if coming to a conclusion.

She laid a hand on Abigail's quilt-covered shoulder and leaned closer. "It will be all right." Such assurance from one who had none for herself.

Abigail looked out from her hiding and nearly smiled. Hope dampened her dark lashes. "*Toda.*"

"She said thank you." Hiram nodded once in agreement.

Elizabeth rushed back to the depot, hoping to find her belongings still there and wondering if things would ever be all right for her again. *Go home and wait*, had been Erma Clarke's encouragement after the humiliating debacle with their employer. Though Erma was Elizabeth's only friend in Denver, her directive was easier heard than followed.

This homecoming was not what Elizabeth antici-pated, though it certainly was ignored. That small wish had been granted.

But the waiting part would no doubt prove more difficult because it involved, well, *waiting.* Something at which she had never excelled.

The mail bag and her trunk and small crate sat like orphans on the platform's edge. No thieves in Olin Springs to abscond with them, as might have been the case at Denver's Union Station.

Alone once more in quieter surroundings, she fingered her reticule, sodden but still dangling from her wrist. Little sparkle if any shown from the dirty glass beads, though if the light hit at just the right angle, one or two still winked.

Her gloves were gone.

She slumped against her camelback trunk, stealing a moment's rest before trekking the few blocks to Mrs. Snowfield's boarding house across the tracks. From her low vantage point, she could just make out the cupola atop the mansion. That's what she and Sophie Price had called the ornately scrolled, two-story house on Saddle Blossom Lane when they were girls. At the moment, she didn't know which was more foolish, their girlish conjecture of secretly meeting suitors in the romantic cupola, or that ridiculous street—

A low growl vibrated through the cord of her reticule and shimmied up her arm. Jumping to her feet, she faced an enormous beast that had clamped onto her bag.

"Oh no you don't!" She slapped the cur, snatching her once-lovely accessory from its drooling jaws.

Quick as a snake, it reclaimed its prize with a sickening rip. The tear unbalanced her, and she tumbled backward into the dirt along the tracks.

Clearly the winner in the tug-o-war, the brute shook her reticule in triumph, flinging coins and beadwork for yards. A rouge pot rolled beneath the platform.

She didn't know whether to swear or scream.

"Pearl!"

Pearl? The tawny four-legged thug looked past the depot, ears flattening at the commanding tone.

"Down!"

It dropped to its haunches, the ruined bag dangling from its mouth.

6

Elizabeth rubbed her wrist. A fine homecoming, indeed

"Give it back." A scowling stranger approached from beyond the platform, his long legs making light of the distance. The mongrel inched closer, giving Elizabeth a woeful look, then opened its mouth and released her reticule as well as its atrocious breath. She gagged.

With a whine, the animal dolefully watched its master stop before them.

The man bent over and took Elizabeth's elbow. "You all right, miss?"

Most unladylike, she spread her feet to stabilize her footing and gripped his hard hand, pulling herself to a standing position. He did not immediately release her fingers, and she looked up into laughing gray eyes framed by a mask-like layer of soot.

He smelled of wet clothing and smoke. Or was it she who smelled? Snatching her hand away, she dusted her backside, long past caring about deportment. "Does this beast greet all train passengers so vigorously?"

The man tipped his hat up, and morning light glinted off the star on his vest. Quite unlike the stout little lawman she remembered, a point in her favor.

"Only the beauties."

His attempted flattery stung, in spite of the humor that danced in his eyes. Surely she hadn't run from one lecher into the jurisdiction of another.

"My apologies, miss. I had no idea Pearl was loose until I heard you holler."

At that, she sniffed. Ladies did not holler. But neither did they work bucket brigades or sprawl in the dirt on their backside.

She glanced at his Colt .45 long barrel. The man took his job seriously.

Re-securing her hat pin, she wondered why she hadn't thought to use it against her attacker. "Accepted."

"Beg pardon?"

"Your apology. I accept it."

A tilted nod. "My pleasure."

Too much pleasure, to her way of thinking. He'd been entertained by the exhibition with his dog.

She turned toward her trunk and crate. Another coin slipped from her mangled bag, and he picked it up with several others and offered them to her.

"Wilson, miss. Garrett Wilson. Sheriff and apologetic dog owner."

Witty too. Taking the coins, she discounted his breadth of shoulder and confident stance. A similar confidence had once enticed her to make a very poor decision, but she was wiser now. "*Mrs.* Elizabeth Beaumont."

"I don't recall seeing you in town before. You weren't planning to take a room at the hotel, were you?"

Nosy or protective of his territory, at least he didn't know her. She let her gaze linger on the camelback, hoping he'd take the hint. Independence was one thing. Dragging a heavy trunk to the boarding house by herself quite another.

He bit. "This yours?"

She bit her tongue. One trunk, one passenger.

"It is." She'd been deliberating, as well as resting, when the lion-dog attacked, considering which to take

8

first—the trunk or her treasure. Valuing the means of her livelihood over her meager wardrobe, she reached for the crate.

The sheriff was quicker. He wrapped one arm around it and rested it against his gun belt.

"I'll be happy to bring this along—and the trunk— if you'll just point me in the right direction. After slinging water and tangling with Pearl, I imagine you're spent."

Either he'd seen her in the bucket line, or she *looked* like she'd been in the bucket line. Probably the latter. "I am far from spent, Sheriff Wilson."

Mother had warned her about her temper, relentlessly insisting Elizabeth display humility and grace. However, good manners paled in the burning glow of assaulted sensibilities, overriding her need of help. With both hands, she took hold of the crate. "Thank you just the same, but I shall take care of my own affairs."

He studied her a moment, amusement spattering green flecks across his gray gaze as he took in her hat and face, her dirty jacket and torn skirt. But he did not release the crate.

She tugged in a one-sided struggle that drew her closer.

Watching her from mere inches above, he stood stalwart. Dark stubble shadowed a jaw as strong as his hold, and a small scar on his left cheek ticked into a dimple-like crease. His mouth opened as if he would comment, then clapped shut.

He let go.

She fell to her southern side again, the heavy crate adding injury to insult.

Without hesitation, he offered his hand, brows slightly raised.

She glared and shoved the crate off her lap. "I think not."

"Suit yourself." He took a step back, touched his dirty hat brim politely, and strode away.

The yellow monstrosity that had started the whole affair rolled out a deep-throated *woof*, and trotted after him.

Elizabeth pushed up using the crate, reminding herself that she'd been bucked off snottier colts—only slightly taller than the sheriff's dog. But this time the bruising reached deeper, all the way to her pride.

Mother was right about that particular trait preceding a tumble.

A few colorful beads lay in the dirt around her, but she let them lie, gathering only the rouge pot from beneath the platform. Anger, fatigue, and humiliation warred for preeminence as she glanced around.

A hatless man stood at the narrow gap between the depot and the express office, writing on a small pad.

He caught her watching him, and ambled off still writing.

A reporter for the *Gazette* taking notes on her standoff?

She hefted the crate and turned for Saddle Blossom Lane—as ridiculous a street name as Pearl was for that monstrosity of a dog. If the scribbling gent really was a reporter, surely the fire was a bigger story than her surreptitious return.

Shifting the crate against one hip, she limped away.

Cade would have a wild-horse fit the moment he learned she'd come home but not to the ranch. She disliked the prospect of squaring off with her big brother, but refused to let him plot her future. On the other hand, he *had* assisted her financially after Edward's abandon—

The remaining syllable came growling up from her chest much like the dog's departing remark.

It took great restraint to keep from glancing behind her. No need to see if Sheriff Wilson and his sidekick were watching her progress. She could feel his smirk, the lout.

Give a man a gun and a badge and he thought he ruled the world.

Dust danced around her shuffling steps and clung to her damp hem like a bad reputation. Who was she kidding? The residents of Olin Springs had memories like elephants. They didn't need to witness her arrival to know that she'd returned. Alone. Without a husband. Tongues would wag faster than that yellow dog's tail for a ham hock.

She'd need a running iron to change the brand she'd acquired.

The ornamental brackets and wide eaves of Mrs. Snowfield's elegant home came into full view, exactly the sanctuary Elizabeth sought. Perhaps the elderly widow had someone to assist boarders with their belongings. Someone not prone to supposition and a flapping jaw.

The Snowfield grounds took up a generous acre. In the morning's fresh light, the mistress stood at her wrought-iron fence, leaning over the decorative spires as she craned her neck and dabbed her forehead with a hankie.

Elizabeth was sweating like a lame pig.

The gate swung open. "My dear Betsy, what happened? I heard the train arrive last night and when you didn't come—and then the fire. Oh my lands, I was worried sick about you. And look at you. Let me help you with that box."

"It's quite heavy. If you could open the front door for me, that would help."

As wispy and lithe as ever, Mrs. Snowfield fluttered up the veranda steps and held open the ornately carved door.

Elizabeth made it to the oak staircase and set the crate on the second step before plopping down beside it.

Her new landlady closed the door with purpose and turned, hands on her narrow hips. "My dear, you look as if you walked all the way from Denver and then helped fight the fire."

Just what Elizabeth needed—a reminder of her bedraggled appearance. She unpinned her hat and laid it atop the crate. "You're half right."

"Let me get you some refreshment and then you can tell me what happened." Whisking down the hallway, Mrs. Snowfield called over her shoulder, "Your room is on the second floor, first one to the right."

Clearly, there was no one to help guests with their belongings. But there was indoor plumbing and a bathing room. Elizabeth had confirmed that bit of rumor in her letters when making arrangements to board with Mrs. Snowfield. At a dollar per day, certain amenities were expected.

A thick floral runner carpeted the stairs, and Elizabeth welcomed its cushion beneath her weary feet. Rather than share refreshment and information, she preferred to take a long nap and soaking bath, but the latter must wait until she had her trunk.

At the open door to her room, she stopped with a gasp. The furnishings were as lovely as anything Denver had offered, though she'd not enjoyed the opulence of the Windsor Hotel. She set the crate and her hat on a writing desk at the curtained window, then tossed her ruined reticule onto the four-poster bed. The embodiment of her emotional state, it too, had come home in tatters.

An in-laid rosewood bed table and washstand complemented an imposing wardrobe and dressing table. The elegantly carved mantelpiece bore keepsake boxes, cut-glass dishes, and painted figurines. The cheval mirror accentuated the grime clinging to her torn skirt, and she opened the wardrobe in search of a clothes brush. Lavender sachet wafted out, and she nearly burst into tears at the long-lost luxury.

Matured by betrayal and thinned by the formerly unknown experience of true hunger, she counted on the residents of Olin Springs not recognizing her as the impulsive rancher's daughter they'd once known. Not until she was employed, providing for herself, and no longer in need of her brother's assistance.

And her plan did not call for sitting mildly by and *letting* things work out.

Pushing aside blue damask curtains, she lifted the window. A hesitant breeze replied, tainted by the smell of wet ash, but a clear view of the depot lay beyond the tree tops. Perhaps a mile or so in the hazy distance rose the nearest ridge, around which the railway curled.

Exhaustion drew her to the bed, where she fell onto a matching damask counterpane and feather tick, judging by the absence of lumps and crunching husks. Just pure, downy comfort. Oh, to skip dinner and simply sleep...

"Betsy, dear. Are you all right?"

Waking with a start, she elbowed up. *Betsy* again.

A gentler light filled the room, and her hostess stood in the doorway, concern bunching her dark brows. Oddly, those brows had not faded to match the cloud of white atop her head, and they accentuated the woman's worry.

"I must have dozed off." Elizabeth threw her legs over the edge, embarrassed that her landlady saw she'd not taken time to remove her soiled clothing before flopping across the bed.

"Well, yes, you did doze. It's almost suppertime." A forgiving smile. "But you must have needed it, I dare say. Come down when you're ready and we'll have a bite. It will be just the two of us this evening. Sheriff Wilson has a late meeting."

"Excuse me?" Surely Elizabeth had misheard.

Mrs. Snowfield paused at the door. "The sheriff, dear. When he delivered your trunk, he said to go ahead without him."

Elizabeth choked, her raw throat burning as she coughed until she couldn't breathe.

Mrs. Snowfield rushed to the washstand, filled a tumbler with water from the pitcher, and handed it to her with a sharp slap on her back. "Goodness, child, whatever is the matter?"

CHAPTER 2

Garrett smacked his hat against the side of his leg, then slapped it onto his head and strode down the alley toward his office. That dark-haired gal owed him two bits for hauling her trunk to Snowfield's. And he owed himself a bath, but the washbasin at the back of his office would have to do for now.

He shed his shirt and took to his hair with a soap cake, dirtying the basin's water to near black by the time he finished with his face, neck, and arms. A clean shirt, though worn, felt like the start of a new day, and he tossed the soiled one on a chair with his other trousers waiting on a trip to the laundry house.

Why'd she have to be so all-fired uppity? He'd seen her in the bucket brigade last night, slinging water with the men, and had gone looking for her this morning. Too bad he didn't find her before Pearl did. Things might have turned out different. Then again, maybe not. She was a snippy thing.

And of course she'd holed up at Snowfield's. With the hotel still smoldering, she didn't have much choice.

He grabbed the comb from his washstand and raked his wet hair back, then tucked in his shirt. He looked and felt considerably better. Better than *Mrs.* Elizabeth Beaumont had when she limped away from his offer to help, head high and that confounded crate as close as an infant. And he'd felt almost guilty lettin' her haul it all the way by herself.

His grandma had raised no heathen, but there was a limit to the abuse a man could take when he was trying to be gentlemanly.

And there was probably a limit to the meals he'd enjoy now at Snowfield's. As in few and far between without the new boarder's vinegary attitude setting his teeth on edge. Snowfield's beat Bozeman's café six ways to Sunday when it came to laying a table.

Hoss Bozeman had cooked for a trail boss before he opened his eatery, and it showed. Depending on the length of Mrs. Beaumont's stay, good food might be scarce as rooms at the hotel.

Garrett tethered Pearl to her picket out back, rubbed her ears, and went back inside leaving the door open. Maybe he'd sleep in a cell tonight since Snowfield had one too many customers and he currently had none.

He propped the front door back with a chair and a prayer for a draft. It'd been hot as blazes lately, a fact that had fed the flames at Olin Springs' only hotel. Two ground-floor rooms survived, and one was the parlor. If it weren't for Snowfield, he'd for sure be bunking in an airless cell.

Catching a cool breeze at the jail was near impossible with the way it was built like a stockade and trussed up in the center of Main Street. Pearl grunted, and Garrett shot her a look down the narrow walkway fronting three cells. The dog would have been fine if not for that fandangled shiny bag on Elizabeth Beaumont's wrist. Or was it Betsy? Snowfield had called

16

her Betsy when he lugged the trunk in the back door and left it in the kitchen.

He huffed. Didn't matter what name she went by so long as she didn't cross his path with that high-falutin' attitude. She was entirely too kind to a man's gaze. A regular misdirection, she was, and not one he intended to follow again.

He pitied her husband.

Pearl barked, a rare occurrence. Poor girl always had been partial to doodads, and Garrett couldn't rightly blame her for running after one. But grabbing it while it was still attached to its owner? It irritated him to admit the woman was right. The recall of her ruined suit and general disarray graveled him further, as did a reluctant regret that he'd deliberately let her fall a second time. But her arrogant struggle for the crate was more than he could tolerate. It was as if she didn't trust him.

He took a handful of jerked beef from a bag in his desk drawer and walked back to Pearl. The bones she got from Snowfield's table might be as few and far between as his suppers.

After returning to his desk, he wrote out his thoughts on the hotel fire and categorized things he'd noticed, including the fact that the fire started on the second floor. Talk about forming a hose team had swirled as thick as the black smoke last night, and he'd been invited to an impromptu meeting this evening at the bank. Charles Harrison wanted to form a volunteer brigade. As the bank president, he had a vested interest. It wouldn't be a bad idea, but first, they needed a hose and reel.

An itch under Garrett's collar said the meeting was also connected to another recent event. The arrival of Anthony Rochester, *Esquire*.

Rochester's store-front office butted up against the feed store, an odd combination. He'd hung a shingle out front, his name underscored with *Attorney at Law*. Nothing wrong with the law, though Garrett suspected that he and Rochester were on opposite sides of it. Something about the slicked-down man in his fancy striped suit smacked of a carpetbagger fixin' to fleece the flock.

Garrett shoved away from his desk, locked the front door, and went out the back. Good a time as any to make his rounds, look in on the hotel, and check with the express agent about a telegraph he expected from his old friend George Booth. Rochester claimed to hail from Kansas City, and if that was true, Booth would know.

The Kansas lawman would also know why a big-city lawyer had set up shop in a small Front Range cow town

By late afternoon, Garrett's stomach was huntin' his backbone, and he figured Bozeman could run a decoy. Beans and beef satisfied his hunger but not his taste buds. They sorely missed Maggie Snowfield's table. For a fella not yet thirty, he was gettin' mighty soft.

The old trail cook had wrapped up a soup bone for Pearl, and back at the jail, Garrett dropped it in the chipped wash basin she ate from. She licked her jowls and looked up at him with obvious affection, as if he'd just given her a four-bit steak.

At his desk, he leaned back, crossed his boots on the blotter, and settled in for an hour. The Regulator on his wall ran five minutes fast. When it chimed, he'd have time to get to the bank by six and then some.

He pulled his hat down over his eyes and folded his arms, chasing a contradiction that darted in and out like a worrisome horsefly. It tempted his self-control near like that sparkly bag had tempted Pearl.

He had looked twice, and then he'd looked again just to make sure. And the evidence had been the same each time.

Mrs. Elizabeth Beaumont wore no wedding ring.

Somewhat refreshed after washing and changing out of her ruined suit, Elizabeth had also recovered from coughing up her lungs at Mrs. Snowfield's casual announcement. The news of a certain fellow tenant rattled her to the bone, but she started for the stairs, grateful that she didn't have to share a table with Laughing Eyes tonight.

That dog probably lay at his feet and begged for scraps.

A bitter snort escaped. Surely Mrs. Snowfield didn't allow the creature on her premises, much less under her roof and table.

It wouldn't *fit* under her table.

Not that Elizabeth disliked dogs in general. Fond memories of Blue and other ranch dogs over the years had been a comfort during her more depressing days in Denver. But she and Pearl had gotten off to a start nearly as bad as the animal's breath.

The savory aroma of roast beef hit her at the third step from the landing. She hadn't had a home-cooked meal in more months than she cared to count, and the appetizing perfume squeezed her memory as well as her empty stomach. It smelled like supper at the ranch before Mama and Daddy's accident.

Stuffing the prickly recollection in a dark corner, she followed her nose to the dining room, where a linen-topped table awaited with only two place settings facing each other. Were there no other boarders?

Sliced roast, freshly baked bread, and gravy served as centerpiece. A hand-painted china tea-pot boasted flowers similar to those on a black-lacquered Sholes & Glidden machine she'd once used, and a matching cream and sugar service stood nearby. All were delicate evidence of Mrs. Snowfield's earlier life with her wealthy and now departed husband.

Somehow, Elizabeth felt she'd come to sanctuary.

Her hostess swept into the room with a cut-glass dish full of red jam.

"Please, sit at either place, dear. We don't stand on propriety here."

Elizabeth's mouth watered. She chose the chair offering a view into the kitchen and immediately regretted it. Her trunk sat near a windowed door that led to what appeared to be a porch. Gratitude warred with her bruised hip.

Mrs. Snowfield sat across the table and signaled her intentions with folded hands. "Shall we offer thanks?"

Elizabeth held her tongue.

"Dear heavenly Father, thank You for bringing Betsy home safely and for Sheriff Wilson's kindness to

20

deliver her trunk. And thank You for Your provision of this food. In our Lord's name, amen."

Two out of three wasn't bad. Elizabeth spread the linen napkin across her lap.

"So tell me, Betsy, how was the train ride from Denver? I haven't ridden the train in years. No need, you know. But I hear the cars are as nice now as any that Daniel and I rode in during our various travels." She took a breath, picked up the platter of sliced meat, and offered it to Betsy.

"About that, Mrs. Snowfield—"

"Posh." A slender hand swatted the air. "Call me Maggie, dear. *Mrs. Snowfield* sounds so stuffy, don't you think? My word, I've known you all your life."

At that, the woman flashed a curious glance her way.

Elizabeth took a generous helping of meat and a slice of warm bread, then reached for the rhubarb-currant jam. Tears pricked and she pulled back. Perhaps coming home during berry season had been a bad idea—ripe, as it was, with memories of hunting the precious jewels with her mother.

Blinking rapidly, she held the napkin to her lips and gathered her emotions.

Mrs.—*Maggie*—poured her a cup of chamomile tea and then one for herself. "Sugar or cream?"

"No, thank you. Only with my morning coffee." She sipped the hot tea, calmed by its comforting aroma. "If you insist that I call you Maggie, please, call me by my given name, Elizabeth."

Maggie stirred sugar into her cup, and the spoon chirped lightly against the saucer as she laid it aside. "As you wish, dear. But might an old woman satisfy her growing curiosity and ask why? Betsy fits you so well."

The dark brows stood guard over clear, blue eyes.

Settling her cup in its delicate saucer, Elizabeth sighed. She needed an ally, and her old friend Sophie Price might never speak to her again once she learned that Elizabeth had come home without letting her know.

But the fewer people who knew, the better. The more time it would give her to get situated before contacting Cade.

And she trusted Mrs. Sno— Maggie. Changing a familiar name might be harder than she thought.

"Your letters asked only that I not tell anyone of your return." Maggie forked off a piece of tender meat. "And I abided by your wishes."

"I do so appreciate it. It means more to me than you can know."

The woman glanced up without raising her head, as if to say, "Prove it."

Stalling for the right words, Elizabeth spooned jam onto the edge of her dinner plate. That's where she'd start. At the edge.

"Betsy was my childhood name. Since then, I've chosen to use Elizabeth. I'm a different person than I was." She topped a corner of her bread with the ruby delicacy and bit it off along with the additional words screaming for escape.

"It's hard to come home again and not be remembered for who you were, dear."

Maggie's quiet comment drifted gently across the table but found its mark with pointed precision.

Elizabeth chewed it over and swallowed. "That's just it. I can never again be who I was. Who I was before I left. I'm branded. I'll always be seen as the ungrateful daughter who ran off with her beau after her parents' funeral, leaving her brother alone to take care of the family ranch and explain to everyone how his good little sister went so terribly bad."

Maggie laid her fork down and pinned Elizabeth with hard, glaring judgment. "Anyone who thinks so should be horsewhipped."

Surprised by the elderly woman's vehemence, Elizabeth struggled to regroup, but her throat pinched her words into a whisper. "It's true."

"It's not the whole story, dear. People rarely know the whole story."

There was little to be said in defense of gambling one's future on the promise of love. Elizabeth knotted her napkin in her lap. "Edward left me."

Exactly what she'd intended to not say.

The muted ticking of the mantle clock punctuated the silence, poking holes in Elizabeth's resolve. "I wouldn't go with him to the Dakota gold fields, so he filed for divorce and went without me. He said I was too dowdy for his tastes anyway, and he didn't know what he'd been thinking when he proposed our elopement."

A less than flattering epithet darted past Maggie's pursed lips, if she heard correctly.

She said nothing and instead drained her tea cup.

Maggie quickly refilled it. "He will be at the head of the line."

She glanced sheepishly at her hostess. "Line?" The only line she could think of involved grimy men and buckets of water.

"As I said, dear. Horsewhipped."

Elizabeth immediately saw who stood behind Edward and shuddered. The image of stick-thin Maggie Snowfield chasing Edward Beaumont and Braxton Hatchett with a buggy whip pushed her tottering soul over the edge.

Maggie reached across the table and held her palm up in invitation. Elizabeth joined it with her own.

"You are not the first person to make a poor decision in the wake of grief. Nor are you the first woman wooed by promises of love and then abandoned to the lure of easy fortune." Maggie's eyes dimmed briefly, then flared to life with a squeeze of her fingers.

"So, *Elizabeth*, I am even more pleased than before that you entrusted your homecoming to me and my humble abode. If you'd gone to the ranch, as I'm sure Cade will insist you must once he hears of your return, you would have been rarely seen and rumors would have propagated like the lilies around my veranda. This way, you are facing the music and shall make your reappearance in strength of character, holding your head high."

Any more of such supportive talk, and Elizabeth might melt off her chair into a puddle of tears.

"Though I'm sure your appearance in the bucket brigade last night has already set tongues to wagging about the identity of the young woman not put off by custom and hard work."

Elizabeth palmed her hand down her throat, still raw from breathing smoke and irritated further by her earlier coughing fit. "Rather obvious, was it?"

"Covered as you were in soot and soil, I should say so. Now." She squared her frail shoulders as if taking on the world. "You must have a skill. I know you can break and ride any horse on your family's ranch just as handily as Cade, and I remember you outshooting him and every other man at the county fair one year. What were you—fourteen?"

Elizabeth flexed her right hand, recalling the single shot from her father's Winchester rifle that raised cheers from every woman there.

"But it won't do for you to join a Wild West Show or hire on at the livery. Do you sew? Can you teach music? You played beautifully at church when Mrs. Pottsinger took ill. What about cooking?" Maggie paused to sip her tea. "Of course there are more menial tasks, such as cleaning and doing laundry, but I hate to see you take that route."

"I am a type-writer."

The woman's thin cheeks blossomed like primroses. "Really? Oh, how marvelous. You must have learned in Denver. I've heard about those machines. Do you have your own? Is that what was in the heavy little crate?"

Impressed by her confidante's ability to string questions together so rapidly, Elizabeth smiled for the first time in a long while, encouragement pricking a tender spot behind her ribs. "I'm going to call at the bank tomorrow, and possibly the Western Union office. If the telegraph agent doesn't already have his own machine, he might be interested in my help. Do you know of any other business that could use my services?"

Maggie thinned her lips in thought and then raised one finger. "There is a new attorney in town, at the north end of Main Street on this side."

Elizabeth wadded her napkin into a tight ball. An attorney. Even here.

"You might visit him tomorrow after checking with Mr. Holsom—he's still in the express office—who, I'm sure will be happy to see you. But whether or not he has need of a type-writer, only he can tell you."

Maggie picked up her plate. "I'll clear these dishes, then help you with your trunk. Surely between the two of us, we can get it up the stairs. If not, I'll ask the boy down the road. He helps the pressman set type at the newspaper and has other odd jobs, but he's usually home by dark."

Mention of her trunk dipped Elizabeth's mood again, drawing her back to the necessity of sharing a roof with the sheriff. The alliteration amused her, but he did not. Neither did the idea of visiting a lawyer. She'd had quite enough of the breed.

However, avoiding Sheriff Wilson at meals might be her biggest challenge, for he certainly would not have a meeting every morning and evening, and she had no intention of missing out on Maggie's cooking and companionship.

Eager to help, Elizabeth took her dishes to the kitchen and set them by the sink. "How long do you think it will be until the town is a-buzz with my return?"

Maggie laughed outright. "Oh, I'm sure it has already begun. The sooner you face, it the better, dear.

Let the old biddies stew. You're safe here with me, you know. And with Sheriff Wilson. I dare say, he seemed rather protective of your trunk, though he declined to carry it upstairs when I told him you were resting."

Suspicion wiggled from the back of Elizabeth's mind to her tongue. "How did you know it was my trunk?"

"He described you to a T." Lowering her chin and voice, she comically mimicked the man. "'An independent, becoming young woman with a temper.' I knew it had to be you." Maggie laughed again and caught both of Elizabeth's hands in her own. "I would have been upset too, dear, if that man's monstrosity of a dog had stolen my reticule."

"He *told* you about that?"

"He most certainly did. But that's not all he told me." With an impish look, she lifted her apron from the back of a kitchen chair and tied it on. "He was disappointed to learn that you were married, but no words were needed for me to hear it. I read it in that handsome face of his all on my own."

Warmth seeped into Elizabeth's skin.

"Off with you, now. I can't have my guests helping in the kitchen." Maggie shooed her into the dining room. "While you're unpacking tonight, you can think about how you're going to break it to him."

Elizabeth stopped at the doorway, her throat tightening with the question she already knew the answer to. "Break what to him?"

"The truth, dear."

CHAPTER 3

T ruth was, sleeping in his chair tied him in knots.

Garrett dropped his feet to the floor, rolled his right shoulder, and rubbed the back of his neck. Cell bunks were softer, not by much, but this way he always woke just before the Regulator's soft chime.

The first tone trailed the thought.

He let Pearl in the back door and set a bowl of water by her mat. "Guard," he growled.

She pulled her jowls into a possum grin and wagged her tail. A so-called gift from Booth when Garrett took the job in Olin Springs, it was a toss-up as to who owned whom.

As he locked the front door and then angled across the street toward the bank, he mulled over the reasons for his requested presence at the meeting.

One reason was inside, leaning against the new safe, hands in pockets and a polished shoe cocked against the enameled cast-iron door. Rochester.

Harrison laid his spectacles aside and rose from his desk chair when Garrett walked in. "Sheriff Wilson." The big man rushed around the end of the counter and offered his hand. "Glad you could make it."

Ranch-born and raised, Harrison usually didn't hurry anywhere.

Garret slowed his breathing and his movements. He glanced around the room before returning to the uncharacteristically nervous bank president. "Happy to oblige, Charlie."

He nodded to the attorney.

Rochester dropped his foot to the floor and slid his hands in his pockets. "Sheriff."

Mayor Overholt, short and flustered, arrived a moment later with Jim Holsom, the Western Union agent, close on his heels,. Fred Reynolds from the mercantile joined them, and finally the barber, Bartholomew Ward. One face he expected to see and didn't was Clarence Thatcher, the hotel owner. Probably still calculating his losses.

Miller Pike couldn't leave the saloon open, and Hunt Fischer hadn't sent his reporter. Either that or he wasn't invited. Seemed like they'd want the press to know.

Garrett helped Harrison gather extra chairs from the back room while Rochester stood smoothing his thin mustache with his thumb and forefinger and staring out the front window. He then took a chair to the wall opposite Harrison's desk, affording himself a view of everyone there as well as the front and back entrances. Rochester remained standing.

Harrison cleared his throat. "Thank you all for coming. I'll keep this brief because I'm sure you'd all like to get home to supper."

"We here to talk about a fire brigade?" Ward's question turned every head and drew Harrison off course.

"We surely need one," Reynolds offered.

Everyone began talking at once—everyone but Rochester.

Overholt raised his hands as if the gathering were a city council meeting. "We need to spread word for volunteers. Where's that newspaper man?"

"And raise money for a pump and hose," Reynolds said.

Rochester coughed just enough to catch the bank president's attention.

Harrison ran a hand over his thinning hair. "Those are fine ideas, Mayor, Fred. Thank you for suggesting them. Perhaps you both could get the ball rolling by signing up volunteers and gathering donations." He tugged on his vest, searching the group as if looking for someone. "Mr. Thatcher didn't make it, I see. That's unfortunate, since the hotel is one of the reasons I've called you all together." He glanced at Rochester, then looked away with a frown and raised a hand toward the attorney. "Actually, it was Mr. Rochester here who thought it would be a good idea for us to meet."

Garrett's stomach tensed. The lawyer straightened, tall yet half the bulk of Harrison, who returned to his chair and fell into it with resignation. Garrett's mind clicked through possibilities like tumblers on a safe lock.

Rochester nodded. "Thank you, Charles. Gentlemen. As Mr. Harrison has so aptly stated, the hotel fire was a costly tragedy, not only for Mr. Thatcher but for the entire town." Addressing Garrett, he added, "Any luck, Sheriff, determining the cause of the unfortunate conflagration?"

Rochester's choice of words grated on Garrett. "As an attorney, Mr. Rochester, I'm sure you know that luck has no hand in it at all."

The overdressed man smiled. A snake-oil salesman if ever there was. "Of course, Sheriff. Your investigation—"

"Is still under investigation."

"So you don't consider this an accident."

A few men mumbled at the attorney's deliberate conjecture and glanced back at Garrett.

He held his posture and expression steady, as well as his tongue.

"I see." Rochester spread his coat flaps, revealing more of his brocade waistcoat and a gold watch chain, then pocketed his hands. "Well, gentlemen, be that as it may, this growing community will continue to do just that—grow. And it is my opinion that fire insurance would be well worth the investment to help victims such as Mr. Thatcher if such an unfortunate incident were to occur again."

From a tube on Harrison's desktop, Rochester withdrew and unrolled a large map of the state, webbed with heavy, dark lines.

"I have here a map of the Denver & Rio Grande Railway in our state, showing its connections and extensions to all principal cities and mining regions. This map is hot off the press, if you will, from Chicago. Please note this particular spur." He pointed a clean fingernail to the end of one short black line. "This is the latest railway extension to be added."

Ward leaned forward, his head tipped back to read through his spectacles. "That's Crested Butte. There's no train to Crested Butte."

Based on Rochester's smirk, Ward had played into the setup. "The railway extended its reach to Gunnison in June and to Durango in July. It's on schedule to link to Crested Butte by November."

The telegrapher scoffed. "Snow'll keep that from happening."

"Tracks are already laid. In six weeks, the train will be pulling in at the new depot there."

He let the news sink in. A fisherman setting the hook.

"Seven hundred and seventy-six miles of track covering Colorado and the Territory of New Mexico, with another seven hundred under construction. A veritable web blanketing the mountains."

"What's all this got to do with us?" Reynolds asked.

"With more railroad comes more business for you and the mercantile, Mr. Reynolds. Progress. And with progress comes trouble. I'm here to help the fine citizens of Olin Springs when that trouble arrives."

The hair rose on the back of Garrett's neck. He fingered the rawhide thong that held his holster to his leg. Was Rochester predicting the future, or planning trouble in order to line his own pockets?

"We've had a depot here a couple years and ain't had no trouble," the mayor said. "What makes you so certain we will now?"

Rochester let the map roll up on itself with a snap. He returned it to Harrison's desk and his hands to his pockets before addressing his audience. "I've seen it before. A quiet little town welcomes the railroad and all goes well for a while. But eventually—sooner rather than later—trouble follows. More people. A greater stress on the infrastructure, increased demand for housing, et cetera."

Garrett could name a few Kansas towns that fit the description. Abilene, for one, a decade ago.

"This fire insurance you mentioned." Reynolds shifted on his hard oak chair. "Where would a businessman find such a thing?"

"I can help you with that, Mr. Reynolds. And any of the rest of you who are interested. I have associates in Kansas City who specialize in such coverage. And like I said, that's why I'm here. To do all I can."

That last phrase cut two ways.

An hour later, the group disbanded, more somber than when they'd arrived, aside from Rochester who looked like a coyote fresh from the chicken house. Harrison had a few more furrows in his forehead.

And Garret had the distinct impression he'd just watched a slick operator shoot fish in a rain barrel.

~

Elizabeth unpacked her trunk, using two wardrobe shelves for unmentionables and petticoats, and the uppermost for her bedraggled traveling hat and a modest straw. She laid her leather portfolio on the floor of the center compartment and hung three dresses above it, a deep rose blush, a summery yellow, and a more practical forest green. A brown woolen skirt and two white shirtwaists made up her professional attire, and she hoped to add to her collection in time. Though considered quite meager in Denver, her clothing was more than adequate for Olin Springs, and the unpleasant weight of fashionable demands lifted from her shoulders.

Truth be told, she missed the days of her girlhood, when riding skirts and boots were her less cumbersome, everyday apparel. But one did not change the past. The present, however, was another matter.

She laid her wrapper and gown across her bed and went downstairs to start a kettle of water. Piped hot water was not one of Maggie's luxuries, but Elizabeth had no complaints. Warming tepid tap water in the bathing room was an easy chore compared to hauling water for her family's copper tub as a child.

Childhood memories pressed in of Cade grousing about having to use her "old" water during their Saturday night preparations for Sunday morning services. One more sorrowful tug from days that had ended so suddenly and completely.

She'd often regretted not taking her riding boots with her when she left that wintery afternoon. Her wide-brimmed hat and leather gloves. Her beautiful mare, Blanca. As if Edward would have allowed it.

Such thoughts had not accompanied her flight from the church following her parents' funeral. Only a naïve young woman's dreams of promised love and provision—dashed immediately upon the courthouse nuptials in Denver.

Shame heated her face and neck, or was it the kettle steaming on Maggie's massive kitchen range? With a quilted hot-pad, she hefted the large kettle and carried it to the bathing room adjacent the kitchen. Wainscoting encased the cozy closet, with rose-covered wall paper above and a thick oriental rug next to a deep soaking tub. A person could submerge themselves completely. She set the plug, turned the porcelain-handled faucet to fill the tub, and poured in the boiling water. Then she lit a lamp on a small side table, raised the wick against the approaching night, and dashed upstairs for her wrapper and gown.

Anticipation lightened her steps, and at the top of the stairs she noticed a door at the end of the landing that didn't match those for all the other upstairs rooms. It had a glass knob, and she immediately wanted to test it. But water was running. She'd investigate later.

At her dressing table, she let down her hair and brushed out the tangles. If only her life could be unpinned and straightened as easily, the painful knots smoothed. Demoralized first by her husband and then her employer, she had little use for men at the moment. If Sheriff Wilson believed she was married, so much the better. Why should it matter to Maggie?

She gathered a towel from the towel horse by the washstand and her bar of lavender soap, then hurried downstairs, anticipating a warm and leisurely bath.

Maggie must have retired for the evening, for she was not in the sitting room when Elizabeth looked in on her way past. Nor was she in the kitchen or the odd room at the rear of the house.

Curiosity got the better of Elizabeth and she peered through the door into a porch with screens rather than glass windows. She'd not seen the like even in Denver. A single bed and chest of drawers took up one end of the narrow room, a washstand and chair the other. Oddly enough, she envied the evening breeze that filtered through the airy space, though it was not nearly as well-appointed as her room upstairs. Perhaps it served as an overflow when the Snowfield home was full of boarders, though without shutters, winters might prove chilling for its resident.

At the bathing room, she hesitated briefly. The door was closed. She'd left it slightly ajar, hadn't she? Perhaps not. She gripped the knob and stepped into the small square space, turning to secure the lock.

The sound of splashing water brought her around to a man sitting in the tub, water sluicing off his chin, neck, and bare chest.

Stumbling back against the door, she clapped a hand over her mouth, muffling a cry.

Sheriff Garrett Wilson's pewter eyes sparked with mirth, not one ounce of shame or disgrace on his face. Nor did he attempt to cover himself. Instead he laid his dripping arms along the tub's edge.

"I wondered who had drawn a warm bath for me." He glanced at the towel and soap in her other hand. "Did you intend to wash my back as well?"

If the soap was not her last cake of lavender, she would have shoved it in his arrogant mouth and drowned him on the spot.

Gathering her wits, she reached behind for the doorknob and twisted. It failed to give way.

He chuckled.

"I believe you locked it, Betsy." His hands gripped the sides of the tub as if to help him rise. "Would you like my assistance?"

Fuming, she spun, twisted the lock, and dashed out. His laughter chased her down the hallway, up the stairs, and into her room where she slammed her door and fell across the bed with a pillow over her flaming ears. Mortified. And furious.

The next morning, she awoke in the same position. Her gown, towel, and wrapper lay crumpled beneath her. She pushed the pillow away, sat up, and sighed.

So much for a fresh start.

After tending to her morning ablutions at the washstand, she finished by twisting her hair at her collar. How satisfying it would be to twist a certain man's neck into a similar knot.

Her skirt, shirtwaist, and high-topped shoes completed her professional appearance. She fingered the red-enameled lapel watch pinned to her bodice, then braced herself to face the omnipresent and hopefully dressed Sheriff Wilson at breakfast.

She was starving. Not as literally as she had the last twelve months in Denver, but she needed sustenance before pounding the boards for a job this morning. If she were lucky, the sheriff would have already eaten and left.

As usual, luck made no appearance on her behalf.

He sat at the head of the dining table as if he were master of the house rather than a tenant. Why was she not surprised?

When she entered the room, his dimpled scar popped into place and he rose. "Good morning, Betsy. Bracing day, isn't it?"

She glared, willing metaphorical daggers to life. No luck there, either.

She took the same seat she'd occupied the evening before, near the opposite end of the table.

Maggie bustled in with a large silver tray of hot-cakes, bacon, and eggs.

Elizabeth feared she might swoon at the aroma. She reached for the china teapot in the center of the table and filled her cup. Coffee would be better, more invigorating, but that required opening her mouth and requesting it, which she was determined not to do in present company.

Maggie disappeared into the kitchen and returned with another cup and saucer and the coffee pot. "You're not alone in your morning preference, dear. Garrett starts his day with strong coffee as well."

He grinned. "Good for what ails you."

If Elizabeth were deaf or invisible, she would not have to respond to Maggie's kindness. She was neither.

"Thank you." At least she didn't have to respond to *him*.

Maggie took the chair across the table and folded her hands. Elizabeth followed suit, and from the corner of her eye, saw that Sheriff Wilson did the same. So the scallywag prayed.

Maggie offered a brief prayer offering more thanksgiving, then passed the platter of eggs and bacon to Elizabeth. "I trust you both slept well."

Elizabeth helped herself and held the platter out toward the end of the table while she stared at the butter dish.

Would he not just take it? Her hand began to shake in its strained position. Resigned to setting it down, she lowered the dish.

He quickly took it with a little tug that pulled her gaze to his.

Greener in the morning light, his eyes left her feeling baited.

She jerked her focus back to her plate.

"Since this is such a family-like setting and I've asked you both to call me Maggie, I suggest that we dispense with formal titles and address each other accordingly. Wouldn't you agree?"

Elizabeth added sugar and cream to her coffee, then downed a most unladylike gulp of the hot, rich brew.

"Suits me fine, Maggie. How 'bout you, Betsy?"

Caught in the downward motion of placing her cup in its saucer, her hand jerked at his use of her childish name and hit the edge of the dish. Coffee splashed a brown spot on the linen tablecloth.

"I'm so sorry." She dabbed the spill with her napkin, glancing at Maggie. The woman seemed bothered not one bit. "But I prefer Elizabeth, if you don't mind."

Sheriff Wilson failed to keep his humor at bay. "But Betsy suits you."

Was it the man's personal goal in life to rile her?

"Oh, that's my fault, dear," Maggie said. "I shall make a more concerted effort to use Elizabeth, as you asked earlier. But I warn you, I may slip from time to time, remembering you with your flying pigtails on that white horse, outshooting your brother."

The sheriff's fork stopped halfway to his mouth.

Elizabeth reached for the hotcakes. The sooner she ate and left, the better.

"I thought you weren't from around here."

A simply stated remark, free of curiosity or inquiry. She ignored it, her heart drumming in her ears.

Maggie met her gaze, then patted her mouth with her napkin. "Garrett, if you have opportunity in the next few days, would you mind helping me with the shutters on the porch. I feel an early autumn coming on, and I don't want you catching your death out there in a surprise snowstorm."

He slept on the porch? In a nearly empty house? "How many other boarders do you have, Maggie?"

"Just the two of you at the moment."

Elizabeth plated her silverware and tucked her napkin beneath the plate's edge. "If you'll excuse me, I need to be on my way. Thank you for a lovely and filling breakfast."

"You are most welcome, dear." Maggie raised her teacup. "I look forward to hearing how your search turns out."

The sheriff stood as she did, mischief rippling his features. "The bathing room's all yours this evening—Elizabeth." He dipped his head in deference.

Embarrassed anew, she walked slowly from the room, determined not to reveal how intensely she wanted out of his presence.

"Oh, I forgot to discuss the arrangements."

Elizabeth picked up her pace at reaching the hallway. She was not about to discuss any arrangements with the sheriff present, particularly after he had fairly flaunted his muscular arms and broad chest last night. Not that she'd noticed.

Hiking her skirt, she dashed up the stairs and escaped into her rented room. She'd been in town less than twenty-four hours and coming home had already turned out to be more of a challenge than she'd bargained for.

CHAPTER 4

G arrett didn't need another challenge, but he fully intended to call Elizabeth Beaumont Betsy every chance he got just to see her light up like a penny firecracker.

Pearl whined and clawed the inside of the heavy office door as he opened up, happy as usual at his return. She tried to squeeze out, but he pinned her against the doorframe with his knee. "Not this time, girl. Hold your horses."

She followed him to the back, where he led her outside to her rope.

"Sorry, but you've got to stay off the street. Who knows how many fandangled lady's bags could be out there, luring you into a life a crime."

Maggie had sent him off with a bowl of scraps from the kitchen, and he set them in the shade with fresh water. "Maybe we'll go for a ride this evening." He rubbed the dog's ears.

She rewarded him with a wet lick to his hand.

If he let her, she'd work him over nearly as good as last night's tub-soaking.

He chuckled, remembering Betsy Beaumont's horror-stricken face—so worth the effort of getting in the tub before she returned. He'd known darn well who'd drawn the bath and lit the lamp.

The hardest part was playing innocent. That, and getting outside in his soaked trousers and socks without swamping the entire kitchen after she'd run off.

Yeah, completely worth it.

Something about that gal drew the ornery out of him. Maybe it was the determined set of her jaw or the way she kept her own counsel and didn't chatter like a jay. Allowing her pluck at jumping in on the bucket line, it wasn't all that hard to imagine her outshooting the men at the annual rifle match. He just had to figure out who her brother was, and the best place he knew of for thinking was the back of his horse.

He locked the front door. As he headed for the livery, the unmistakable slap of the batwings at the Pike Saloon stopped him. A mite early for a fight.

A man tumbled over the hitching rail and into the street.

"Don't come back!" Miller Pike's bellow preceded his bulk through the swinging doors. He stopped on the boardwalk, his meaty hands clenching and unclenching.

"Trouble, Miller?" Garrett ambled that way.

"Done took care of it, Sheriff." He pointed a beefy finger at his former customer. "But that youngster comes back to my establishment, and you can haul him off to yours."

At that, the fella glanced up at Garrett with a boyish face, white and worried. He wore no gun, and his farmer's hat said he should be tending a plow, not tipping a glass.

Garrett's insides went cold, and remorse slid icy fingers down his spine.

"Too early to be drinking—both you and the day." He darkened his tone, aiming to turn a lad away early rather than drag him off later, dead. "Where you from, boy?"

The young drunk struggled to his feet, pointed out of town, and double-stepped to keep from toppling over.

"You best be headed that way."

He waited for the kid to find the boardwalk and head south. Didn't need some freighter running him over in front of the townsfolk.

Or a stray bullet bringing him down.

Garrett shook off the encounter and the idea of riding, and crossed to the hotel. Sawdust tinged the air and hammers rang. He reset his hat and walked through the doorless entrance looking for Clarence Thatcher and a clue.

Thatcher and another man were trying to paste green-and-gold flocked wallpaper on the lobby walls, one of a few rooms that still had a ceiling. Garrett would rather skin snakes.

"Clarence." He dipped his chin to the other gentleman, who was wrangling a narrow length of paper twice his height.

"Sheriff." Thatcher slapped paste on the wall and took hold of one edge of the paper. "I'm tied up at the moment, as I'm sure you can see."

Suited Garrett fine. In fact, better than fine. He'd ask questions later. "I'm gonna look around."

"Be my guest."

The other man laughed. "Guess you can't do that, can you?"

Thatcher cut him a hard look, and the other fella's grin fell to the floor along with the paper.

Garrett took to the singed staircase that was mostly intact, with one or two boards burned through here and there. The worst of the damage was on the second floor, which confirmed Garrett's hunch that the fire had started there.

Thatcher's decision to work on the ground-floor rooms first made sense. Easier to get them livable in quick time. But up here, it'd take more than wallpaper to cover the damage. Walls were charred clear through, other than the outside walls of the northeast corner.

A fire he'd witnessed in Abilene had started downstairs in the kitchen and burned up the whole place in fifteen minutes. Literally *up*. Different than this.

Garrett chose his steps carefully, staying close to support beams and away from checked flooring. Only a blackened iron bed remained in the corner room above the lobby. From his precarious vantage point, he could see most of the second floor lying atop the first. Mangled beds had fallen through. One area appeared to be nothing but ash. He made his way back down for a closer look.

Maybe it was the time of day, the angle of the light, or the fact that this end of the hotel hadn't been cleaned out by carpenters yet. An odd shape poked up through the ash. He worked his way across the charred remains to the lump and picked it up. His guess—the brass burner of an oil lamp.

~

Confident in her simple attire and straw hat, portfolio under one arm, Elizabeth marveled at how

Main Street had expanded in the last six years. Apparently the *Olin Springs Gazette* was prospering, based on the large Gothic print painted across the building's false front. The livery was no longer at the end of the street, for several storefronts had sprung up beyond it, including a saddle shop. New stables stretched behind the livery toward the stockyards near the railway.

Even the church had a neighbor to the north—a modest home with a sign hanging at a right angle to its picket fence: *Library.*

At the bank's entrance, she drew a steadying breath, then stepped inside.

Nothing had changed, other than the teller whom she approached. "Good morning. I am Elizabeth Beaumont, and I'd like to speak to Mr. Harrison, please."

The sober man looked her up and down with obvious suspicion, but dipped a nod and walked back to the president's desk. Harrison paused in his paperwork, then peered over his eye glasses in her direction.

She was banking on him not recognizing her.

A snicker nearly escaped at the turn of phrase, but she tucked it away as he rose from his chair.

"May I help you,"—he glanced at her left hand clutching the portfolio—"Miss Beaumont?"

A half-truth, but she'd take it. "I'm here to see if I might be of assistance to you, sir. I've recently arrived from Denver, where I was employed as a type-writer for several legal firms." *One* legal firm—less than a half-truth. She opened the portfolio and presented the

45

evidence. "I am quite proficient, as you can see by these samples of my work, and I have my own machine."

The firm set of his mouth gave her the answer she didn't want to hear, but he politely looked through her work, nodding appreciatively.

"Indeed." He fingered back to one memo in particular and read through it again before squaring the papers and returning them to the portfolio she'd laid on the counter. "I can see that you do fine work, Miss Beaumont, but I can't use your services at the moment. Perhaps a few months from now you might check back."

He removed his eye glasses and gave her a more penetrating appraisal. "You say you're not from Olin Springs? Something about you seems vaguely familiar."

"Thank you for your time, Mr. Harrison." She'd said nothing of the sort, nor did she intend to add to her little white lies, piling them up until they were as black as her type-writer ribbon. Clutching the portfolio to her shirt front, she stepped back. "A few months, then. Good day."

She quietly shut the door behind her, expelling a tight breath and ruing all the times she'd insisted her father take her to town with him. Only once or twice she accompanied him inside the bank, but she was the female version of his very image, especially now, so thin. The connection would no doubt come to Harrison in the middle of the night or during a meal or in conversation with local businessmen. She expected no less.

Continuing past the hardware store and other familiar sites, she took a side street back to the depot and Western Union, where she slowed her steps and drew up her most confident posture before opening the door.

Mr. Holsom looked up from his desk. "May I help you?"

"On the contrary, sir, I believe I may be of help to you." Elizabeth offered her hand across the countertop as he approached with curiosity crinkling his forehead."

"Betsy?"

Drat.

"Elizabeth, now. Elizabeth Beaumont. It's good to see you, Mr. Holsom."

Apparently pleased to see her, he smiled and pushed his visor higher. "Well, I'll be. I didn't know you were in town. Here to visit Cade?"

"In good time." Telegraphers typically knew everyone's business, which was exactly the reason she had not communicated with Maggie via telegraph. She wasn't surprised at his response. "First I'd like to secure employment."

Holsom's expression went limp and he pulled his visor back down, reaching for a scrap of paper from a nearby stack. "A telegram, then. Is that it?"

"No. I'm here to see if you can use a type-writer. I even have my own type-writing machine and several samples of my work." She opened her portfolio on the counter and fanned the papers to show a collection of letters, memorandums, and other communiques. "As you can see, I am quite experienced."

Mr. Holsom worked his mouth as if chewing marbles and lifted the corner of each paper, giving it a brief review. "That you are. Nice work, young lady." As

Harrison had done, he squared the papers into a neat stack and closed the portfolio.

Elizabeth's heart plopped onto her hastily eaten hotcakes.

"If I had need of a type-writer, I'd be sure to hire you. But as it stands, I just don't need the service right now. Maybe if the town grows like they say it will. Maybe then I could give you a little work."

He slid the portfolio toward her.

"Might I ask who *they* are?"

His puzzled look followed.

"They who say the town will grow."

"Oh." He chuckled. "Had me there for a minute. Well, that new attorney, Rochester, for one. He's been telling everybody that Olin Springs is about ready to bust wide open with new people and new prospects. His office is near the end of Main on the east side if you want to stop and check with him. Right next to the feed store."

She thanked Mr. Holsom and left, regrouping outside on the depot boardwalk. Olin Springs may have expanded its Main Street, but it was not as progressive as she had imagined. After a half-dozen years in Denver, the last two as a type-writer for Gladstone, Hatchett and Son law firm, she had forgotten how quaint and wholesome a town she'd come from.

Disheartened but not enough to quit, she returned to Main Street and the newspaper, doubtful that the editor would need a type-writer. A type-setter, perhaps, but that was a completely different skill, and based on Maggie's mention of a neighbor boy, the editor already had one. She prepared to be turned down a third time and opened the door.

A bell clanked as she stepped inside, and a middle-aged man came from the back of the long, open room. His bib apron was inked nearly black, and he wiped his hands on a rag as he approached the counter.

"Mr. Fischer, the editor, isn't in, but if you want to place an ad or have a news item, I can take it down for you. I run the press." He extended his stained hand. "Ben Witherfall."

At Elizabeth's hesitation to shake his blackened fingers, he quickly withdrew them with shy humor. "Sorry, ma'am. I forget sometimes."

"What time do you expect Mr. Fischer to return?"

"Hard to say. He's over at the café trying to drum up—I mean, he's checking in on the latest happenings. Depends on what he finds this morning." Hopefulness brightened his face. "Do you have news for the paper?"

"No. I am a type-writer newly arrived from Denver, and I'm inquiring about his need of my services. I have my own machine."

Doubtful, he rubbed his forehead, leaving a black smudge there. "All our writing is printed on the press. But I'll let him know you stopped by." He took a small square of newsprint from a cut stack and handed it to her with a pencil. "If you'd like to leave your name and how he can reach you, I'll pass it on to him."

She wrote out the information and slid it across the counter.

He read it, then smiled briefly. "Nice to make your acquaintance, Mrs. Beaumont. I'll be sure Mr. Fischer gets this."

Elizabeth detested the surname, but there was nothing she could do about that.

She continued along the west side of Main Street, entering any place of business she thought might offer employment. By the time she crossed the street at the opposite end of town, she'd been turned down five times, recognized twice, and referred again to the attorney.

There was nothing to do but make her way back up the street. She should have gone there to begin with, as Maggie had suggested, but the bad taste that lingered from Gladstone and Hatchett made her hesitant to work for a law firm again.

However, if her plans to survive independently of her brother were to succeed, she needed work. She knew of many attorneys who were quite reputable and offered honest service, but doors had closed after Mr. Hatchett's destruction of her reputation.

In addition, the cost of living in Denver consumed a type-writer's wages like winter consumed fall, a reality that had sealed her decision to return to Olin Springs.

Glancing up from the boards, she neared barred windows. At the sheriff's office, she quickened her pace and hurried by the open door, praying she'd not be spotted by the man or his dog. It was more of a panicked plea than a real prayer, for she was rusty and out of practice. She'd not prayed for quite some time. Complying with Maggie's wishes at the dining table didn't really count.

Safely past with her person, pride, and portfolio intact, she crossed an intersection and slowed as she approached the shingle bearing the attorney's name. Her reflection in his curtained front window caught her eye, and she lifted one hand to her chignon.

A tall, angular man coming out the door stopped short and grabbed her arm to keep from colliding with her.

His shrewd eyes quickly took her measure, and she clutched her portfolio tighter and stepped out of his grasp.

Bending at the waist, he gave a brief bow. "My apologies. In my hurry I neglected to look for passersby. Please forgive my brutishness."

A familiar, litigious tone crawled beneath his words.

She could turn and leave, but she needed work. Her grip on her portfolio tightened. "Mr. Rochester."

His thin mustache pulled a near smile as he dipped his head, still watching her. "At your service." With a flourish, he opened the door for her to enter. "How may I be of assistance to you this fine morning?"

She stepped inside, sensing the flutter of useless wings, similar to those of the fly in the spider's parlor.

CHAPTER 5

G arrett smashed the black widow with his boot.

Snakes, coyotes, even outlaws gave him no pause. Anything he could draw a gun on. But that brittle snap of thread had chilled him when he'd picked up the broom. He found the shiny black ball dangling in the corner with its red hourglass a fitting target.

After dashing the web and egg sack with the stiff broom straws, he finished cleaning the cells, eager for a good cold snap. But it'd be nigh on eight weeks before winter killed off the widows and sent snakes to their holes.

Maybe it'd do the same for Anthony Rochester.

Garrett had spent most of the morning speculating on the lawyer's motives and the bank president's preoccupied manner last night, but nothing added up. Just as he was about to dump the cold coffee from the pot on his stove, the Beaumont woman fairly ran by his open front door. He watched from the threshold as she crossed the side street, then followed from a distance. Sure enough, she plowed into Rochester himself, and then went into his office.

Garrett walked that way, slowed at the attorney's window, and met up with heavy curtains just high enough on the big front glass that Garrett couldn't see a thing other than his own reflection.

What was she searching for, as Maggie Snowfield had mentioned at breakfast, and why in the world would Maggie send her to Rochester?

He turned down the alley and again at the depot, stopping at the express office. Holsom had no telegram from Booth yet, but he sure enough coughed up some interesting information when Garrett mentioned Elizabeth Beaumont.

"Betsy Parker, you mean. She sure has grown into a fine-looking woman." Holsom thumbed his visor up. "You weren't here when her and Cade's parents died that winter—'75, it was. Worst blizzard in twenty years, some of the old timers said. Sad situation."

The news could have knocked Garrett over with one of his broom straws. He'd heard Cade had a sister but had never met her, nor did he expect to. The questions just kept piling up.

"Both died, you say?"

"Buggy accident, it was. The colonel must have thought he could drive headlong into a blizzard rather than wait it out in town."

The colonel had to be their pa.

"Neither Cade nor Betsy were the same after that. Fact is, Betsy up and ran off with that Beaumont fella. Based on all the money Cade wired, she was living in Den—"

Caught in the error of his ways, Holsom clapped his jaw shut and tugged his visor down.

Garrett tapped his knuckles on the countertop. "Let me know when you hear from George Booth."

Holsom jerked a nod. "Will do, Sheriff."

Craving more coffee, Garrett returned to Main Street, intent on the café. Bozeman's brew could cut axel grease, but it was either that or The Pike Saloon. He took a seat at the far window table, his back against the wall and his eye on Rochester's door. No telling if the gal was already gone or still in there.

At lease he knew why Maggie Snowfield called her Betsy. But why the name change?

She hadn't out and out lied to him about where she was from, but she'd come darn close. And why wasn't Beaumont with her? She was hiding something, and it might be in that crate she guarded like a treasure chest. It was heavy enough, but he doubted it held gold coin.

Bozeman brought him a cup and left the coffee pot on the table. Too early for dinner, Garrett was the lone customer. A few folks passed by outside, men giving a nod when they caught his eye, but Garrett was otherwise occupied, chasing an idea around the back of his brain.

Maggie needed his help with the storm shutters, and she'd want to wash them before he hung them, just like last year. With Betsy in town, right now was the perfect opportunity, giving him time to steal upstairs. He swigged his coffee, scalding his throat and taste buds, left a coin on the blue-checkered cloth, and made tracks to the boarding house.

Around back, Maggie was throwing a pail of water on two shutters she'd already hauled up from the basement and set against the back of the house. A more determined woman he'd never met. Except maybe Elizabeth Betsy Parker Beaumont.

54

"Why, Garrett." She smiled. "What good timing you have. Can you bring up the rest? We might get this chore completed before supper tonight."

He tugged his hat down. "Be right back."

The narrow door next to the bathing room stood open, and a soft light glowed from the basement. He tromped down and returned with two shutters under each arm, reaching the top of the stairs as Maggie came in the back door.

"You're a dear. Just lean them against the house with the others." She mixed water and vinegar in the pail and dropped in a heavy brush.

He shook his head at the little lady who could near outwork a grown man. No telling what she'd have him doing next, but he'd wager that chopping firewood was on the list. He backed through the door, then stopped and turned on the stoop before taking the five steps down, where he leaned the shutters against the bottom of the porch with the others.

Maggie kept a ladder and tools in an old buggy shed out back, and when he returned with them, she was busy dousing and scrubbing.

Seizing the opportunity, he calmly went inside, then hurried through the kitchen to the hallway and took the stairs two at a time. Chancing that Betsy's room was the first on the right, he knocked and waited a moment. What he'd say if she came to the door he had no idea, but he wouldn't just barge in on her.

The memory of her doing just that last night, and the stone-cold shock on her face, drew a chuckle. He twisted the knob and peeked in. A might fancier than his quarters, but he hadn't wanted to bunk upstairs. He needed to be able to leave at a moment's notice without waking the whole house, and he didn't take to lace curtains and flowers all over the walls and bedding.

The crate in question sat on a writing desk in front of the window, the lid pried up.

Checking his back trail, he glanced at the landing and stairs, listening for Maggie's footfall in the kitchen. Nothing. He ducked inside, and opening the weighty little box, he found the last thing he expected.

~

Anthony Rochester's narrow shotgun-style office held a large oak desk with an ancient leather chair hunched behind it. Two captain's chairs languished in front. A worn leather writing pad, ink pot and fountain pens, and a shallow, walnut box of letterhead adorned the top.

The nicest articles in the room were the man's suit and a brown velvet curtain across his window, hung just low enough to allow some sunlight in above it.

Only two framed certificates decorated the walls.

Rochester's touch at her elbow made her flinch.

"Please, be seated." Light but persistent pressure urged her toward the tired chairs.

She chose the one closest to the door, settling on its very edge.

He took his position behind the desk, planted his elbows on the writing pad, and steepled creamy white fingers. An image of Sheriff Wilson's rough, weathered hands flashed in her memory.

"How may I be of service, Miss…"

"Beaumont." Fighting for her nerve, she straightened her back even more and laid her portfolio across her lap. "Mrs. Elizabeth Beaumont."

"Of course, Mrs. Beaumont."

She didn't miss his glance at her left hand. Oh, why had she sold her wedding band in Denver?

For the same reason she was sitting in this office. Money.

"How long have you been in business here, Mr. Rochester?"

He flipped a hand, making light of his meager surroundings. "This is all temporary. My permanent furnishings should be arriving any day on the train." He leaned forward. "But I'm sure you're not here to discuss my décor."

So much for niceties and straightforward answers. "I am a type-writer looking for work, but I can see you are not set up for an assistant or employee, so I won't take up any more of your time." She rose.

His arm swept theatrically across the room. "Please, don't be put off by appearances. I most definitely could use someone with your capabilities, though I expected to hire a man here in Olin Springs. Your employment here would be seen as progressive." He indicated her portfolio. "Have you a sample of your work?"

Choosing what she believed was her least-important example, she laid it on his desk.

"Come, come, Mrs. Beaumont. Let me see all your work." His smooth hand waited, pale palm up.

She gave him the collection, revealing more of herself than she wanted, but retained her portfolio and again took the seat's edge.

He read each page thoroughly, frowning at a few as though troubled by their content. At others he nodded appreciatively, and at one he simply stared, but she couldn't see which one drew such concentrated attention. Then squaring the pages as everyone else had, he handed them back. "Nicely done, Mrs. Beaumont. Obviously, you have worked for another legal firm. Have you letters of reference?"

Her heart threatened to crash through her ribs, and maintaining her composure cost a fair amount of energy. "Not at the moment." Sudden departures from self-indulgent employers left little time for supportive correspondence.

"Perhaps I can contact someone at Gladstone, Hatchett and Son to vouch for you. I'm sure you understand."

"Certainly."

Experience told her he was reading her like an open ledger—every move, every blink of her eye. She held her hands immobile atop her portfolio, her posture poker straight. "Contact Miss Erma Clarke and she will see that your inquiry gets into the proper hands." Which would be Erma's.

"Might I assume you also possess stenographer skills?"

Precious few. "Yes." She could always practice at the boarding house.

"And you understand the utmost importance of confidentiality."

Her pulse ricocheted from temple to throat. "Indeed."

He continued to wait, poised, like a spider at the corner of its web. Suddenly he leaned back. "Very well.

I shall telegraph Gladstone, Hatchett and Son today. Should I receive a favorable reply, when could you begin?"

He'd snatched her tongue as surely as that yellow mongrel had snatched her reticule. She slid her work into the portfolio, stalling, raking her brain for a reason she could not work for him. None came, other than an edgy discomfort.

"I am waiting to hear from others, but I will get back to you." Such a bold, pathetic lie.

She rose a second time.

He followed suit, eyeing her with a challenging expression. "I assure you, you would have your own desk and a proper machine within the week."

"I have my own type-writer." As soon as the words escaped, she regretted them, fearing she appeared desperate.

His right brow arched. "I see. Very well, then. Until we meet again."

For the second time that day, she wanted to run from a room because of a man, but she walked calmly to the door.

"Mrs. Beaumont?"

She gripped the door knob and turned slightly to find him half the distance to her.

"Are you not curious about the salary I offer?"

Frankly, she was not. Perhaps cleaning and doing laundry weren't as bad as Maggie warned. Or she could swallow her pride and go back to the ranch. She raised her chin in false bravado. "Of course."

He smiled. "Twelve dollars a week."

Surprise tightened her hold on the knob, but she schooled her expression at hearing his offer match what she'd made in Denver.

"Thank you. Good day."

After closing the front door behind her, she clipped along the boardwalk, two heartbeats for every footstep. She'd done more play-acting in the last twenty-four hours than in all her life. And told more lies. Circumstances were not at all as she'd hoped they'd be. Nor had they been in the last six years.

At the corner, she turned for the boarding house, slowing her steps and her breathing. The pleasant grounds that skirted the Snowfield home just ahead helped ease her fretting. Maggie must employ someone to tend to the roses and lilies, and the crowd of apple trees gathered below the house.

A breeze slipped by, and Elizabeth turned her face to the blue expanse above, filling now with towering clouds—an armada of tall ships sailing into port. A summer storm would soon break the heat and wash the dusty streets.

If only it could wash away her misgivings as well.

Rather than go immediately to her room, she fell into a corner of the quaint swing suspended at one end of the wide veranda. She unlaced her boots and lifted her stockinged feet beside her, the action setting the swing in motion. House wrens and sparrows twittered nearby, flitting between a feeder she'd not noticed earlier and a giant elm that shaded the end of the house.

As a young girl, she had paid little if any attention to Margaret Snowfield herself, simply aware of the woman's mansion-like home, so out of place in Olin Springs. Now it was a refuge, and as Maggie had suggested, Elizabeth did feel safe under its wing. Gratitude had made few if any appearances in the last several years, but it welled quietly within her now.

A sudden gust whipped around the corner, hushing the birdsong and rattling the rosebushes. Clouds scuttled past the sun, and in the weakened light, she shrank from the prospect of working for Anthony Rochester.

Was it merely his profession that unsettled her so? He'd said or done nothing inappropriate and, in fact, had behaved himself most gentlemanly. Perhaps that was it. Edward's similar manner had once lured her off course, and she vowed never to be led away again. That and her hasty departure from Denver had formed the foundation of her return to Olin Springs, where she hoped to find her footing once more if given the chance.

If Miss Clarke remembered the generous offer of support she made before Elizabeth left the Hatchett law firm, Rochester would receive a favorable reference letter, appearing to be from the elder Hatchett himself.

She shuddered at the implication.

But Anthony Rochester could be her chance at a new beginning. And she was willing to take that chance in spite of her reservations.

CHAPTER 6

Garrett didn't believe in chance. Everything happened for a reason.

He hefted the final shutter into place and, bracing it with one arm, drove a long screw into a hole in the frame. Three more screws secured the window, and he climbed down from the ladder and stood back to inspect his work. Still couldn't figure why his landlady didn't hinge the shutters back against the house like everyone else did.

But Maggie wasn't like everyone else in Olin Springs, and neither was her house.

"Lovely." She clasped her small hands like a young girl. "You came back at just the right time."

Exactly. No chance to it. He'd helped his landlady and learned more about the mysterious Elizabeth Betsy Parker Beaumont all at the same time.

"It's so warm out, I'll make sandwiches and a pitcher of lemonade if you care to wait. Or do you have duties in town to attend to?"

Garrett stuck the screwdriver in his belt and folded the ladder. Her offer of lemonade cinched the deal. "They can wait."

"Wonderful. I'll bring a tray out to the veranda. With the breeze, it will be more pleasant outdoors than in the dining room."

She gathered her pail and brush and rushed up the stairs, true to her state of constant motion.

Garrett returned the ladder and tools to the old carriage house and took his time poking around inside. Not exactly a barn, but used as one, with a couple of stalls that sported busted boards and feed troughs needing repair. Fixed up, it'd be a decent place for horses to winter.

A hooded jump-seat buggy sat in dusty neglect, its tucked leather seats dull and dry. Saddle soap, some oil to the wood, and he could have it looking in its prime. He'd not paid attention to it in the year or so he'd lived there, but had often wandered out to the pasture where a bay mare grazed. A small enclosure with a trough and pump at this end and a shallow creek cutting across the far corner, it had more than enough grass for the old girl.

Maybe if he offered to groom and grain the mare, fix up the so-called barn and buggy, and pay extra, Maggie'd let him board his gelding here as well.

It was worth a try.

He hung his hat on a fence post, pumped water into the trough, and stuck his head under the flow for a quick dousing. Pulling back, he flung his head, speckling his shirt and vest with water. He shoved his hair back, then dried his face and neck with his neckerchief, remembering earlier days in another town with George M. Booth.

Good days that ended in a bad way, pushing him back to the cattle drives and ultimately the job in Olin Springs. *The trail is no place to end your days*, Booth had prodded, *busted up, lonely, and poorer than Job's turkey. Nearly three decades alone are more than any man should tolerate.* Though Booth was still riding single and pushing sixty.

Resetting his hat, Garrett walked back past the carriage house and around through the orchard on the south end of Maggie's house. The architecture reminded him of the homes of wealthy mine owners, timber giants, and Wyoming cattle barons. Maggie never talked about her departed husband and how he'd made his money, just a rare mention of her "dear Daniel." And as far as Garrett knew, they'd had no children.

In spite of Booth's harping, Garrett knew the old marshal was right. He didn't want to end up with no family other than Pearl and Rink.

Maybe that was why Maggie took to Betsy so. Which, he admitted grudgingly, he could as well if it weren't for her infernal arrogant attitude, subtle lies, and obvious dislike of his dog.

Mounting the front stairs, he slowed at finding her curled up asleep on the porch swing. Her black lace-up shoes stood primly beneath the white slatted swing, and she lay tucked between its ends, one arm bent under her head, her expression guileless. Nothing about her hinted at the she-bear who'd fought it out with Pearl.

Two rockers and a small table fronted the house. Hanging his hat on the far rocker that angled toward the swing, he planted himself there to study his fellow boarder. He leaned forward, elbows on knees, as if he could peer inside that pretty head to what drove this gal like cattle before a hard storm.

And that's the way she found him when her eyes flew open at Maggie's unexpected announcement.

"Perfect timing again, wouldn't you say, Garrett?"

He straightened abruptly and coughed back a comment.

Betsy shot up like a startled rooster.

Maggie set a tray on the table. "Imagine the chance of finding you both out here enjoying the breeze." She poured two glasses of lemonade and gave one to each of them with a small napkin.

"I promise a hot meal this evening, but for now there are plenty of sandwiches here for you, plus the lemonade. Enjoy yourselves."

She then disappeared through her front door, closing it soundly. As if telling them to stay out.

Garrett's mouth watered at the lemon slice floating in his chilled glass, and he knocked back half the drink with one gulp.

Betsy held hers and the napkin in one hand, the swing seat with the other, and fished for her shoes with her feet.

He couldn't stop a chuckle.

She glared.

Which made him laugh outright. He walked over and took her glass. "I'll hold this while you get yourself shod."

She reached for the glass. "Don't bother."

He jerked it back, spilling cold lemonade on the floor. "My apologies, Mrs. Beaumont. Let me make it up to you." Then he topped off her glass from his own, some of his ice tumbling in.

But the chilled glass in his hand had nothing on the frosty woman in the swing.

~

Elizabeth pulled knots in her laces, trying to get her shoes on in front of a man rude enough to sit and watch her. But it was either struggle in front of him or walk in her stocking feet around the end of the house to the back. Maggie had probably locked the front door after her abrupt departure, and Elizabeth refused to beg admittance by knocking.

She leaned over to better reach her shoe and the swing dipped. Too late to counter the move, she toppled out.

Sheriff Wilson had her in hand before she had her wits.

"Are you all right?" Genuine alarm creased his brow.

His gentleness stunned her as much as the bare wooden floor, and she couldn't help but compare his concern with Anthony Rochester's smug appraisal.

With a hand on each arm, he helped her stand.

She instinctively gripped his forearms, as solid and strong as they'd appeared in the bathing room. The memory warmed her neck, and she lowered her hands and her gaze. "Thank you for your help. Again."

She carried her shoes to the other rocker. "Don't you have something better to do than watch me put on my shoes?"

He chose two roast beef sandwiches from the platter and sat in the swing, rocking it in great sweeps, his feet planted squarely on the veranda floor. "Now that you mention it." Raising one sandwich in a mock toast, he shoved the whole thing in his mouth.

Honestly. He'd fit right in at the ranch with Cade and Deacon.

A quick dart pinged her conscience. She should send word to Cade that she'd arrived. Which meant she must be employed first. Which meant she must decide about Rochester.

She pulled on her right boot, snugged the laces, and tied a neat bow.

Sheriff Wilson was still watching her. At least he chewed with his mouth closed.

As bold as he was, there was nothing lecherous in his perusal. More brotherly annoyance, if anything. Oddly enough, he did not make her uncomfortable. He simply watched, as if he were observing someone pass by his office.

What did he think about all day behind that metal star? Bandits? Outlaws? The price of bullets? She glanced at his gun, worn low and tied down, then picked up her left boot and went to work loosening the laces. "Do you happen to know the new attorney in town, Anthony Rochester?"

The sheriff continued watching, his expression unchanged. He swallowed the last of the second sandwich, finished his lemonade, and rested the glass on his knee, relaxing back against the swaying swing. "Do you happen to know Cade Parker?"

Surprised, her fingers fumbled. She stared at her shoe, stalling for an answer the second time in one day, as she slipped her foot inside, tightened the laces, and tied them off. Straightening with as much grace as possible, she met him head on. "I asked first."

His mouth ticked up on the scarred side. "Why do you ask?"

Infuriating man. How foolish to think she'd glimpsed compassion a moment ago. She leaned back in the rocker and picked up her lemonade. Two could play this game.

"Lovely afternoon, don't you think, Sheriff?"

"Garrett."

With him clearly in the corner of her eye, she focused her attention on Maggie's roses, blushing with their last amber and ruby blooms of the summer. Snow could be falling in six weeks—she'd seen it happen before. An azure sky one day blotted out by a blizzard the next.

A hearty gust blew through the open space, affirming her recollection, and caught the hem of her skirt and the sheriff's damp hair. He fingered it back with a broad, brown hand.

He needed a haircut.

She needed an answer.

Without employment, her small savings would vanish in a month. Cade would insist she return to the ranch. But he was married, and sooner rather than later, the two extra bedrooms would be filled with children.

Another dart snagged behind her ribs. She'd not thought of babies during those first few years in Denver. Not until she began seeing less and less of

Edward and realized she would more than likely end up on her own.

It was just as well. She couldn't afford to raise a child alone. Nor would she limp back to the ranch and live off Cade's generosity. He'd done enough. She would take care of herself.

The sheriff rose and in one long stride, stood before her, the toe of his boot skimming her skirt hem. Towering like a tree, he picked up the lemonade pitcher and refilled both glasses.

He emptied his to the dregs, leaned down as he returned it to Maggie's tray, and bore into Elizabeth with gun-metal eyes.

"He's a snake, Betsy." His voice had sunk with deep caution.

Unable to breathe, she held his gaze until he turned away. Down the front steps and across the street, his long, steady gait took him back toward town.

He turned the corner, and hand to her heart, she drew in as much air as her lungs would hold. She'd won the game, but not the prize.

As if on cue, Maggie flitted out through the front door. "Need more lemonade, dear?"

Elizabeth suspected the woman had watched—and listened—through the parlor window. "I have plenty, thank you."

Maggie took the other rocker with a deep sigh and gazed off in the direction of town. "So Garrett has returned to his office."

"He didn't say." A lot of things.

Another gust danced across the veranda.

Maggie lifted her face to it, inhaling deeply. "Garrett got my shutters on just in time."

Elizabeth looked at her sideways, curious about what Maggie did or did not know. Her tension stretched as wide as the clouds piled high upon themselves, denser and grayer than the earlier white-sailed ships. They were not the only storm churning. Sheriff Wilson was stirring into her background, for whatever reason. Perhaps he'd seen through her ruse, learned the facts elsewhere, and was now challenging her to be forthright.

"How did things go for you in town, dear?"

Another personal squall, though more pressing. "Only one person needs a type-writer, but I didn't give him an answer yet."

Maggie picked up the last sandwich, took a small bite, and pinned Elizabeth with bright expectancy.

"Mr. Rochester offered me a substantial salary."

"And you didn't accept right away?"

"I told him I'd let him know."

The older woman flashed a questioning glance but held her tongue.

Elizabeth sighed. Who else did she have to talk to? "He's checking my references. But something about him makes me uneasy. I can't put my finger on it, but on my way back this morning, I even considered cleaning and doing laundry—though I would never ask to do laundry here. I've not played the piano in years, and I doubt I could make enough teaching music to pay my board anyway."

"Posh." Maggie brushed sandwich crumbs off her lap. "You can do so much better than domestic service." She set the rocker in motion. "To be honest, I don't know anything about Mr. Rochester, aside from his impeccable manners and deportment. I've not needed an attorney's assistance for several years now, but I can ask the ladies at my next Library Committee meeting. Someone might know something more about him."

Stilling the rocker, she picked up the tray and balanced it on her narrow lap. "What did Garrett say?"

Maybe Maggie hadn't been eavesdropping after all. Or maybe she was playing her own game. How else would she know that Elizabeth had asked him about Mr. Rochester? "He said the attorney was a snake."

Maggie rose. "Then perhaps you're right to distrust Mr. Rochester. Garrett would tell you the truth."

Elizabeth sniffed. She'd believe a man spoke truth when he did so to his own detriment, but she'd keep her opinion to herself.

And yet, those gray-green eyes...

Maggie took the tray to the door she'd left slightly ajar and nudged it open with the toe of her shoe. "He spent more time here today than any day since he's been boarding." One dark brow arched beneath her snowy topknot. "Last year it took him weeks to get around to my storm shutters. That's why I asked so early this time."

Catching the questioning tilt of her landlady's head, Elizabeth folded her hands over a sudden flurry in her stomach.

CHAPTER 7

Pearl's tail swept up a flurry where she sat waiting behind the jail. Garrett turned her loose and watched her follow her nose from building to bush, scouting for just the right spot. Her search was as disjointed as his curiosity about Betsy Beaumont. He didn't have time to get sidetracked by some gal who hedged the truth and refused to give him a straight answer. And he sure didn't need her getting tied up with that attorney before he figured out exactly what the fella was up to.

He set out a bowl of fresh water and left the back door open.

At the front, someone tapped on the window.

He unlocked the front door.

"Afternoon, Sheriff." Holsom stepped inside and handed him a folded telegram. "Just arrived."

"Much obliged." Garrett fished a nickel from his vest pocket and gave it to the express agent for his trouble, then waited for the curious fella to leave.

Easing into his desk chair, he read the last line first: GMB.

Above it, brief and to the point, the six-word reply carried code from earlier days:

> Opened box. Found snake. Gold
> toothed.

Evidently, he and Booth had the same opinion.

A lesson he'd learned from his granddad rose up clear and sharp in his mind. Garrett had been eight years old, lying on his belly with a rifle aimed at a rattler coiled under his grandparents' house. He was more familiar with the shotgun, but Grandpa said they didn't need a hole in the kitchen floor.

Be wise as a serpent and harmless as a dove, the old preacher said. He was one for quoting the Good Book at the oddest times. *Watch him, son. A snake never takes his eyes off his prey.*

Garrett squeezed the trigger.

~

That afternoon, Elizabeth lifted her Remington from its crate, centered it near the front edge of the writing desk, and set the crate against the wall. With a hankie, she cleaned dust from the black finish on all exposed parts and gently wiped each ringed key, beginning with the numbers along the top row and continuing to the lettered keys of the second row— Q W E R T Y...

She took a blank sheet of paper from the back of her portfolio, then flipped a lever on the Remington and slid the sheet between the feed roller and rubber platen, rolling the paper in and straightening it along the top edge. A chair from a corner of the room seated her perfectly in front of the desk, at just the right height. She locked the type-writer into lower case, then straightened her skirt around her legs and poised her fingers above the keyboard. As if it were a piano.

Depressing the *Upper Case* key with the little finger of her right hand, she struck the letter E with the middle finger of her left hand and quickly released both keys. The rest of her name followed precisely and cleanly, like individual notes of a melody. A touch of the wooden bar beneath her thumbs added a space before the next word.

A knock at her door halted her practice. "Come in."

Maggie peaked around the door's edge, a slave to curiosity. "I heard clicking."

Elizabeth smiled at the childlike admission and waved her over. "I'll show you how it works."

Facing the desk again, she lifted the lever at the back of the machine that locked the letters into upper case and typed a few words. Then she lowered the lever, returning the letters to lower case, and continued, her fingers flying evenly over the keys, pausing only to press the *Upper Case* key occasionally with the little finger of her right hand, or to pull the carriage-lever gently forward and push it to the right.

"But where are the words?" Maggie leaned over the machine, squinting into its workings. "How do you know if you pressed the correct letters?"

An old confidence lifted Elizabeth's heart. "I always hit what I aim at." But to appease the woman, she rolled the platen until the type came into view.

Her name appeared first, followed by what she'd added for Maggie's benefit. Not a mistyped letter anywhere:

```
Elizabeth    Madeline    Parker
Beaumont
COME, THOU FOUNT
Come,  Thou  fount  of  every
blessing,  tune  my  heart  to
sing Thy grace.
```

Maggie's hand rested on her breast. "Oh, child, I remember your mother playing that hymn so beautifully and singing with all her heart."

So did Elizabeth.

At supper that evening, Maggie could speak of nothing but Elizabeth's demonstration. If only there were several boarders and not just one quiet man who flicked her an occasional glance, eyes amused. She was not funny. Had never been funny, and it took her back to the days of Cade's taunting when they were children.

"You should see her," Maggie boasted. "Calm as a sleeping baby's breath, yet quick and sharp and accurate." She cut into her fried chicken leg and poised her fork before popping the bite in her mouth. "She hits that for which she aims."

The scar twitched. "So you're saying she's a crack shot."

"That she is. Why, I remember one summer—"

"I'm sitting right here." Elizabeth glared at Garrett, challenging him to speak *to* her and not about her as if she were a child to be seen and not heard.

He scooped a mound of mashed potatoes, returned the spoon to the serving bowl, and resting his arm against the table's edge, looked at her full and long. From hair to chin. Lips to eyes. "Yes, you are. And most becomingly, I might add."

Maggie twittered.

Elizabeth tapped her foot against the carpeted floor, wishing for a hole into which she could fall.

After coffee and a generous helping of hot apple pie, Garrett excused himself, thanked Maggie, and left through the front door.

Elizabeth struggled for a deep breath, her corset straining against the meal and her frustration. She'd best curb her appetite or she'd be spending her salary on a new wardrobe. A salary that, at that instant, she chose to accept.

"Did you get enough, dear?" Maggie collected serving dishes, balancing two along one arm.

"More than enough, I'm afraid. I can't eat like this at every meal, or I'll be rolling onto Main Street and through the door of Mr. Rochester's office."

Maggie picked up her own plate and gave Elizabeth a surprisingly neutral look. "So you've decided."

"My options are rather limited. No one else in town needs my services. If he receives my references and the position is still available, I have no other choice."

Maggie's gaze warmed. "My dear, you *always* have a choice."

She disappeared into the kitchen.

Elizabeth could only disagree. Where was the choice if she had no control over the circumstances? The fount of blessing had dried up. Her parents were dead, Edward had abandoned her, and Hatchett had disgraced her and let her go. Poverty lurked at her door. Where was her choice in any of those situations? Rather than making things happen, she was stuck with making the best of what did happen.

Discouragement congealed like the white pan gravy in Maggie's china gravy boat.

A dull breeze shifted the lace curtain at the end of the room, signaling additional betrayal. The storm had circled Olin Springs, possibly dissipating. Clouds without rain.

Elizabeth laid her silverware across her plate, unaccustomed to heaviness of limb from overeating. She needed fresh air, a vigorous walk.

Avoiding the sheriff's retreat, she took the back door next to his now-enclosed quarters.

Evening's long, blue fingers reached across the grounds, flirting with the light breaking through distant clouds behind her. *Foreboding,* her mother had always called the odd mix of light and dark. As a child, Elizabeth had thought she was saying *for boating.*

The memory brought a smile.

She approached a small barn. Slanted light washed its graying boards, and crickets called, stirring the taste of home long left behind. A pasture rolled out beyond the old building. She continued toward the fence, and a bay mare lifted its head and pricked its ears.

Just beyond the horse, a glint of light winked. No wonder the grass was so lush and green, unlike the tall, sturdy range grass of Parker Land and Cattle. The narrow fall of a stream cut across one back corner and meandered south, disappearing onto neighboring property.

The bay also meandered, telegraphing its intention every few steps with a flicked ear, working its way toward her. Latent joy bubbled up, a reminder of carefree days riding her beloved Blanca, gentling colts in the home corral with Cade, and frustrating him with her inborn knack for the job.

A clearing throat turned her sharply.

Tall and back-lit, the silhouette was several yards away. Not close enough to make his footfall heard, he'd let her know he was there.

"Evening." Garrett's voice flowed deeper than before, blending with the shadows, and he joined her at the fence with a polite distance between them.

She lifted her hand to the mare that stood with outstretched neck, whiffling at the newcomers.

"She hasn't come to me like that, and I've lived here almost two years."

Pride tugged, and Elizabeth tamped it down. No need to be arrogant. "People say I have a way with horses."

"Cade Parker one of 'em?"

She'd walked into that one with eyes and mouth wide open.

Rubbing the mare's head, she reached up under the forelock. Why dodge the matter? He obviously knew the truth, or part of it. "The first one. Besides our pa."

He set his hat farther back, pulled something from inside his vest, and clicked his tongue.

The mare looked over, nostrils flaring in and out, testing the scent. Then she walked unhurriedly his way and lipped a carrot from his palm.

Elizabeth scoffed. "Bribery gets them every time."

"So will kindness."

An odd thing for a gunman to say. She slid a glance at his profile. Stern, sharp-planed. He'd seen other than kindness in his time. But he was proving more surprising at each turn.

"When it's accepted."

Case in point. Apparently, he also hit what he aimed at.

She dodged. "How did you end up with a dog named Pearl? Rather than Pirate or Purloiner?"

He allowed a small laugh, almost a pleasant sound. "You have a knack with words."

A compliment or a dig, she couldn't tell.

"She was an irritating little thing."

Elizabeth looked at him straight on. "Little?"

He gave an easy smile.

She fought to not return the gesture, so genuine was his reaction to her puzzlement.

"For a half-breed Irish wolfhound, she's on the smaller side," he said.

"She's not the right size or color for pearls. That's like naming this bay Ivory."

"It's not about color."

Elizabeth was losing her bid for neutral conversation, along with her patience.

"As a pup, she was an irritant. I figured I could let her be a burr under my skin or smooth her over with kindness. Like a pearl in an oyster."

And how would a lawman know about oysters and pearls unless he was more than he appeared to be? She pulled her arms close against her waist.

"She's lived up to her name. Turned out to be a real charmer. Unless something shiny catches her eye."

Elizabeth snorted, then slapped a hand over her mouth. Ladies did not holler, sprawl, or snort, yet she'd excelled in all three since that dog came into the picture.

The sheriff chuckled and rubbed the mare's neck. "I'll gladly pay for the damages."

"That won't be necessary, Sheriff."

"Garrett."

He said it more to the horse than to her.

She crossed her arms, fisting her fingers where he couldn't see them.

"And what if I insisted?" Was he inviting a showdown? Would he next challenge her to a shooting match, a riding contest? Did he break broncs and brand cattle?

She turned for the house. Thunder rolled off the nearest ridge, dragging the storm back to Olin Springs. A fat rain drop splashed her shoulder.

"Elizabeth."

Reflexively she stopped at the warm tone, thought better of it, and continued on.

He was at her elbow, again soundlessly, as if he were part Ute. A second drop struck her forehead, but she faced him, half curious about what he'd say next.

He raised his hand to touch her arm, but caught himself and drew it back. Unlike his commanding presence, his voice came gentle. "Be careful with Rochester."

His comment snagged her as surely as a prickly pear, and she stood caught by his dark look. Another fat drop, then another. Lightning pierced her peripheral vision and she flinched.

He gripped her arm and they ran for the back door, drenched by the time they reached it.

CHAPTER 8

Garrett drenched his hotcakes in blackberry syrup, then cut into the stack of three. Betsy's chair sat empty and lonesome, and Maggie kept looking toward the door to the hallway, her expectation as clear as the sunshine through the dining room window.

The storm had washed a week's worth of dust from the air and cleared a few things in his mind as well. "Have you ever thought of renting out your pasture?"

Maggie acted as if she hadn't heard him, but he knew for a fact she could hear a whisper in a windstorm. Probably knew he'd sneaked into Betsy's room, but he waited for her to sip her tea. He'd learned as a lawman that if he didn't fill the silence, the other person usually did.

"No, I haven't. Lolly's had that pasture to herself as long as we—I've lived here." She covered her single cake with currant jam. "Why do you ask?"

He hadn't mouthed the mare, but he'd put her at twenty-five, if not older. Without exercise, she was growin' a grass belly, and a little company might do her good. "Would you consider letting me board my gelding here? Plenty of feed for two horses, three even. I'd pay extra, make repairs in the shed, and polish up that old buggy."

Maggie cut a small bite off her cake and thoroughly chewed it before taking another. He'd have wolfed it all in two.

The mantle clock kept time with the woman's jaw, ticking the rhythm of the pancake's demise. He finished his coffee and tucked his napkin under his plate, something he'd seen Betsy do. Blasted woman was as irritating as Pearl had been.

He pulled the napkin out, dropped it on top, and pushed from the table.

Maggie looked at his plate, then up at him. "I think we could work something out. Would you drive her once in a while?"

The mare. Right. He ran his hand over his mouth, not liking the picture of himself in a buggy, taking a spin through town. Maybe on a back road. For Maggie. "Once in a while."

Her head bobbed twice. "All right. If you'll do all you say, you can keep your horse here for no extra fee. But if they start fighting,"—she leveled a hard glare—"he'll have to go back to the livery."

"Fair enough." Garrett set his hat and tugged it down. "Appreciate it, Maggie."

She rose and picked up her plate and the coffeepot. "Why didn't you think of this last year?"

He had no idea. And he didn't like the accusation in her voice. "Didn't occur to me." He touched his brim. "See you this evenin'."

He didn't miss the irony of moving Rink in with a female, a situation similar to his own, though he wasn't no gelding. George Booth would laugh him into the next county.

Out the front door and through the gate. He stopped to latch it and glanced up at Betsy's window. Opened, curtains pulled aside. Unable to resist the taunt, he slid two fingers along his hat brim in salute, then turned toward town with a grin.

~

Elizabeth stood back from the window, glad she'd parted the curtains and certain the sheriff couldn't see her. She gasped when he looked up as if he could.

Her heart lurched. What was it about that man that put her on edge, on guard, and on pins and needles all at the same time?

Thank goodness, he was gone.

Her yellow cotton day dress spoke of spring rather than advancing autumn, but her wardrobe was as limited as her employment options. She twisted her hair into a bun, smoothed her skirt with a final glance in the cheval mirror, and went downstairs.

Maggie had insisted Elizabeth enjoy the bathing tub last night after coming in soaked to the skin from the storm. The bath had warmed and refreshed her, and she'd slept better than she had in months.

An untouched place setting waited, but she picked up her cup and saucer and took them to the kitchen. "Good morning, Maggie."

Pots and pans clanked in a sudsy bath. "I wondered if you'd slipped out early, dear. I have hotcakes in the bread warmer, and it will take me no time at all to scramble up some eggs."

Elizabeth hefted the big coffee pot from the range. "I couldn't eat a bite, but thank you just the same. I'm still full from last night."

She pulled out a chair and helped herself to the hand-painted sugar and cream set centered on the small table.

Maggie dried her hands on her apron and joined her. "The Ladies' Library Committee meets today, and I'll inquire—discreetly, of course—about Mr. Rochester. Bertha Fairfax mentioned something about him two weeks ago, but I paid her no mind." She added sugar to her coffee. "That woman is always fussing about something, but I don't want to ignore her if anything is truly amiss."

Elizabeth's uneasiness stirred like Maggie's spoon—silent, slow, and steady. But she must have work. And if Mr. Rochester hired her, she could always resign if he was anything like someone else she'd worked for.

She sipped her coffee. If he was anything other than above reproach.

"I'm sure all will be well." Frankly, she wasn't sure about anything. She really must get a handle on this habit of lying at the drop of a hat.

"I'll be walking to services tomorrow, dear. I hope you don't mind. But with the weather still warm, I much prefer walking to taking the buggy."

The assumptions of others had always irritated Elizabeth—like a splinter in the finger that one couldn't see well enough to remove. But Maggie Snowfield was not easily put off, and Elizabeth would not intentionally hurt her for the world. "I don't mind at all."

A short visit later, she stepped through the spired gate, determined to face the music Maggie had mentioned. And the best place for a Saturday morning dance was the mercantile.

Purged of dust and residue by the previous night's storm, the air sparkled with promise, winking from dewy grass tips fringing the roadway and shimmering in scattered puddles. She'd not seen a post office during her earlier walk through town, so with the letter she'd penned to Cade last night, she marched toward Reynolds' Mercantile.

Traffic on Main Street was heavier, children bobbing from the backs of farm wagons come to town for groceries and supplies. Pausing at the corner, she waited for an opening, then dashed across the road, up onto the boardwalk, and into the past.

A small brass bell clinked. The scent of lye soap, spices, leather, and dry goods whirled around her, drawing her eyelids down until all she could see were her mother's boots peeking beneath her skirt, her hand tightly clutching Elizabeth's pudgy fingers.

"Mornin', Miss."

Stunned by the impact of memory, she opened her eyes to Fred Reynolds, the spitting image of himself and not a year older, unloading a crate behind the counter. His wife, Willa, attacked canned goods with a gray feather duster.

She glanced Elizabeth's way, continuing to hunt down and dispense with all foreign particles—then jerked to a halt and whirled.

"Betsy Parker? Is that you?"

Willa and Maggie could have been sisters, though Willa's hair had silvered rather than gone white. She set down her duster, pressed her hands against her apron, and approached with wonder and disbelief.

Elizabeth swallowed a soap-cake-sized lump. "Hello, Willa."

The rail of a woman swept her into a hearty hug, then stepped back and dabbed her eyes with her apron hem. "Child, I thought I'd never see you again. But, oh my, you are no longer a child."

Elizabeth could have warded off winter with the heat in her cheeks.

Willa drew in a sharp breath and her glance deflected over Elizabeth's shoulder. "Oh, Betsy—"

Elizabeth turned, ready for the worst, and met the welcoming gaze of a beautiful woman near her own age.

A long dark braid hung over her shoulder, and she reached out with one hand. The other rested against her rounded belly. "Betsy, I'm so glad to finally meet you. Cade has told me so much about you."

Cade? About her? Numbly, she took the woman's hand.

"I'm Mae Anne. Cade's wife." She glanced at their joined hands.

Elizabeth realized she was squeezing and released her grip. "Please forgive me. It is an unexpected pleasure to meet you, Mae Ann."

She'd been prepared to dance, but she hadn't envisioned this partner. An involuntary glance darted toward Mae Ann's condition. "Is Cade with you?"

Gentle laughter brightened brown eyes. "No, he's at the ranch, getting ready for roundup and fit to be tied that I insisted on driving myself in." Absently, her hand caressed her protruding belly. With the other, she touched Elizabeth's forearm.

"You must come out to the ranch. I know he'd be thrilled to see you. So would Deacon."

Elizabeth's heart gave way. How she'd missed that old cowboy and his orneriness, as full of love and wit as a hive was of honey.

Mae Ann glanced out the window as if looking for someone. "Are you, um, visiting?"

"Not exactly." Elizabeth fumbled in her skirt pocket and drew out the letter. "I'm here to stay, if all goes as hoped. I'm employed here in town." Or she would be soon. "I've written to Cade and was about to post it. Would you mind?"

Mae Ann reached for the letter. "I'd be happy to."

"It explains everything. I hope. He wasn't exactly— he wasn't expecting me. Not on any specific day, that is. He knew I was returning, but he didn't know when. Things just worked out…"

Perspiration warmed her brow and she felt like a child trying to excuse her tardiness to the teacher. "You're as lovely as Cade wrote in his letters."

Did Mae Ann know about the money he'd sent? "I'll come out to the ranch, just not…yet." Her gaze flicked again to the precious bundle hidden beneath discreet folds.

Mae Ann leaned in and lowered her voice. "The baby is due near Thanksgiving. So our celebration may be light, if I'm abed and unable to get around. But please, consider this an invitation, and I do hope you'll come sooner."

Elizabeth took her hand. "I'll try. And best to you and the baby. I'm sure things will be, well, they'll be fine. And you'll be fine." She patted Mae Ann's hand. "I really must go."

She turned to find Willa busying herself near enough to hear every word. "Good day, Willa, Mr. Reynolds."

She paused at the door and looked back at the beautiful woman in the blossom of motherhood. "Thank you for giving Cade the letter."

Once more on the boardwalk, Elizabeth was much worse for wear. She should have eaten breakfast. Fingering a few coins in her skirt pocket, she walked to the café, hoping for a pastry and a cup of coffee. And no surprises. Facing the music was as exhausting as any day on a roundup, and dinner was hours away. Her stomach rolled like an empty bandbox.

CHAPTER 9

Freighters rolled by. Farm wagons and buggies. Maybe Rochester was right and more people were moving in.

Garrett scouted the south end of town where, even at this distance, hammering rang out of the Olin Springs Hotel. He planned to look around some more, poke through Clarence Thatcher's brain. Garrett had an itch about the fire that needed scratching. But first, he'd gather Rink and his outfit, and pay his bill at the livery.

Tacked up like he was striking out, Garrett raised the suspicion of his sometime deputy, Erik Schmidt, who pinged his hammer on the anvil, set a shoe around the horn, and gave Garrett a curious once-over.

He pulled up. "I'm not leaving town, just moving Rink to Snowfield's place."

"Is *gut*." The burly, elder German tapped a curve in the shoe. "Business is *gut* too. Lots of people, lots of horses."

The big man's "tap" was an ordinary man's full-out, double-fisted swing, guaranteed to make a rebel rouser think twice about resisting. The prime reason Garrett hired him when he needed extra help.

He rode out of the livery and to the opposite end of Main Street, gathering a few looks along the way. It felt good to sit a saddle again, a condition that came natural to him and the one thing he missed most in his position as lawman. He needed to ride more. Rink needed it too. Would so even more now that he'd be out on grass till snow flew.

Maybe Betsy would ride with him, judging by Maggie's boasting of her skills.

He palmed his face with one hand, irritated that such a thought could ambush him when he had important matters to attend to.

A new hitching post stood in front of the hotel, and Garrett laid reins to the rail. Thatcher was overseeing a carpenter framing in a registration counter in the lobby.

"Mornin'." Garrett offered.

The carpenter didn't look any too happy, and Thatcher's mood matched. "Sheriff."

"I'm not here to visit, Clarence, but I've got a question. Do you remember who was in the last room upstairs on the south end the night of the fire?"

Thatcher frowned and rubbed a jaw that needed to see the barber. "Lost most of my register, so I can't say for sure. But I know a dry goods drummer had come through the day before. Paid up front for two nights. Course, he didn't get the second night, but I never saw him again. Why?"

"How about local folks. Anyone from town take a room?"

"That new tailor, Hiram Eisner, and his wife. They'd been here two nights. But they were at the other end of the hall."

"Anyone else from town?" Just a name. All he needed was a name, the right name, and it'd scratch his itch.

"No. Middle of the week like it was, I had fewer guests. Most folks around here have their own place. Rochester, now, that new attorney. He rented a room for about a week when he first came to town. But I heard he's staying in a spare room at his office."

Garrett ground his back teeth. Not what he wanted to hear.

"Why? You have any ideas about who started the fire?"

"Just working out a theory." Garrett tipped his hat. "Obliged."

~

Snowy powder lifted beneath Elizabeth's nose as she bit into a sugar-dusted *bear sign*. Nibbling and chuckling, she made her way back to the boarding house, savoring Hoss Bozeman's thunderstruck look. He'd thought he was pulling a fast one, but the joke was on him when she flicked not an eyelash at the name he gave his pastries.

She'd grown up eating Deacon's bear sign on roundups. The best doughnuts she'd ever had.

All considered, the day was a success. No one in Bozeman's café seemed to recognize her, including Hoss. Someone else had owned the place when she was growing up, and customers were scant this late in the morning. Willa Reynolds had, of course, and sweet as she was, she could be counted on to set the gossip bell tolling longer and louder than tomorrow morning's call to worship. Before Pastor Bittman got the front door open, everyone who had known Elizabeth would know she'd returned.

At the moment, she faced Maggie's front door glass, squinting at her reflection, brushing around her mouth for traces of powdered sugar and greatly relieved that Cade would know tonight that she was in town.

It wasn't that she didn't want to see her brother, she simply wanted to be established first. Yet it was cowardly of her to ask Mae Ann to deliver the letter rather than riding out to the ranch herself. But that would require hiring a buggy or finding someone to let her ride their horse.

And she wasn't about to ask Sheriff Wilson for help.

She opened the door and walked straight into the delectable aroma of seasoned chicken. Maggie's humming funneled down the hallway, drawing Elizabeth to the comfort of the kitchen.

"It smells so good in here."

"Oh, you're home." Maggie smiled over her shoulder while rolling out a pie crust on the table. "I wondered how long you'd be gone today."

"Are you sure I can't do something to help?" Her sense of accomplishment fueled the need to continue, though she'd rather not attempt anything like actual cooking. Not exactly her strong suit.

"Oh, no. My residents don't do any of the work. You're paying for all this, you know." Maggie brushed her brow with the back of her flour-covered hand. "Unless, of course, it's something I can't do on my own and you happen to be six feet tall and very strong."

And handsome.

Elizabeth nearly stomped her foot, grateful that she hadn't voiced the thought.

Maggie threw her a sparkly-eyed glance. "He is quite handsome, isn't he?"

If her landlady read minds, Elizabeth was in a fix. "Well then, if you don't need my help, I'll fetch my sewing kit and try to make amends with my reticule."

"A clever turn of phrase, dear. You should be writing for the newspaper."

"I noticed their newly painted storefront. Business must be good."

"Oh, it is. Mr. Fisher himself goes door-to-door seeking subscriptions, advertisements, and news. He probably knows more than the bartender at the Pike and all the ladies in my library group put together."

Elizabeth's mental cataloguing of her landlady's exploits expanded to include not only a buggy-whipping scene, but one of the woman dragging information out of the Pike's bartender. Elizabeth wouldn't be surprised if she had campaigned for the women's suffrage referendum four years ago. Given Maggie's fervor, it was surprising that it had failed.

Upstairs, she rummaged through her trunk for her small sewing kit and picked up the ruined reticule. Already the days were skimping on sunlight, and soon darkness would lock her indoors. She retired to the veranda, choosing a more stable rocker over the lulling swing.

Fluffy clouds clung to the northern mountains, and bits and pieces had broken off and floated down toward Olin Springs's wide, grassy valley, suggesting another evening storm. The guarding elm tree ruffled in a slow breeze, and her anxiety eased a bit.

Maggie's inclusion of her in the mention of home had touched a place in her heart long neglected, and it raised a sigh in her breast.

By contrast, there was the totally inexplicable Sheriff Garrett Wilson who simply raised her perplexity. The mere thought of him affected her reflexes, and she jabbed the end of her middle finger on a loose needle. She held the wound to lips rather than stain her skirt or reticule—as if that mattered.

Half the beads were missing and the velvet was stiff with dog drool. Disgusting. But the bit of navy fabric presented just the creative challenge she needed, thanks to Pearl.

What an absolutely incongruous name for that half-breed dog.

She left her kit on the side table, then carried her reticule around the house and out to the small pasture, lifting her face to the breeze. It teased at her hair, loosening strands that tickled her nose. Succumbing to a childish impulse, she pulled the hair pins from the knot at her neck, and let her hair fall.

How long had it been since she'd felt such freedom?

The mare met her at the fence.

Elizabeth slipped her pins into her skirt pocket, her reticule cord over her wrist, and lifted the pump handle, cupping her hand beneath the flow. "It's cold, girl. Invigorating, right?"

The horse whiffled the water as it fell through Elizabeth's fingers, and tossed her head in agreement. Elizabeth laughed, grateful to be away from the city and close to the land again.

She worked the handle and held her bag beneath the clear water, regretting for the millionth time running away with the wrong man. How could she have been so foolish? In spite of the searing pain of losing her mother, she should have known the fire was hotter than the frying pan.

Dirt and slobber washed away at her kneading, and soon her reticule glistened, lovely again in spite of its missing beads and a large tear. She shut the pump off, smoothed the velvet nap in a singular direction, and turned the bag inside out. The mare lifted her head and whinnied.

~

In all his days, Garrett hadn't seen anything prettier.

He slowed Rink to an easy walk, and the gelding's ears pricked toward the bay and the woman by the trough.

Her loose hair rippled about her shoulders like shadowed prairie grass, inviting his fingers to pull through its length.

Rink tossed his head. Either an answer to the mare or his opinion of Garrett's distraction.

Betsy watched them until he drew rein at the fence and dismounted. Rink reached for the trough, and Garrett pulled him up short, removed the headstall, and let him drink.

"He's beautiful."

He leaned into his horse as if whispering a secret. "Don't take it personal. She meant it as a compliment."

Laughter, the first he'd heard from his fellow boarder, fell like a clear stream pouring into a shallow pool. It caught him by surprise.

"Is he really so easily offended, or would that be his owner's interpretation?"

She moved in and ran her hand down Rink's neck and over his shoulder as if judging his worth by her touch.

Garrett stepped back, out of temptation's reach. "You have a good eye."

She flicked that eye his way, applying her judgment to him. "Daddy had a small band of mares. Cade and I worked the youngsters, trained some for buggies, others for riding."

"*You* broke horses?"

Another sharp-eyed appraisal, more scathing than the first.

Where was his poker face—and voice—when he needed it? "I mean, you broke horses."

She slid along the gelding, her left arm draped easy over Rink's hind quarters as she stepped around to the other side. Not her first time handling horseflesh.

"I like to think of it as gentling rather than break-ing," she said. "A broken horse—like a person—isn't much good for anything."

Surprises just kept piling up.

"So what moniker did you choose for this regal roan? Surely not Diamond or Glaze or Gunmetal."

"What makes you think I'd call him some fandan-gled name like that?"

"Well, you did name that monstrosity of a dog *Pearl*. I expect you'd have something equally imaginative for your horse."

He cleared his throat and coughed out the name.

"What?" Her challenging eyes barely cleared the gelding's withers.

"Rink."

She stared.

He frowned.

"And what's the story for this name?"

Wasn't any of her business, but she was being sociable. He looped a rein over Rink's neck. "I named him after my grandfather. Only thing he hated more than sin was his given name. Said he'd rather be called Rink. It stuck."

"Sin?" Her voice rose at the end of the word.

"He was a preacher."

"What was his given name?"

Garrett sized her up, gauging her willingness to trade information, whether she'd be party to give and take. "Why'd you choose Elizabeth over Betsy?"

She moved to the gelding's neck, hiding her expressive eyes. "Always a lawman, answering a question with a question."

"Only the unanswered ones."

She puffed out her irritation but stood her ground, Rink between them like a barrier. Her arm came up under the gelding's neck and she ran her hand down along his chest. Easy. Confident. As familiar with his horse as if it was hers.

"I had a horse once."

The admission wasn't what he'd been waiting for, and if the night hadn't been as quiet as it was, he'd have missed it altogether.

"What happened to it?"

"I don't know. Maybe she's still there, at the ranch. In a way, I don't want to find out, because if she's gone…"

He heard the fissure in her voice, the first, tiny opening into the Betsy side of her. He tugged Rink back, removing the wall.

Though she stood not two feet from him, she was somewhere else, staring off over his shoulder and into the past, thumbing her empty ring finger.

"Blanca." Her dark eyes shifted to his. "Not very imaginative of me. No story to go with it. But I thought it fit her at the time."

A young girl's white horse. "Better than Ivory."

She almost smiled and glanced at Snowfield's bay mare before walking back to the house.

He led Rink into a stall, unsaddled and brushed him down, then gave him a can of oats. Her answer wasn't what he'd wanted, but he was satisfied for the time being with one more piece of the puzzle that was Betsy Beaumont.

Everything he touched in the buggy shed, from the stall door to the saddle racks in the tack room, puffed up a dust cloud. Must've been decades since anyone had used this place.

Satisfied that all was well, he made sure the barn door to the pasture was open so the mare could come in if she wanted, then headed for the house.

Slapping his hat on his leg, he stomped the dust off his boots. It seemed like he dirtied up the place every time he walked into that fancy dining room in his work clothes. But the togs he wore were all he had, other than the leftovers he sported when these were stiff enough to stand up on their own. Didn't matter what he looked like when he had an appointment out back of the jail with the washboard and a soap cake.

Didn't matter what he looked like, period—if he kept his horse groomed, his jail clean, and his jaw shaved.

A quick scrape of his hand proved he'd slacked off there some.

Another shirt and trousers wouldn't take that much from his steady pay. Maybe a new vest. Out of respect for Maggie and her fine house, of course. In fact, he could use a haircut too.

First thing Monday morning, he'd pay Bartholomew Ward a visit, then check out that new haberdashery that Hiram Eisner opened up on Main Street.

CHAPTER 10

First thing Sunday morning, Elizabeth wrote a quick note telling Sophie Price when and how she'd arrived in Olin Springs, apologizing for not letting her know ahead of time. If Sophie and her family showed up at church, she'd give her the note. If not, she'd post it the next day.

She tucked the letter in her skirt pocket, and checked the mirror, assuring herself she was as put-together as possible. Satisfied, she folded a fresh sheet of paper from her satchel, and took a pencil from the desk drawer. Pastor Bittman's sermon would be the perfect opportunity to practice her stenography.

Garrett was not at breakfast, and Elizabeth offered thanks for small blessings. He had a way of pressing in where he wasn't wanted, and last night she'd let down her guard. A foolish thing to do. Admonishing herself to be more careful, she focused on Maggie's light fare of oatmeal and toasted bread.

On the way to church, she worked to keep up with her landlady, who dashed off as if she were marching to glory. They were the first to arrive at the chapel besides Pastor Bittman, his wife, Millie, and a darling daughter toddling down the aisle toward her mother. Elizabeth suspected Maggie had planned things accordingly.

"Betsy." Pastor Bittman's welcome touched a wellspring that threatened to overflow. "It's so good to see you again. I do hope you'll be staying for a while."

"With me, Pastor. Elizabeth is boarding with me for the time being."

He appeared to pick up an unspoken message from Maggie's brief explanation and smiled accordingly. "Home is a good place to be."

Odd that he classified Maggie's house as home instead of the Parker ranch. Or perhaps he meant Olin Springs in general. Regardless, Elizabeth was grateful for his acceptance. Two blessings in one morning.

The welcome from Pastor Bittman and later Millie steeled Elizabeth for tsking head-shakers who would no doubt make their opinions known. She followed Maggie to a pew halfway to the front on the left side. After a few matronly parishioners frowned their disapproval in passing, Elizabeth relaxed. Their judgmental glares were not as hard to bear as she'd feared. Either that or they were constrained to behave with Christian charity inside the church.

"Since you've no Scriptures, dear, you may share with me." Maggie's whisper was a tender gesture.

Elizabeth had a small book of prayers that she'd taken from her mother's dressing table before the funeral, but the family Bible was all she'd ever known growing up, and she assumed it was still in her father's desk.

As if returning to a familiar trail through a forest, she instinctively knew when to stand during the service or bow her head in communal prayer. Words to hymns long left unsung came to her lips without reading the hymnal, but most surprising of all was the rich baritone that rolled over the pews and people behind her. She knew without looking that Garrett Wilson was the one who lifted his voice with such controlled strength and gentle warmth.

When Pastor Bittman directed everyone to the next hymn, she suspected Maggie had somehow requested the number. Each stanza held a tender glimpse of Elizabeth's childhood, but at the third, her voice diminished to a whisper. "Prone to wander, Lord I feel it..."

With a tingling rush across her skin, she knew she was not *prone* to wander, not at all. For she'd already proven that she had.

~

The next morning, Elizabeth rose early, dressed in her simple business attire, and secured her straw hat above her knotted hair. She tucked Sophie's note in her skirt pocket, then brushed her fingers across the Remington's white keys before going downstairs.

Too nervous to eat, she appeased Maggie by accepting a cup of coffee.

"I want to be clear-headed and sharp this morning, and I can't do that if I fill up on your wonderful cooking."

Maggie saw through the flattery and set a biscuit and jam in front of her. "You need your strength as well as your edge, dear."

Garrett Wilson had eaten and left, and for that Elizabeth was grateful. In the name of clear-headedness, he posed a stumbling block, particularly now that she knew what he called his horse and how well he sang. The man was an enigma.

After a brisk walk to Anthony Rochester's office, she entered to find him writing.

He laid his pen aside and rose, smug satisfaction darting across his features.

"Good day, Mrs. Beaumont. I do hope you are bringing me good news."

She pulled the door quietly closed. A small walnut table and matching chair sat against the opposite wall, lined up precisely with Mr. Rochester's desk. Her pulse shortened its stride to a fitful skip. No turning back.

He came around his desk and adjusted the angle of one of his captain's chairs, offering it to her, then returned to his own, leaning back in quiet perusal.

Only then did she realize she'd left her portfolio on the writing desk in her room. Perched on the edge of her seat, she had nothing to occupy her hands, so she folded them in her lap, straining for an air of ease.

"Is your position for a type-writer still available?"

"Indeed it is." A thin brow arched like a drawn bow. "Are you willing?"

To do what? "And the salary is unchanged?"

He nodded slowly, with an obsidian hold.

She could bolt for the door before he left his chair.

"Did you receive a reference from my previous employer?"

He slid a telegram from beneath his desk blotter. "Sterling," he said, unfolding it and glancing over the message before returning it to its hiding place.

She would give her first day's salary to read what Erma Clarke had written. Forcing calm into her fingers and her heart, she stood and pressed her hands to the sides of her skirt. "Then I will get my type-writer and return shortly."

"Magnificent." He got up and ushered her to the door, a light touch at the dip of her waist as he reached for the knob.

She went cold, repugnance gripping her by the throat. His fingers seemed to linger near the lock before turning the brass knob.

Almost imperceptibly, his head bent closer to hers. "I look forward to your return."

She drew back at his breath on her hair, his cologne strong and biting.

"We've much to do."

She crossed the threshold, one leaden step in front of the other. *Do not run.*

A left turn took her the length of his curtained window, her heels ticking against the weathered boardwalk, carrying her closer to the street corner. *Do not run.*

Once safely beyond his view of the side street, she hiked her skirt and bolted for the boarding house.

~

Garrett held a cup of charred coffee, elbows cocked on the blue-checkered cloth of Bozeman's corner table. The new chambray shirt chafed.

The door to Rochester's office opened and Betsy stepped through. She hadn't been inside five minutes. Did she tell the crook no?

Silently, the coffee cup touched the cloth. Garrett's hand slid to his holster, an old habit brought on by the chill at his neck that always flagged trouble.

Betsy walked to the corner, ramrod straight, head rigid, lacking the grace and ease she normally moved with. At the cross street, she glanced over her left shoulder, closest the building, stepped around the corner, and ran.

Garrett's heart slammed into his throat and he launched to his feet, rocking the table and spilling the coffee.

Bozeman looked up from where he was wiping down the counter.

Garrett tossed him a coin and hit the door in full stride, one eye on Rochester's place, the other on Betsy. If he blew through the attorney's door, he'd tip his hand. He had to find out first what had happened. But he couldn't chase her down and frighten her even more. If he hailed her, she'd know he'd followed her. Which was worse—his aching need to know or her ire if she learned he'd been watching?

He picked up his pace at the alley, trotted across and up the block, then paused at Snowfield's street. Betsy was fighting with the gate. He walked her way, shortening his stride, becoming as nonchalant as he knew how.

"Is it stuck?"

At his question, her head jerked up. Fear flashed in her rounded eyes, then relief. Her shoulders sagged and she stopped fumbling with the iron clasp. One arm hugged her waist, the other went to her throat.

His trigger finger flinched. "Let me help you with that."

He fully expected her to reject his offer and continue battling the gate, but she stood waiting. Her chest rose and fell as if she'd run all the way from the other end of town.

She didn't move back as he approached. He had to lean into her lavender scent to reach the latch, and he came close to reaching for her instead. Drawing her close and holding her until her breathing slowed and her color returned.

The clasp flipped up, and he pushed the gate inward.

She hurried through but stopped at the steps, hands gripping her skirt in preparation to climb. The tops of her black lace-ups showed. "Thank you, Sheriff."

No sneer. No retort or deflecting half-truth. Just honest gratitude before she rushed up the steps and through the front door.

But it was still *Sheriff.* He had to get her to talk.

~

Elizabeth fell back against the closed door to her room, shoving her hat askew and sucking air like a winded horse. She held both hands out in front of her, palms down, and they trembled like aspen in an autumn breeze. How would she be able to work with her hands shaking so?

It had been worse than she expected. The confinement of the small office, cramped even further with the additional table and chair. Mr. Rochester's black, all-seeing eyes. As if he knew.

She curled her fingers and walked to the mirror, appalled by the pallor of her skin. "You need this job," she scolded. "Get ahold of yourself. This is not Denver. And Anthony Rochester is not Braxton Hatchett."

At the washstand she removed her hat, rolled up her sleeves, and splashed tepid water on her face and arms. Droplets spotted her white shirtwaist, but they would dry. She repinned the bun at her neck, and rather than attempt dabbing on rouge with shaking fingers, she pinched color into her cheeks.

Nervous energy made light work of loading her Remington. Hat in place and crate in hand, she started downstairs.

Garrett Wilson stood like a wooden Indian at the front door, its beveled glass a halo to his rigid shoulders. What was he doing? Serving as self-appointed doorman?

A blanching suspicion passed through her. He'd seen her run from town.

She was so very good at doing all the things she should not.

Unable to hold the railing, she descended slowly, her gaze flicking between the next step and the sheriff— feet spread, arms crossed, hat low. His impervious posture appeared a dare as much as anything. What she did or did not do was no concern of his, and he'd better not try to prevent her from leaving.

With temper tightening her hold on the crate, she considered ignoring him and leaving through the back door. But that was wishful thinking at best, recalling his long, galloping stride. He'd get there well before her.

Instead, she braced herself for his inquisition, resentful of, yet grudgingly calmed by his presence.

He relaxed his arms and came toward her when she reached the bottom of the staircase. "I'll carry that for you."

It was neither request nor offer. Simply a stated fact, as if he'd said, "The sky is blue."

Without argument, she allowed him to take the crate from her. He hitched it under one arm and opened the front door.

She raised her chin, assuming a stoic, professional demeanor. "I'm going to Mr. Rochester's office next to the feed store."

She descended the front steps before him.

His boots echoed across the veranda in her wake.

"I know where it is."

He didn't sound exactly pleased, but she was not in the sheriff-pleasing business. She was in the survival business, and at the moment, that meant working for Anthony Rochester, Esquire.

Fumbling with her empty hands, she hid them in her skirt pockets and discovered the note she'd written to Sophie. She'd intended to take it to Reynolds' Mercantile before she went to Mr. Rochester's office earlier.

This time the gate latch yielded, and she stepped through. "I must make a detour to the mercantile. I have a letter to post."

He stood like a tree inside the gate, shaded, unreadable. "On one condition."

Irritation wiggled up her spine. Now he was making deals? "Which is?"

"You call me Garrett."

His plain, hard tone left no room for argument.

Clenching her jaw, she drew a deep breath through her nose. "Very well."

She continued on, expecting him to follow, which he did not. Stopping, she faced him, her jaw tight. Had those tall boots sprouted roots right there in front of Maggie Snowfield's spired fence?

His head rose a notch. That was a look she'd seen before. He wasn't bluffing.

Annoyance puffed from her lips, but low enough that he couldn't hear it. "Very well, *Garrett.*"

A smile threatened, softening slate eyes in a surprisingly appealing way.

She turned around before she smiled back into that face with a dimpled scar.

~

At Main Street, Betsy turned south for the mercantile. Garrett easily moved ahead of her and opened the door. Fred Reynolds looked surprised to see him, but didn't speak to it. "Good morning, Betsy. How can I help you?"

She glanced at the mail slots behind the counter. "Does Todd Price ever stop by and check the mail for his family?"

"Regular as clockwork. At least when he's in school. This is his last year, and some days he doesn't ride in. Helping his ma work the farm and all."

Betsy drew a folded letter from her skirt and turned it over to reveal *Sophie Price* in elegant script rather than blocky print from the type-writer.

"I'd like to leave this for Sophie, if you don't mind. I'll be glad to pay postage."

Reynolds waved that off and took the letter. "No charge, Betsy. It's just good to have you back home after all this time."

She looked down at her empty hands and her voice quieted. "Is there by any chance a letter for me from Cade?"

He sobered some. "No. Not yet. But if he came to town to mail it, he'd probably just come find you. Unless he sent it with Todd, of course."

She offered a polite but empty smile. "Of course. Thank you."

As they left, she looked up at the clinking bell, melancholy dousing her usual fire.

A pin pricked Garrett's chest, and he slid his right hand beneath his vest. The badge was intact. He was not.

Betsy kept her eyes down on their way to Rochester's office, walking so slowly that Garrett nearly had to shuffle to stay with her. Tiny beads of sweat popped out on her temple, and with one hand, she fingered her collar.

A raw urge to protect her tightened like a cinch around his lungs.

"You all right?"

She stared straight ahead, not exactly focused on anything, but lost in a place he couldn't see. He wanted to help her but didn't have the slightest idea what to do other than haul her type-writer to Rochester's. And sit in there with her, making sure the lawyer didn't get too close.

That'd be the day.

Dad-blasted woman had his brain in a knot. Her fiery-eyed ire was preferred over this. He swiped his hand across his mouth and jaw. "We could get a cup of coffee at the café."

She looked at him, her face mirroring thoughts that tied her to some other time. Then she jerked her head quick-like. "What? I'm sorry. What did you say?"

He swallowed. "You want some coffee? Café's just a few doors down."

"Oh." Her pace picked up some. "No. Thank you. I need to get to Mr. Rochester's."

Like she needed a three-legged horse.

Speak o' the devil, the man himself was peering through his window, the dark curtain giving the appearance that the top of his head was floating. A definite frown sank his expectant look, and he moved to the door as they reached his office.

"Mrs. Beaumont, I do apologize. I would have been happy to carry your type-writer for you." An ice house couldn't hold the glare he shot above Betsy's head.

Garrett warmed to the challenge. "No need, Rochester. Got it handled."

Betsy went to a small table against the far wall, and Garrett set the crate on top.

"Thank you, Garrett." She did not look up.

Rochester sniffed behind him.

Garrett tipped his hat. "My pleasure, Elizabeth."

He left her fussing over the machine and the attorney steaming around his collar. Best morning he'd had in a spell.

CHAPTER 11

Elizabeth sat spellbound, her view from the small table confined to the brown velvet curtains and a strip of daylight above them. She might as well be in jail. With Garrett Wilson.

A slightly disturbing thought.

She had avoided looking at him when he left because she didn't want him to leave—also disturbing. He'd called her Elizabeth.

Shaking off a sense of abandonment, she adjusted her Remington against the table's edge, placed her hat behind it, then glanced across the narrow room. Her new employer was watching her, tracing his thin mustache with thumb and forefinger as if considering how to consume her. She'd rather face the foul-smelling Pearl, but she had to give this job a chance.

"You mentioned that you had quite a bit of work for today. What would you like me to begin with?"

He hesitated a moment, then picked up the box of stationery on his desk and brought it to her. It barely fit beside her type-writer.

Next he gave her several hand-written letters. "Print these out for me. Or type-write, whatever you call it. Let me know if you can't read my writing."

He returned to his desk, gathered a few papers, and, without a word, left through a door at the back of the room, which he closed behind him.

She relaxed in her chair. Not sure how she would let him know anything, as he had suggested, she was grateful that he wouldn't be sitting there watching her work or standing over her shoulder.

Each letter was written in bold, pointed script, sharply slanted to the right with a slash over every *i* rather than a dot. Not only had she learned to typewrite, but thanks to her mentor, Miss Clarke, she'd learned to recognize handwriting patterns and quickly decipher nearly illegible penmanship.

She held a sheet of fine letterhead to the window's light, revealing a clear watermark near the bottom edge. At the top, *Anthony D. Rochester, Esq.* arched in heavy print over a larger, more ornate underscore: *Attorney at Law.* The overall effect made quite an impressive statement, as attorneys were wont to do.

She chuckled at the stuffy phrasing used so often by Miss Clarke, but the woman was spot on. Fitting a sheet between the roller and platen, she fed it into her Remington, leveled the paper, and started on the first letter to a Mr. Charles Hayworth of Kansas City, Missouri.

After the fifth letter, she walked to the window and pressed both hands into the small of her back, arching against tight muscles. A shadowless street agreed with her lapel watch that it was just after noon, as did several people coming and going at the café two doors down across the way. Her stomach rumbled a reminder of the breakfast she'd declined, a timely word to the wise for tomorrow.

The door at the back of the room opened, startling her.

"Finished already?"

Unfamiliar with his tone, she neutralized her own as she returned to her table. "Five are completed if you care to review them." She held out the crisp sheets, but he ignored them as he lowered himself into his chair. Reluctantly, she crossed the short distance and laid them on his desk.

His manner was much brusquer than it had been earlier that morning, to her great relief. Taking her seat, she positioned a clean sheet of letterhead in the machine.

True to his calling, Mr. Rochester had quite a dramatic flair with his words. His punctuation was precise, his grammar pristine. She merely copied what he had written, making few corrections.

In two hours' time, she finished the remaining letters—seven in all, two of which were quite lengthy and required two sheets. Several of the letters were addressed to local businesses regarding property ownership, or leases, taxes, and such. The two longer letters were addressed to Kansas City and mentioned contracts to follow. She felt they were written in a form of code. Each one said basically the same thing, referring to various flowers and blossoms.

She had no idea what Rochester was talking about.

Mid-afternoon slanted through the narrow gap above the curtains, increasingly bright and irritating as the sun dropped toward the mountains, shining directly in her eyes. Of all the stores on Main Street, the cobbler directly across the road did not have a second floor or a false front. Afternoons would be painful until the sun traveled farther south on its way to winter.

"Will there be anything else today, Mr. Rochester?" She stood and laid her work on the corner of his desk, then placed his original handwritten letters in a separate stack.

He continued to read from a thick book opened before him, possibly unaware that she had spoken. Quite a feat in a room so close.

It occurred to her that he had no law library. No shelves upon shelves of leather-bound tomes, as common in an attorney's office as shoe lasts in a cobbler's shop. She scooted her chair in, toed the crate against the wall, and picked up her hat. "Very well, then. I will see you tomorrow."

He looked up as if surprised. "Pardon me if I don't see you out."

"I am an employee, Mr. Rochester. There is no need to see me out."

"Tomorrow, then. Nine o'clock."

She gave a courteous nod and stepped out onto the boardwalk, drinking in great gulps of semi-fresh air as she closed the door. Though muddled with dirt, horse manure, and axel grease, the street was a flowing brook compared to Mr. Rochester's stagnant office.

She arrived at the boarding house well before supper, so she went straight to her room. From the wardrobe shelf holding her petticoats, she retrieved her small leather journal and an embossed box with her Esterbrook Lincoln pen, a cherished gift from Erma Clarke at the Denver train station.

Even now she could feel the warmth of the woman's gloved hand as she pressed the slender box into Elizabeth's. *You may be an exceptional type-writer, but every writer needs an exceptional pen.*

Erma may well have saved Elizabeth's life, taking her side in the fray and helping her get her things to the station. She'd certainly saved her sanity.

Eager to record the information while it was still fresh in her mind, Elizabeth pushed the curtains wide for the last rays of sunlight, and sat down at the small desk. She dipped her gold-nibbed pen in the ink from the desk, opened the journal, and left one blank page between her new entries and those from Gladstone, Hatchett and Son.

September 3, 1881, Olin Springs, Colorado
Curious Correspondence for Anthony D.
Rochester, Esquire
Mr. Charles Hayworth of Kansas City,
Missouri

Eleven more entries followed, as well as the flower or blossom mentioned if one was included in the letter. Red bud, poinsettia, quince. *Hanabi* was the only unfamiliar variety.

She capped her pen and placed it in the desk drawer. While the ink dried on the page, she opened her trunk, pushed several winter items aside, and pressed a point near the right corner at the bottom of the trunk. Her journal slid into the tight space where it fit neatly atop her other Remington.

After returning everything to its previous order, she drew the curtains and went downstairs.

She was starving.

Garrett's mouth watered as he came through the back door and left his hat in his room. Even blindfolded and hog-tied, he'd have been able to find his way to the dining table. He tucked the day's newspaper beneath his arm, grateful that he had neither constraint, and followed his nose to a spread that looked more like a church potluck than supper.

Chicken pot pies, biscuits, butter, and preserves. A mess of green beans with bacon and onion, sliced tomatoes, and fresh berry cobbler. He moaned in anticipation.

Betsy took her place looking pale and spent, which merely riled his curiosity over what she'd done all day in that stuffy office with that overbearing peacock.

Maggie set a tea service at Betsy's end of the table, then came back with the coffee pot and filled his cup.

"My dears, I hope I did not fail to make it clear that I serve dinner promptly at twelve o'clock every day of the week."

Even though it was the woman's way, it rankled Garrett every time she included him as a *dear*.

In the silence that followed, he could almost hear her cock one brow.

"Well, did I?"

"Clear as Pike's watered-down whiskey. Not that I imbibe, mind you," he said, coughing around the words. How was it she could make him feel guilty for something he didn't do?

Betsy made no sound or sign.

"I am not fond of throwing all my preparations to the chickens, hence this heavily laden table this evening.

117

So if you are not going to come to the board, please let me know ahead of time."

Betsy pressed her napkin to perfectly clean lips.

"And Betsy—pardon me—Elizabeth. No breakfast. No dinner. Does that Mr. Rochester not let you leave for a meal?"

Garrett's hackles rose.

"I'm sure he does, but I didn't think of it today." She poured herself a cup of tea. "I was busy with his correspondence."

"Well, if he doesn't, I will see to it that he changes his mind."

Garrett stifled a remark. At the steel in Maggie's voice, he had no doubt she would.

"I see you brought the newspaper with you this evening, Garrett. More news of President Garfield's condition since the shooting?"

"A small article reprinted from the *Rocky Mountain News*." Garrett helped himself to a hearty serving of pot pie, suddenly regretting bringing the paper. It had been his ace in the hole, a diversion if conversation turned to Rink and Pearl.

Now he felt like a turncoat betraying the innocent. "Not much, really, other than a different picture of the hotel fire."

"There must be something that inspired you to bring it. What did Mr. Fischer have to say about our fine community this week?"

He glanced at Betsy, who kept her head down, studying each bite she took as if it were her last. The newspaper had been a bad idea. A very bad idea.

Maggie reached across the table, palm up, demanding. She could be a federal marshal. Better yet, a judge.

He handed it over.

Unfolding it, she held it beside her, skimming the headlines. By the movement of her eyes, she paused at the fire photograph, then dropped to the bottom-right corner of the front page:

Surreptitious Arrival of Former Resident

She refolded the paper and dropped it beneath her chair. "You are correct. Not much."

She cut him a scolding look, but kept her thoughts to herself. Betsy missed the whole thing.

After he finished a second serving of everything, Maggie scooped blackberry cobbler onto a small plate and set it in front of him, then did the same for Betsy and herself. "The Library Committee met today and enjoyed a nice tea."

Betsy returned from wherever she'd been. "Did you speak to Mrs. Fairfax?"

"I did, and both you and Garrett may be interested in what she had to say."

Garrett doubted that he'd care what Bertha Fairfax or any of the other matronly library supporters had to say, but manners kept his opinion contained and his mouth shut. Except when he was filling it with cobbler.

"Mrs. Fairfax has been paying Anthony Rochester a rather steep monthly premium for fire insurance on her home."

CHAPTER 12

A fire sparked in Garrett's eyes, and he nearly choked on his cobbler. Elizabeth momentarily considered dousing him with her tea. She hadn't seen rage ignite so instantaneously since her father.

The difference, however, was in Garrett's self-restraint.

"How long has she been making payments?" He wiped berry juice from his mouth and clenched his teeth while waiting for Maggie's reply. The bulging muscle in his jaw gave him away.

"A month. Bertha said she was reluctant at first, but after the hotel fire, she was only too happy to have already insured her property."

"Why is she paying Rochester and not sending premiums to an insurance company?" Elizabeth asked.

Maggie scraped up her last bite of cobbler. "I posed that very same question." Plating her silverware, pushed her dish aside, and poured herself a cup of tea. She glanced at Elizabeth, teapot in hand. "May I warm your cup, dear?"

Garrett cracked his knuckles beneath the table, his jaw flexing like a pumping heart.

Elizabeth scooted her teacup toward the center. "Thank you."

"What'd she say?" Garrett's tone was as hard and cold as the old skating pond in winter. Something besides insurance premiums fueled his dislike of Anthony Rochester. Perhaps the same something that had motivated him to haul her Remington to the attorney's office this morning.

"Bertha's exact words were, 'Mr. Rochester said he was here to do all he could, and helping make things easier on me was one of them.'"

Garrett mumbled into his coffee cup, but Elizabeth was certain she heard, "I'll bet."

"And the other ladies," she added. "Have any of them bought fire insurance?"

Maggie stirred sugar into her tea. "Two or three. Much of the meeting was taken up by discussion of insuring the library, and the great cultural loss we would all suffer should the old house go up in smoke."

It was difficult to watch the shadows shift across Garrett's face and keep an eye on Maggie's expression at the same time. Elizabeth felt as if she were looking through a stereoscope without benefit of the two scenes meshing.

Garrett stood. "Thank you for supper. I have some work at the jail this evening."

"I'll leave the back door unlocked for you," Maggie said.

Not allowed to help in the kitchen, Elizabeth retired early. The day's events replayed through her mind in rapid succession. As she sat at the dressing table brushing her hair, she reviewed Garrett's obvious displeasure at their landlady's news, his relentless determination to escort her to work, and what he'd said several days ago about Anthony Rochester.

The snake image disturbed her, and she tugged her wrapper close and blew out the lamp. Before crawling into bed, she tip-toed to the window. As if someone would hear her. Ridiculous. She parted the curtains she'd drawn earlier, looking as far as she could angle to the south. In the next block, Rink stood saddled and tied behind the jail, gleaming in the moonlight as if he were nickel plated.

Odd that Garrett had ridden the short distance and not walked.

Leaving the curtain parted, she climbed into bed, understanding in a visceral sense why he would ride any distance, given the chance. She ached to do the same since returning to Olin Springs, to feel the strength of a fine animal beneath her, wield the power associated with a mere flick of her fingers or inflection of a knee. She longed for Blanca and feared that Cade had sold her.

The next day dawned decidedly cooler. Elizabeth laid out a light cape before going downstairs, but left her heavier petticoats and warmer stockings in her trunk, saving them for the snowy months.

That morning, and for the remainder of the week, she ate a filling breakfast and returned at midday for dinner. Mr. Rochester made no objection to her leaving, and on Friday at noon told her she did not need to return until Monday. However, he paid her for a full week, an act he probably considered generous. She did not. Indebtedness and favors led only to unwanted pressure in the future. But since he paid her with a check, she could not refuse the extra half-day's wage.

Before leaving town, she opened a savings account at the bank into which she deposited half her earnings. The other half went into her mended reticule. Much of the day remained, so she stopped by the livery and inquired about the price of renting a horse, then strolled the length of town perusing store windows. She visited the Eisners' tailor shop and haberdashery and congratulated the couple on their recent opening.

The hotel flaunted its unpleasant aroma before it came into view, and the noise of reconstruction drowned out all sounds of traffic as she approached. She'd love to know if the owner had purchased fire insurance from Mr. Rochester. Perhaps in her position, she'd soon find out.

Crossing at the saloon positioned conveniently across the street from the hotel, she glanced over the batwing doors into the shady interior. No out-of-tune piano music, its operator possibly sleeping away the day in preparation for tonight's revelry. She often heard the rowdy evening choruses from her open window in the Snowfield home.

The jail sat squarely in the middle of the next block, as if centering the town like the hub of a wheel. A flatiron held the front door open wide. The morning's chill had burned off beneath a warm midday sun, and Garrett might have regretted the fire in the stove that she saw as she hurried past the doorway.

"Hold up!"

Halting at the deep command, she regretted her response—as if he had the right to tell her what to do.

Heavy iron scraped across the plank floor, followed by boot steps and the stout door closing soundly behind her.

"I'll walk with you."

It would be rude and petty to ignore his offer and walk away. But honestly, the man had no idea how to request. He simply announced.

"We don't want to keep Maggie waiting dinner on us, do we?"

Elizabeth was no longer part of a *we,* and she resented the familiarity it insinuated. She and the sheriff might be the only two boarders Maggie Snowfield had, but they were not a *we.* She charged ahead.

His long stride kept easy pace. From the corner of her eye, she could tell he was more relaxed this afternoon. Not the tense, angry man who had stormed from the supper table Monday evening.

"What brings you to this end of town?"

She'd seen little of him during the week, other than at meals, and she resisted the amicable companionship he seemed to be offering now. Her affairs were none of his concern. "Just seeing the sights."

He scoffed.

His reaction was so similar to Cade's when they were children that she had to take tight hold of her skirt to keep from slugging Garrett in the arm.

"Do you have siblings?" The question popped out without her permission.

Another one-syllable sound equivalent to what his horse would make, and then a complete sentence. "Why do you ask? Do I seem like a big brother?"

"Hardly."

More like a big irritant. That actually qualified him for the big-brother category, now that she thought about it. But *brotherly* was not how she viewed him. Not at all. Exasperated by her reactions to his warm voice and simple kindness, she quickened her pace.

He matched it. "You must be hungry."

She looked straight ahead.

"Either that or you're in a race."

Hiking her skirt and sprinting would be completely unacceptable. Unless she tripped him first.

~

"Garrett, I've used the last of the fresh milk and would appreciate you riding out to Travine Price's farm for me tomorrow. That is, if you don't have any outlaws to chase down."

His mouth was full of beef stew, and he'd bet a week's wages Maggie had timed her assault.

"It's the perfect opportunity to exercise Lolly, per our agreement." A quick glance his way followed her weighted reference.

"Elizabeth, dear, pass the biscuits, please. Oh, and I have something for you."

She went to the side board and returned with a letter. "I picked up my mail this morning, and this had come for you."

Maggie Snowfield couldn't have been easier to read if she'd laid her cards face-up on the table.

Reaching for a biscuit, she added, "Forgive me, but I couldn't help noticing Sophie's name on the envelope. What a perfect opportunity tomorrow would be for you to visit her, since Garrett is making the trip anyway. I know you and Sophie were the best of friends in school."

He allowed that Betsy did an admirable job of not spewing her meat and potatoes across the table. Poor gal hadn't seen it coming.

"Two birds with one stone and all that, you know." Maggie gave them each an innocent smile and continued with her meal as if she hadn't just railroaded the both of them.

Looked like he'd be airing out ol' Lolly tomorrow.

Riding to the ranch with Betsy Beaumont wasn't the worst idea he'd ever heard, though he'd prefer to do it without benefit of a buggy. But a deal was a deal.

Friday nights in Olin Springs weren't exactly churchlike, so he spent the afternoon cleaning up the buggy and oiling the harness. The seat was in better repair than he expected.

Later, he stopped by the livery and asked Erik to cover for him Saturday morning. Shouldn't be much trouble, he assured the big man. Most of the drunks would be sleeping off their Friday night frolicking, and not up and around until Garrett returned. He'd leave an extra badge on the desk, and Erik could pick it up in the morning.

A couple hours after dark, two rowdies insisted on spending the night in jail, and Garrett had them bedded down and sawing logs before midnight.

The next morning they were sobered up and thick-tongued enough to leave without much of a squabble. He was glad the farm boy hadn't been one of them.

Counting on everybody to mind their manners while he skirted the countryside with Betsy and ol'

Lolly, he left the front door unlocked for Erik and called Pearl to follow him out the back.

She didn't. The rangy mutt knew he was gonna tie her up. She could tell when he was about to ride, and a buggy made no difference. Her mournful look branded him a louse for leaving her behind.

"All right, you can go."

Danged if the dog didn't understand plain English. This time he was ready for her leaping gratitude. Tall as she was, she'd nearly knocked him down a time or two.

"You'd better not greet Betsy Beaumont that way or she's liable to beat you off with one of Maggie's frying pans."

Pearl dropped to her haunches, sweeping the floor with her ropey tail, eyes bright as torches.

He tied the lead to her collar and walked to the buggy shed, where he tethered her to a wheel for good measure before fetching Betsy.

Good thing.

The second that Betsy saw Pearl, she planted herself in front of him like a fence post.

He nearly ran into the back of her.

"Whoa—"

"I am not riding with that monster."

"Just hold on." He stepped around her, and there sat Pearl on the clean buggy seat, nearly smiling at him. No wonder Betsy balked.

"Get down."

Pearl gave him a hangdog look as she lumbered to the ground. Then she spotted Betsy.

"No!" Stepping on the rope, he stopped the charge, then half-hitched Pearl to the nearest stall door.

Betsy hadn't moved. She looked more like an *Elizabeth* now with her straw hat perched atop her rigid head, reticule clutched at her waist, staring holes clear through him. He could almost feel a breeze.

"You can't be serious."

"What?"

Her eyes narrowed to slits.

He tugged his hat down and brushed dusty paw prints off the leather seat. There were entirely too many females trying to wrangle his life.

Satisfied, he wiped his hands on his trousers and offered to hand her up. "You comin'?"

She sure was uppity for a ranch gal, something he'd like to hear more about on their trip to the Price farm if he could pry it from her perfect lips.

He switched hands, offering the cleaner of the two. "You got something against dogs?"

She gathered her skirt, accepted his hand, and climbed to the seat. "Not if they have manners."

"Pearl has manners."

Betsy snorted. She'd done so several times since he'd made her acquaintance. *That* said rancher's daughter more than anything else about her.

He untied the dog, coiled and tossed the rope in the buggy, and headed out, avoiding Main Street and driving along the road that fronted the depot. Pride was a merciless master.

At the outskirts of town, he set the old mare to an easy trot, surprised at her smooth gait. Pearl charged past them like a runaway train, but she'd keep him in range. Her manners might be wanting, but her loyalty wasn't.

Betsy's stiff posture relaxed after a mile or so, and she drank in the countryside like a drunk took to liquor. She wouldn't appreciate the appraisal, but he could sense the near desperation without even looking at her. It radiated from her like heat from the jail's potbelly stove.

He chuckled at his poor comparisons, neither of them something a lady would liken herself to.

"What's so funny?" She gave him that uppity down-her-nose glare even though he topped her by a few inches.

"Just a wild-hare thought."

"About Maggie Snowfield's 'two birds with one stone'?"

He laughed outright. "Picked up on that, did you?"

"I thought Maggie was above such machinations. Travine Price is not the only woman in the county with a milk cow. Why, Willa Reynolds probably knows of one closer. I wouldn't be surprised if she and Fred had a cow themselves. They do sell butter at the mercantile, you know." She brushed at her skirt, smoothing wrinkles from her lap. "But it will be good to see Sophie, and well, your *agreement* with Maggie precluded searching for a nearby bovine."

"And I'll just bet you'd like to know what that agreement is."

A sharp scoff turned her head to the scenery again. "It obviously has something to do with you keeping Rink in the pasture."

He swallowed a laugh. Curiosity crawled her like prickly on a cactus pear. He slowed the mare to a walk. "Lolly needs her exercise, and I offered to drive her out once in a while and clean up the buggy and barn if I could board Rink with her."

Betsy studied the mare, tipping her head to the side. "That seems fair. She does have a grass belly on her, and at her age, exercise will keep her from stoving up."

For certain, the woman had grown up around horses. So why wasn't she on the ranch instead of in town?

He rubbed a spot on the back of his neck, conceding that Maggie was right about one thing. The outing *was* a perfect opportunity—one he had no intention of passing up.

"Since we're clearing the air, I figure it's my turn now."

A sharp look arrowed past, just missing his nose. "Your turn for what?"

"Questions."

She huffed. "Ask away. No answers promised."

No surprise there, but it was worth a shot.

"What's the real reason you came back to Olin Springs?"

CHAPTER 13

R eason had nothing to do with it.

Elizabeth had been enjoying the outing, feeding her hungry soul on the scenes of her childhood, and marveling at the graceful ease with which that otherwise gangly dog loped across the grassland. She'd let her guard down again, in spite of her resolve, and Sheriff Garrett Wilson had picked it up and run off with it, the opportunistic lout.

How had she allowed herself to get into this fix? She folded her hands in her lap. "That's really none of your concern."

Sitting so close, his silent chuckle vibrated through the seat.

"In my line of work, I make everything my concern. Especially a woman who is on her own."

"How magnanimous of you." That was just the kind of attitude that got her back up. As if she couldn't take care of herself. "Truth be told—"

"Which you haven't done since you got here."

Her head snapped his way.

"Have you." Not a question.

Trapped as surely as if he'd thrown her in jail, she turned away from his ever-present badge and holstered gun, and watched the dry grass and stony roadway slide by. She was imprisoned in a narrow buggy with a man she didn't know asking about her past and doubting her veracity. If Pearl wasn't gamboling about, Elizabeth would have gladly walked the rest of the way to the Price farm.

"You lied to me."

"I beg your pardon."

"You're not married."

"Who told you that?"

He reached for her left hand.

She tucked it under her arm, but he grabbed her wrist and pulled. His rough hand held hers aloft, and he ran his thumb over the faint line circling her ring finger.

She jerked away, but not before his strength and warmth made an unwanted impression. And not far enough to outdistance Maggie's warning to tell him the truth of her divorced state.

Divorce was such an ugly word.

However, she'd never said she wasn't divorced.

Legally, she still bore her married name. Emotionally, she never had. But she wore the unseen yet definitive boundary of matrimony like a shield in certain circumstances, such as in the offices of Gladstone, Hatchett and Son and Anthony Rochester.

With Garrett Wilson, it had been merely habit to pronounce the *Mrs.* in front of her name when she arrived in town, and *Beaumont* rather than *Parker*. Now might be the time to correct the misconception.

"The question is, why? Why would you come back to your hometown, lead everyone to believe you're married, and not go home to the family ranch?"

Or not. She buried her burning fingers in the folds of her skirt and blinked away the frustration that threatened to do more than threaten. "Don't you have better things to busy yourself with? Like hunting down real criminals?"

"Tell me one thing."

She stared straight ahead.

"How long has it been since you've been home?"

She wanted to defend herself. Explain her reason for leaving like she had, her reason for staying away. Her reason for returning now. But she couldn't justify herself to herself, let alone, to him. Let the facts speak for themselves.

"Six years."

Without further inquisition, he raised the ribbons and snapped Lolly into a trot. The rolling grassland and scattered scrub oak that had drawn her back to better days now fled past as if running from her. What power words had to dampen one's spirit—a truth she had too quickly forgotten.

After some time, the Price windmill bloomed like a steel flower on the horizon, and Garrett drove as if he had every intention of passing by the turnoff.

"You've never been out here, have you?"

He shot her a frown.

"Turn here."

Lolly drew up beneath his quick hand and backed a few paces.

Elizabeth fully expected him to chide her for not letting him know sooner, but he said nothing. She may have finally succeeded in silencing him.

Oddly enough, she wasn't sure if she liked that.

He slowed as they drove into the yard, where a familiar buckskin stood at the hitch rail. She'd know that horse anywhere.

Straightening and checking the position of her hat, she looked around at the outbuildings and barn and squinted to see between the corral rails.

Travine Price stood at the derrick tower, her head tilted back, one hand on her aproned waist and the other blocking the sun. At the sound of their arrival, she turned to scrutinize her visitors. Ruthless winters and endless farm work had etched their stories in deep lines. But the eyes—her eyes still said Travine Price was a beautiful woman where it mattered most. On the inside.

"Mornin', ma'am." Garrett slowed Lolly to a stop and touched the brim of his hat. "Sheriff Wilson and—"

Travine rushed to the buggy. "It's not Todd, is it?" Her worry flashed between Garrett and Elizabeth as she searched for an answer before hearing an explanation.

He jumped down. "No, ma'am. Far as I know, he's fine and working hard at school. I'm here for Margaret Snowfield. She'd like some fresh milk for her boarding house, if you have extra." His usual attendant humor was missing, and as he faced Elizabeth, the small scar lay cold against his cheek. "And there's someone to see your daughter."

Now she was merely *someone*.

Puzzled, Travine looked again at Elizabeth until recognition dawned and her hands reached out. "Oh, Betsy, look at you! All grown up."

Elizabeth climbed down into Travine's embrace— the closest thing she'd felt to a mother's love in a long, long time.

134

A creaking whir scratched across the morning, and they all looked up as the windmill began its slow and steady turn. A tall, angular man made his way down from the platform, his back to the onlookers until he stepped to the ground.

Elizabeth's heart nearly burst through her bodice.

The man offered his hand to Garrett, his silvery mustache not as bushy as she remembered. Then he turned toward her and the years fell away.

She was a young girl learning to gentle a skittish foal. Older, at the fallen cottonwood, aiming for tins lined up like soldiers on the dry, white bark until she pinged them from their perches. And older still, sneaking her carpet bag into the back of the wagon, caught by his sad, knowing eyes. Not a word. Just a slight shake of his head.

She'd never said good-bye.

Wild horses, they say. Wild horses could not have kept her from him, and he caught her up and swept her off the ground in his tough old arms, as strong as they ever were. A catch in his chest answered her own quaking breath.

"Deacon," she whispered. "I've missed you so."

Gently he set her down and held her at arm's length, his old blue gaze misty with memory. "A fine woman you've become, Betsy girl. A fine woman."

She'd never be Elizabeth to Deacon. Only his Betsy.

"Well now, come inside, all of you." Travine swiped a quick hand across her eyes and shooed everyone toward the house. "I'll get that milk out of the root cellar, Sheriff, and then we can all have a cup of coffee and some of my apple fritters."

Elizabeth fell in beside Deacon, his long arm draped around her shoulders. Garrett followed a step behind.

She glanced back and caught a glint of gray light, fleeting but there nonetheless. Gentleness had settled around his mouth, and he looked at her as though he'd never seen her before.

What had happened to his lawman's calloused questioning?

~

Garrett knew Deacon Jewett was Cade Parker's foreman. He'd seen him in town a time or two, but this welcome at the Price farm was unexpected. Elizabeth Betsy Parker Beaumont was a passel of unanswered questions.

He and Deacon washed at a bench behind the frame farm house.

"When'd she get in?" Deacon's rusty voice did a poor job of hiding his feelings.

"Couple weeks ago."

The old cowboy dried his hands on the roller towel, then stepped back for Garrett to hunt a dry spot.

They entered through the kitchen, filled mostly by an old cook stove and a large table, where the sweet aroma of coffee and fritters drew everyone together. Cups and saucers waited.

Mrs. Price poured coffee round the table, but with Deacon, she laid a hand on his shoulder and poured slowly, stretching out the time she stood there. Garrett glanced at Betsy, who'd also caught the gesture.

"Sophie's at the ranch, checking on Mae Ann." Taking a seat at the end of the table nearest the stove, Mrs. Price pushed a plate of fritters toward Deacon on her right. "Cade's as nervous as a goose at Christmas. This being their first child and all."

"I saw Mae Ann at the mercantile a week ago," Betsy said. "She appeared happy and healthy, and just as sweet as Cade mentioned in his letters."

"So Cade knew you were coming home?"

Deacon cut a look at Betsy, but he missed the shade that drew across her face.

"Not exactly." She studied her fritter. "He knew I would be returning, he just didn't know when."

Garrett bit into a fried pastry, hiding his reaction to her partial explanation.

Silence settled like a blanket, and he helped himself to another fritter.

"Deacon rode over early this morning to fetch help for Mae Ann, and Sophie said she'd go." Mrs. Price's weathered cheeks pinked. "When he saw the windmill wasn't turning, he stayed to work on it for me."

It never ceased to amaze Garrett that in the face of silence, a person's nerves would drive them to say more than was necessary. Except in the case of Betsy Beaumont.

Deacon coughed and fidgeted. "Weren't nothin' much."

Betsy rolled her lips and kept her head down.

Garrett could have eaten a half dozen fritters but reined himself in at three.

"Thank you, ma'am, for sharing your fine cooking with us, but I best get that milk to Mrs. Snowfield."

She sprang up like a much younger woman. "Oh yes, I nearly forgot. I'll be right back."

When the door closed sharply behind her, Deacon zeroed in on Betsy. "You gonna stop by the ranch?"

She dallied with her coffee cup and flashed him a questioning look.

"It's all right, girl. Cade got your note. He ain't mad. Just distracted with his missus in the family way and all."

Betsy's shoulders eased and her eyes puddled, but she managed to maintain a calm front.

"Won't be much outta your way," he offered.

Garrett stood and took his cup and saucer to the sink. "We've got time."

He stepped out the back door, giving Betsy some time with Deacon, then met up with Mrs. Price at the buggy. He gave her Maggie's money, took the two quart jars she'd brought, and set them in a basket under the seat with toweling bunched between them.

Betsy and Deacon came out, and the old cowboy handed her up.

Garrett joined her on the bench.

The Price woman stepped in close to Deacon as if she belonged there.

"Thank you, both." Betsy's voice caught, and she cleared her throat and pulled herself up stiff and straight. "I'll see you again."

Deacon jerked a quick nod and may have smiled. Garrett wasn't sure. Mrs. Price dabbed her eyes with her apron corner and waved as they drove out of the yard.

If he didn't know better, he'd think those two were Betsy's parents.

Pearl trotted out from behind the barn, and Garrett hoped she hadn't been chasing chickens. He hadn't heard squawking and she didn't have any feathers growing out of her mouth, but he wouldn't put it past her.

At the end of the farm road, he slid a sidelong glance toward his passenger, who sat staring straight ahead as if eyeing her firing squad.

"I know your brother, but I've had no occasion to come out to the ranch, so you best tell me where it is."

"Northwest as the crow flies, but the next cut off will get you there."

"I suppose Deacon takes the crow's route."

A near laugh puffed out and she relaxed a notch. "Yes, I imagine he does."

"Were you surprised to see it?"

She looked up at him. "You mean Deacon and Travine?"

At least she was talking to him. He had other questions he'd rather ask, like *why* she'd waited six years, but this'd do for now.

She made a soft breathy sound. "Not really, I guess, though I never noticed Deacon taking an interest in Travine when I was at home. But I had other things on my mind in those days."

"You don't say."

Her sass returned and she snapped him an icy glare. Back on familiar ground.

If he hadn't been watching, he'd have missed the thin trail cutting off to the west. He put Lolly to it, and they bounced over the seldom-used track a rough mile or so before a sprawling log barn rose up in the distance like an eagle about to take flight.

Betsy sat up straighter and gripped her hands until her knuckles turned pale.

"Breathe, Betsy. Remember what Deacon told you."

He knew guilt when he saw it, and Betsy Beaumont was wearing it like Lolly wore her riggin'.

A flash of yellow raced toward them, and Pearl tore off to meet the pup Cade had taken off Garrett's hands last year. It was nearly as big as Pearl now, and they greeted each other as dogs do, romping and jumping and whimpering. An older cow dog sat off by itself, keeping an eye on the buggy.

A raw-boned plow horse stood loose-tied at the rail in front of a two-story log house. No saddle. Evidently, Sophie Price could horseback like any other farmer's daughter.

He drew up in front of a stone path to the front door, and before he could get around to help, Betsy gathered herself and jumped down. She brushed off her skirt, tugged and pulled at her clothing and hair, and generally poked herself into a nervous frenzy.

He took her elbow and she froze.

"It's all right. You look fine. More than fine."

She didn't pull away from him, and he could feel the tension singing through her like news on a telegraph line.

"Thank you," she whispered.

She turned for the front door. He expected her to walk right in, but she stopped. As she raised her fist to knock, the door flew open.

CHAPTER 14

E lizabeth's heart flew to her throat and stuck there, choking off what she'd planned to say. It blocked all her words and most of her breath.

Her brother, aged by responsibility and worry, looked stuck himself, and stood staring as their father often had. The resemblance chilled her.

And then he pulled her to him and held on tight, as if she too might fly.

Fear drained away, leaving her light-headed and weak. She clung to him for balance as much as for forgiveness.

Finally, he set her back and focused over her shoulder. "Garrett." His deep voice rolled across the threshold and the years, undergirding her to stand on her own.

"Cade." Garrett stepped closer, and she welcomed the essence of him, as solid as the stone beneath her feet. "Mrs. Price told us Sophie was here checking on your missus."

"Milk," Elizabeth managed, pushing at her hat. "Mrs. Snowfield sent us to the Price farm for milk."

"Come in." Cade stepped away from the entry and gestured toward well-worn leather chairs near the hearth. The smell of home nearly overwhelmed her—

the cooling fire, ancient log walls, old books—and she reminded herself it *wasn't* home. Not anymore.

Garrett stomped his feet on the landing and doffed his hat, then closed the heavy door behind them.

"Betsy!"

The squeal came from the top of the stairs, followed by Sophie Price bounding down and across the room, where she wrapped Elizabeth in a warm embrace. She'd been hugged more today than in all the years she'd been gone. Not at all the judgmental response she'd expected.

Mama's gentle voice curled around her heart in a whisper: *Oh, to grace how great a debtor.*

"Please, sit," Cade said. "I'll get coffee."

"*I'll* get coffee. *You* sit." Sophie drew herself up in an important way, all grown up and taking charge.

So much was different, yet so much was the same. The dichotomy nearly made Elizabeth's head swim.

"But Mae Ann—"

"Is just fine and resting," Sophie scolded as she hurried toward the kitchen.

Cade plowed his fingers through his hair, clearly distracted, then plopped down on the raised hearth. Elizabeth hesitated, clawing her way back through the years, yet feeling it was only yesterday she'd sat in this very room talking to Pastor Bittman about funeral arrangements.

Achingly, she took Mama's chair. Garrett took the other.

"I got your letter, Betsy, but I've been so distracted with the baby and Mae Anne and the mares needing to be brought down. I meant to write, but I couldn't sit still long enough to put pen to paper."

"Don't apologize, Cade. If anyone should be apologizing, it's me." The words came easier than she had imagined, and the tight straps that had bound her heart for so long loosened and fell away.

"As I mentioned in the note, I'm working in town as a type-writer and stenographer, and staying at the Snowfield mansion—boarding house, I should say."

Cade looked up, disheveled hair and concern weighting his features. "You could have come here, you know."

Relief washed through her as he spoke the unspoken, lancing the boil. She softened her voice. "I know, but you have a family now. And I need to make my own way. Face the music, as Maggie Snowfield puts it. Not that I don't appreciate your..."

She stopped, remembering they were not alone and unwilling to air any more laundry in front of Garrett Wilson. He'd seen and heard quite enough today already.

A much larger man than the colonel, he filled her father's wing chair, twirling his hat between his high-pitched knees. With no sign of discomfort or awkwardness, he merely waited as if he had all the time in the world.

"I appreciate you bringing Betsy out today, Garrett."

Cade's comment stirred him from private thoughts. "It was Mrs. Snowfield's idea. Not that I wouldn't have been happy to volunteer..."

Garrett's candid remark added another layer to her curiosity, but she couldn't think about that right now.

"You mentioned the mares. They're still in the mountain pastures?"

Cade shot her a nervous look as though she were their father bellowing and blowing, rather than his prodigal sister feeling her way through the fog.

"With Deacon's help, how many hands do you need?"

He scrubbed his scalp again, digging for an answer. "One or two more would make an easy day of it. But I don't want to go too far from Mae Ann in case she needs me."

A plan spun through her mind, tugging and tightening until it was smooth and sweet as pulled taffy. "I can help."

Garrett's hat stilled.

"So can Garrett." It took all of her will power to not look at him. "Sophie can stay here with Mae Ann—I'm sure she wouldn't mind—and with Deacon, the four of us can find the band and drive them down."

Though she could only feel Garrett staring, Cade did so open-mouthed. He wanted to object—she'd seen that fish-face before—but she counted on his overtaxed brain to tell him that her plan was a lifesaver. The mares couldn't stay in the mountains much longer, exposing their foals to wolves and winter, and there were probably a dozen yearlings that needed handling. There always were.

She put on her best smile. "Besides, a good ride is just what I need."

Sophie returned with coffee and square servings of chocolate cake. "Mae Ann makes the best cake you've ever had, and I'm sure she'd insist we all had some to celebrate your homecoming, Betsy."

At that, Elizabeth glanced sideways to find Garrett watching her. If he could, he'd pick her brain clean, no doubt about it. But she wasn't some old woolen sweater to be plucked and pulled.

He shifted on the chair, turning more toward her brother. "My apologies, Cade, but I can't be gone that long. My fill-in deputy agreed to a half-day's watch, and tonight's likely to be a typical Saturday night in Olin Springs." He looked square at Elizabeth. "And Mrs. Snowfield is waitin' on her milk."

"Pfft." Elizabeth swept the comment away like a fly. "You and I both know she doesn't need that milk any more than she needs another buggy."

Cade shook his head. "Garrett's right, Betsy. I can't ask him to spend the day chasing mares. It takes an early morning start at that, and it's near noon now."

She sagged beneath the truth of his words, but she wasn't beat yet. There had to be some way she could help.

"I'll tell you what I *can* do." Garrett forked a huge bite of cake, leaving his offer hanging above them all until he swallowed and looked up. "I can leave Betsy here, drive back to town, and return before sunup tomorrow. That way Maggie gets her milk, I can still cover the town tonight, and we get an early start tomorrow."

She could kiss him.

Wait—no. Perish the thought!

Fearing that her emotions showed plainly on her face, she dipped her head and pushed at her chignon. A hug. She could hug him. Heavens, what had come over her? But she'd hugged everyone else she knew today, why not an infuriatingly exasperating man who insisted on calling her Betsy and sprouted acts of kindness when she least expected them.

Cade visibly brightened. "That's mighty generous of you, Garrett, but I hate to ask you to take a day away from your responsibilities in town."

"You took that yellow pup off my hands last year. I'd say I owe you one."

Cade mashed the remains of his cake with his fork. "He's more than earned his keep."

Now there was a story she wanted to hear. Unlike her, Cade had never been very good at hiding anything important.

"It's settled then." She finished her cake and coffee, set the plate and cup on the table between the two chairs, and leaned back against a leather wing.

A sudden thought shot her forward. "Are my riding clothes still here?"

Cade nodded, his mouth full of cake and frosting, then followed it with a swig of coffee before he answered. "I let Mae Ann wear them at first. Didn't think you'd mind and didn't know if you'd ever be back." A quick glance from beneath drawn brows told her what he was really thinking. If that was the only scolding he offered, she'd gladly take it.

"Course, she's not wearin' 'em now, and hasn't for a time. They're ready and waiting right where you left them."

That solved one problem.

She turned to Garrett. "Will you let Maggie know what's going on, that I won't be home until tomorrow evening?"

"Planned on it."

His easy-going humor was gone, and she found she missed it.

~

Garrett set Lolly to an easy walk. No sense driving the old girl into the ground on her first day out. Pearl didn't need any such saving, and she loped along the road, stopping every hundred yards or so to look back as if asking why they weren't keeping up with her.

If he couldn't convince Maggie to let him take Lolly out again tomorrow, he'd rent a rig at the livery. Or he could haul Betsy behind him on Rink.

Yeah. That'd be the day, when she willingly wrapped her arms around his waist and leaned against him. The idea struck him as completely pleasurable, particularly after riding next to her in the buggy with her lavender scent swirling around him.

In spite of her reluctance to come clean about her past, leaving her at the ranch was the hardest thing he'd done in a long time. It set him off center, feeling alone and empty-headed—a fine condition for a lawman with a city to watch and a bur under his saddle by the name of Anthony Rochester. Garrett's gut told him the lawyer had a connection to the hotel fire. But knowing something and proving it were two different things.

It was well after sundown when Lolly clopped onto Main Street. Music poured from the Pike, but no one was rolling out beneath the swinging doors.

He drew up at the little barn Maggie called her carriage house, then unhitched the mare and led her inside for a good rub down and brushing. She'd done well for her first trip out in some time, but from the looks of her, she wasn't up to another one tomorrow. He felt for heat in her legs, checked her hooves, and gave her some oats for her efforts before turning her out in the pasture.

Rink sauntered over and welcomed him with a low whiffle against his shoulder.

"We're ridin' out early, fella, with a full day's work in the high country. Maybe comin' back double tomorrow night." His insides got all warm and jittery at the prospect. "The exercise'll do us both good. We've been too long idle."

Pearl stuck her head in the trough, then flung water all over creation. He didn't want to take her back to the jail tonight because he wouldn't leave her cooped up inside all day tomorrow while he was movin' horses.

Stooping eye to eye, he rubbed her scruffy head. "If I leave you in a stall, do you promise not to get in trouble?"

A wet slurp across his face answered the question, and he sleeved off slobber as he walked her back to the barn and closed her in. "No jumping out."

She plopped her hind quarters down at his stern tone and swept a bare arc on the straw-covered floor. Fool dog understood more English than most people he'd jailed.

He grabbed the milk jars, headed for the house, and bounded up the back steps and into Maggie's fragrant kitchen.

She glanced behind him. "Is everything all right?" She opened the warming oven and withdrew two plates of roast beef and potatoes.

"Betsy's at the ranch with Cade and Mae Ann." He set the jars in Maggie's icebox and gulped the coffee she'd poured for him. "I can't stay, but this coffee hits the spot."

"Sit for one minute and I'll pack your meal. The town won't burn down before you get there."

Catching what she'd said, Maggie threw him a worried look, then cut two thick pieces of bread and topped them with sliced beef. She wrapped the sandwiches in a napkin and stacked them inside the milk basket with a generous serving of apple pie.

Looked to be near half the pie, by his estimation.

"You can tell me all about everything tomorrow."

He took the basket. "Afraid not. The Parkers are driving down a band of mares tomorrow, and I'll be riding out early to help them." He raised the basket. "And thank you for this."

Her worried look slowed him at the door. "Betsy's family and Sophie were glad to see her. When I left, they were planning tomorrow's roundup." He walked back to the whip-thin woman and looped an arm over her frail shoulders.

"She's fine. Said to tell you she'd be back tomorrow evening."

Maggie didn't look convinced, and her doubt echoed what had been trailing the back of his mind. What if Betsy stayed at the ranch?

Maggie fussed with her apron, her brows tight as a hat band as she glanced up at him "Well, she'd better."

Yeah, she'd better, aggravatin' woman. He chuck-led nervously, and gave Maggie's shoulders a quick squeeze. "Would it be all right if I leave Pearl in a stall? She promised to behave herself, and we should be back before nightfall."

"She promised, did she?"

His decoy worked, and Maggie took an old bowl from the counter and scraped Betsy's meal into it. "Give this to that monstrosity on your way out. I'll say a prayer for you and Betsy at church tomorrow."

Sunday had slipped up on him again, something his grandparents never let happen. Course, they couldn't with Grandpa standing behind the pulpit.

The streets were quiet, the alley quieter, no strays or vagrants hiding in the shadows. The Pike's piano edged the night with an off-key tune. The man at the keys must have been tone deaf or just plain deaf.

He unlocked the back door to the jail and walked through to his desk, where he left the basket, then went out the front. Heading up the boardwalk away from the din, he walked a circle around the north end of town, checking store fronts. The back-room lights were on at the *Gazette,* Hunt Fischer working on the press. The man didn't sleep much, far as Garrett could tell. His last edition had run a piece on starting a local fire brigade and a second story on the new railroad spur to Crested Butte.

Across the street, Rochester's office was locked up tighter than a miser's fist. Garrett rattled the doorknob to make sure.

The whole town was rolled up like a slicker on a sunny day, aside from the Pike, spilling its tinny music and yellow light into the street. He crossed back at the hotel and stopped in front of its recently replaced window, the single biggest piece of glass in town, shipped in by train from Pennsylvania.

The saloon lights reflected from across the street and quickly brightened as the batwings flew open.

Miller Pike's bulky silhouette had a man by the scruff of the neck, and he dunked the fella in the horse trough.

Pike yanked him out of the water and hollered, "I warned ya next time you showed up here, you'd be goin' to jail."

Garrett strode across the street, a chill climbing his neck. Even in the dim light, he recognized the farm boy.

"Just in time, Sheriff. Got a customer for you, and he's ripped, fool kid. Heeled too. I'll not have some mother's son trying to get hisself gut shot in my establishment."

While the boy leaned on the trough, gasping and coughing, Pike ducked inside and returned with an old cap and ball. "Wavin' this around, he was. I figured he'd either get hisself killed or bust up my new mirror. Either option is bad for business."

Garrett stuck the gun in his belt and found himself short on words and long on memories. He grabbed the boy by the arm and headed for the jail.

The lanky kid stumbled along, sulled up, smelling like the Pike, and dragging his left foot. Hatless and wet down to his waist, not to mention behind his ears, he stared at the ground until they reached the jail.

Garrett's early start tomorrow was looking less likely by the minute.

At the jail, he pushed the door open and ushered the boy inside. "What's your name?"

With no lamp or stove fire, the room yawned like a cave, deep-throated and cold. He grabbed the key off his desk, then led his client to the first cell. The iron hinges moaned an eerie welcome, and the boy trembled either from the soaking, fear, or both.

"Clay."

If Garrett didn't know better, he'd have thought the whisper came from a small child.

"Clay what?" He directed him toward the cot against the outside wall, where the boy slumped onto the thin tick. Faint moonlight filtered through the bars of a tiny high window, brushing the boy's drooped head. Garrett almost pitied him.

But getting liquored up and waving a handgun around in a bar full of less than clear-thinking men didn't qualify for pity.

"Ferguson." A tight breath sucked in through chattering teeth.

Garrett backed out of the cell and closed the door—a deafening, hopeless benediction in the dark.

He found a banked coal in the stove and added kindling, then lit the lamp on his desk. The soft light spread across the office and down the hall to the cells like melted butter on biscuits. Garrett remembered his supper.

He took a sandwich from Maggie's basket, walked back, and held it through the bars. The boy didn't look up.

"Clay." No movement other than shivering. "You hungry?"

Garrett snagged his old shirt from a hook by the back door, then unlocked the cell and laid the shirt and sandwich on the cot next to his pathetic prisoner. Backing out again, he kept his eye on the boy, ready for a sudden move. Serpents and doves.

He shot the boy a side glance. If the kid couldn't feed himself and take off his wet shirt, so be it. Garrett was fairly certain there were no broken bones and even more certain that he was no nurse maid. Nor would he be starving out of sympathy.

He built up the fire, added water to cold coffee grounds, and called it good. Then he settled in at his desk, feet up and crossed at the ankles, a fat slice of apple pie to start off the meal.

If you eat the best first, you'll have the best left.

He chuckled at the truism, a riddle he hadn't understood as a youngster in his grandparents' Texas home. He'd pestered his grandpa 'til the old man explained that whatever he had left was the best he had.

A light scuffing drew Garrett's attention to the cell, where Clay Ferguson stood bare-backed, facing the opposite wall and one arm huntin' the old shirt's sleeve.

Garrett's boots hit the floor. The boy jumped and turned, fear and anger and hatred marring his young face.

"Hold up." He tempered his voice as if approaching a skittish colt. "Come over here and let me have a look at those welts." From what he'd seen, they hadn't yet scarred over and were still red and tender.

"I don't need your pity."

For all the world, the kid reminded him of Pearl when he and Booth had found her at an Abilene garbage heap. "Got no pity to offer. Turn around and let me have a look."

The boy stood where he was, rock rigid and glaring.

"Look, son—"

"And I ain't your son." He shrugged into the shirt and, without buttoning it, plopped down on the cot.

Garrett threw his shoulders back. "Suit yourself."

Stubborn, but alive.

Half the pie and a sandwich later, he stretched his legs out again and settled in for a nap. The Regulator marked the slow, dull seconds, and the stove popped and ticked as its potbelly heated up.

A gruff whisper perked Garrett's ears. "What's that?"

Silence answered, punctuated by the clock's steady heartbeat and then a clearing throat. "Thanks."

Garrett got up and poured two cups of coffee, then slid one through the space beneath the cell door and cocked a boot heel against the wall. Leaning back, he sipped the worst coffee he'd ever tasted. Maggie was turnin' him soft.

Clay limped over and picked up the cup.

"You hurt your leg in a scuffle at the bar?"

The kid's shaggy head turned side to side. "I'm a cripple."

Garrett harnessed his surprise. "Where you from?"

The boy sat down again, arching his back against the dry shirt. "La Junta."

"You ride here?"

A silent nod.

From what Garrett had seen, the boy had cause to be guarded. The napkin lay crumpled beside him. He'd eaten.

Garrett went to his desk, opened the bottom drawer, and pulled out a small jar of salve. He unlocked the door, slid the key inside his vest, and sat down beside the boy who was watching him like the aforementioned serpent.

"Take off the shirt."

The kid's eyes narrowed and he angled his head away, but held Garrett in his sights.

"Works on dogs and horses. It'll work on you."

Another long look, then hard, cracked hands reached up to pull the shirt off bony shoulders. The boy scooted around on the cot but kept his head cocked toward Garrett. Apparently, trust didn't come natural.

"Who did this to you?"

He flinched—either at Garrett's touch or his question.

A couple of stripes cut near to the muscle and drew a quick breath when Garrett pressed the rag against them. He had a pretty good idea who would do something like this to a boy with a limp, and a vengeful gall worked up the back of his throat.

"Think you can ride?"

A scoff.

"I'm leavin' before sunup to help a friend. You're welcome to come with me if you can horseback."

His patient pulled away and turned piercing blue eyes on Garrett. "I could shoot you on the trail, steal your horse and saddle, and clear out."

Garrett took him by the shoulder and turned him back around to finish the job. "My horse wouldn't let you near him, and I doubt you could draw on me with your grandpa's hog leg locked in my desk."

The shoulders went slack.

Garrett put the lid on the jar and stood. "Well? You game?"

"You don't know me from Adam. Why should you trust me?"

He left the cell, the door clanked against its frame, and he tossed the rag on the floor near the back door. "Somebody needs to."

CHAPTER 15

Elizabeth lay awake in the dark, not trusting her senses. Torn between the past and present, she fought a queasy feeling of belonging to neither.

Her bedroom was exactly as she'd left it, aside from dust that lay heavy on the chest of drawers and dressing table. Its dry scent clung to the quilt she huddled beneath and scratched her nose each time she stirred. She'd not shaken it last night, hoping to avoid breathing in the falling particles.

If she were staying—which she wasn't—she'd give the room a good scrubbing and wash the bedclothes.

If only regret could be purged as easily.

She threw back the covers. Her clothes had been just where Cade said they were, and she'd laid them on the foot of her bed the night before, a habit her mother had instilled in her when Elizabeth was toddling at her skirts.

Be ready for the day before the day gets here, Mama had said.

And so she was, shedding her nightgown and tugging into her riding skirt, shirt, and belt. Her boots showed extra wear and her hat was missing, but Cade probably had an old one lying around. After tending to her needs at the washbasin, she tied her hair back with a ribbon, paused at Cade and Mae Ann's door for sounds of stirring, and then stopped at the landing.

The great room seemed smaller than she remembered, but nothing had been rearranged. Her father's desk guarded long wall-hugging book shelves, scattered steer hides covered the smooth plank floor, and Mama's piano stood against the inside wall. Protection for its strings, she'd always said, from the drastic temperature changes this part of the country was known for.

The aroma of dark, rich coffee drew her down the staircase. Deacon.

"I knew you were at the stove." She hugged his waist from the side, and he clamped an arm around her, stirring sausage gravy with his other hand.

"Horned and barefoot. The aroma charged up the stairs to meet me."

Deacon chuckled and gave her a quick once over. "Now that's the Betsy I know. Ready to ride."

"Your forgiveness means everything to me."

His mustache pulled hard to one side. "Never you mind about that now. You're back, and that's what matters."

She pulled away and opened the cupboard door, surprised to find new rose-bordered china, the remains of her mother's ware set back to make room. Only a man in love would splurge on new dishes when old chipped plates and cups served most men just as well.

A tug of envy accompanied the cup she set in its saucer, and she filled it with dark Arbuckle's, spooning in sugar from the old silver bowl centered on the cloth-covered table. Polished to a sheen, it brought Garrett Wilson to mind.

Conflict stirred within her. Exasperated yesterday by his scrutiny, she was excited about riding with him today. Why couldn't he just settle into the same corner of her life as other men? Other than Edward and Braxton Hatchett. Why did he have to stake claim to his own section?

Deacon watched her without watching her, as was his way, and she wondered if he could still read her mind as easily as always. So be it. She had nothing to hide from him, and sat down at the table. "I thought Sophie was coming back today to stay with Mae Ann."

He grabbed a folded towel, opened the oven door, and pulled out a skillet of golden biscuits. "Should be here any minute, but we need an early start. Didn't wanna wait on breakfast."

Barking dogs drew her back to the great room, where she opened the front door to find a buggy and outrider reining in at the hitching rail. Garrett's blue roan was tied to the back of the rig. She closed the door and took her coffee to the fireplace, where she stood with her back to the warmth, facing the door. It was colder up here than in town.

She hadn't seen Pearl with them, thank goodness.

Boots stomped outside and in Garrett walked, followed by a boy a few years older than Todd Price would be.

Garrett's silver-green gaze met her across the open space and her insides fluttered, a completely annoying reaction that served absolutely no purpose at all. She swigged an unladylike gulp of strong, sweet coffee, hoping to drown the sensation.

"Betsy." Garrett doffed his hat. "This is Clay Ferguson. He's come to help."

Clay stood mute as a tree stump.

159

Garrett elbowed him.

"Ma'am."

At least he wouldn't be talking up a storm. "Pleased to meet you, Clay. Have you ridden on many horse gatherings?"

He flashed Garrett a worried look.

"Doesn't matter."

She turned to the voice.

Her brother tromped down the stairs, hair sticking out every which way and looking like he had when he was twelve. But now worry plowed his forehead and fanned his eyes.

"Smells like we're about to eat. Join us." He offered his hand to both men, apparently glad for the extra help whether the boy knew what to do or not. "Thanks for coming."

"Grub's on!" Deacon called from the kitchen.

She smiled to herself.

Cade sat at the head of the table—one small difference she hadn't foreseen, but a most reasonable one. He was the head of the house now. She chose the chair to his left, surprised when Garrett pulled it out for her. Rather than thanking him, she flashed a look at Cade, who had caught the sheriff's gesture. Deacon seated himself across the table, and Clay moved quickly for the neighboring chair which left Garrett beside her.

It didn't matter. She set her coffee cup on the table, careful not to let any telltale flutter reach her fingers. Besides, this way she wouldn't have to avoid looking at him while she ate, a regular chore at Maggie's.

Cade bowed his head, and Elizabeth peeked beneath her brows to see who followed suit.

"Thank you, Lord, for the help you've sent today and this good food." Cade paused and cleared his throat, his voice weakening some, as if he was trying to hold it in. "And thank you for bringing Betsy home."

A lump as big as one of Deacon's biscuits lodged in her throat and she bit the inside of her lip to keep tears at bay. She'd not cry at the table in front of four grown men. Well, three and a half.

Still oblivious to proper manners, Deacon passed the biscuits across the table to her, towel folded around the hot skillet handle. "Eat hearty 'cause I ain't takin a chuckbox. I've got makin's for your saddle bags, but it won't be more'n leftovers."

She helped herself to a biscuit and handed the skillet off to Cade, who took two. Clay glanced around the table and snatched two before passing the skillet to Garrett, who helped himself and then reached back and set the skillet on the stove.

"More's in the oven," Deacon offered.

Sausage gravy, fried eggs, and canned peaches spent little time on the plates.

Cade looked at Deacon, worry pinching his features. "Isn't Sophie coming this morning?"

"D'rectly."

"Is Mae Ann all right?" An indelicate topic to discuss in male company, but this was ranch life and Elizabeth wanted to know.

Cade nodded. "Just resting. She does that a lot more lately."

"Good." As if Elizabeth knew anything at all about such matters. Still, it seemed a sensible thing to do when one was preparing for childbirth.

In less time than she took to sweeten and stir her second cup of coffee, every man had cleared his plate and was outside checking his cinch and stuffing Deacon's *makin's* in the saddle bags. Cade's old dog, Blue, and the yellow hound reminiscent of Pearl whined and sniffed around the men and horses, sensing a ride in the offering.

Garrett unhitched the buggy horse and led it to the corral. From the looks of Clay's gelding, the poor animal had been rode hard and put away wet, as Pa would have said. The boy wasn't far off that mark either. Hopefully, they'd both survive the day.

She wrapped Cade's extra coat tighter and stepped onto Ginger, a little red mare she remembered as willing and sure-footed. Sophie finally rode into the yard on the Price's old plow horse. The raw-boned mare had to be older than Sophie and her brother put together. It walked right up to the hitch rail, with Sophie partially hidden by a high coat collar and floppy wide-brimmed hat.

"Got here as soon as I could." Her crooked smile peeked out beneath her brim. "When Todd heard about the drive, he wanted to skip school and come help, but Ma said no." She glanced at Clay, then gave him a second look like she'd seen a stray dog that needed rescuing.

Honestly, she was as soft as Garrett.

On second thought, Garrett Wilson wasn't soft on anything other than a good meal. She still had a bruise on her backside.

"Thanks for coming, Sophie." Cade swung into the saddle. "There's biscuits and coffee left from breakfast."

Another glance from Sophie made Clay sit up straighter and hold his head square.

"We'll be fine," she said. "Don't you worry about a thing." She loose-tied the mare and walked over to Elizabeth. "Ma says I have a healing touch, and I'm happy to help make her comfortable." She grabbed Elizabeth's hand, tugging her down, her voice a whisper. "That baby's gonna come before everybody thinks. I feel it in my bones—and from the way Mae Ann's bones are carrying it."

Alarm shot through Elizabeth and she squeezed her friend's hand. "Does Cade know?"

Sophie shook her head and rolled her lips as if she were holding in a heavy secret.

"He needs to."

"Not today. We've probably got a few weeks, but for sure not clear into November. The baby won't come while you're gone. Get the horses, then we can tell him tonight."

As much as she didn't want to, Elizabeth agreed. Her brother would try to be two places at once if he knew, and that wasn't safe. He couldn't bring horses down from the mountain with his mind and heart at home.

He and Deacon struck out to the west, away from the brightening horizon. Garrett and Clay followed, and she urged Ginger into an easy lope, intent on catching up with Deacon.

The three of them rode abreast until they topped a ridge that dropped off into a wide park. It stretched long and lazy into the hills, narrowing where a river cut a path to the back country. Snowmelt flooded the pass each spring, but in winter, ice made it treacherous going. Cade was right. They needed to get the mares down now.

With the rising sun behind them, Cade kicked into a lope across the park, startling deer that bounded effortlessly across the meadow. A watery rush of wings and raucous honking sent a gaggle of Canada geese skyward, sunlight flashing off their bellies.

Elizabeth's heart squeezed at the familiar sight so long absent from her daily life. Denver and all that had happened there seemed miles and years away.

Riding into the back country, she consciously threw off everything she could think of from her time in the city. The lack—so different from her life of abundance on the ranch. Cold, lonely nights waiting for Edward's return from his so-called business. An unnamed hunger for warmth and love as much as for food.

She'd known early on that marrying Edward was a mistake, but ingrained in her very fiber was the fact that one did not go back on a promise.

Clearly, Edward did not have the same upbringing.

She looked over her shoulder at Garrett and Clay riding side by side. She imagined their horses' hooves trampling her discarded memories, grinding them into the dirt where she'd dropped them. Lord, let it be so.

By full daylight, they rode single file along the narrow river. As they climbed, the temperature dropped. It would stay cold until the sun rose higher, and even then it might not warm that much.

She envied Cade and Deacon their shotgun chaps.

Garrett raised the collar on his sheepskin coat and pulled his leather gloves from his pocket. The boy had done the same, though the old coat Garrett had given him didn't keep the cold from nipping his ears bright red. Snow hadn't flown yet, but warmer temperatures had—all the way to Mexico. It had to be ten degrees colder up here in the pines than it was at the ranch.

Betsy wasn't suffering. Wrapped in an oversized coat, she sat her horse as if born there, lightly holding the reins.

Naked aspens raced down the gullies, and at the mountain's shoulder they bunched together, bony white, skirting timber stands like skeletons on guard.

A few miles in, the river broke through to another wide park. As they trailed along beside it and into the grassland, Rink's ears pricked at a high whinny, sharp and clear.

Cade pulled up and waited for everyone to join him.

"That's the lead mare. Even though we're down-wind, she knows we're here, and may take the band across the valley." He looked at Deacon. "Skirt the edge and get around behind them if you can. Garrett and Clay, you ride around the opposite side. Betsy and I'll pull back up against the trees and wait for the horses to head this way, then we'll flank 'em toward the pass."

He shifted in his saddle toward Garrett. "It's not like drivin' cattle. Don't worry about strays breakin' out—they won't. They'll band together. It's that lead mare we need to turn. The others will follow her. Once she gets through the pass, she'll remember the feed down at the ranch and head home."

He glanced at Betsy. "I hope."

She must have telegraphed her reaction to the sorrel, for it danced and side-stepped, as if eager to get going.

Clay fidgeted with anticipation and tugged at his gloves, too big on his young hands. Garrett prayed the boy didn't come unseated.

"You don't need to get close the way you do with cows," Cade said. "Give them room. They'll come runnin' at first, but don't chase them. We don't want them stumbling and tearing a ligament. They'll ease up after a while."

"You planning to rest them like before?" Betsy took a short rein on Ginger.

"In Echo Valley, that first park we came through. They should be moving easy by then, and we'll spread out around them until they settle and start grazing. Then we'll meet at this end of the valley and do our own grazing on what Deacon packed for us."

Garrett screwed his hat down. He and Clay took off behind Deacon, and when the old cowboy cut left, they cut right.

Another whinny pieced the cold air, and a dark patch started moving across the grassy park before them. Rink's ears held tight on the drifting mass, and he leaped into a gallop at the touch of Garrett's heel.

Low rolling thunder rose from the valley floor, a couple hundred hooves beating a get-away behind the lead mare. Deacon's mount ran like a racehorse across the flat and soon outdistanced the herd. Garrett and Clay were closing the gap when Garrett spotted a white mare, black foal at her side, running at the edge of the band of fifty or so.

Not much in life was more beautiful than horses running free and wild, heads high, tails and manes dancing behind them like flags.

A bay mare ran at the point, ears pinned, head lunging with each long stride. Deacon closed in, waving his hat, and she veered north to where Garrett and Clay tightened the noose. The mare turned, and soon the bunch was running back up the park toward Cade and Betsy.

The sun had crested the near range, and the horses headed into it, slowing somewhat with Cade and Betsy riding wide. They funneled in at the river, and Betsy tore through the pass ahead of them, she and her little red mare light and swift with the band hard on their heels. For a moment, Garrett's heart galloped away from him as he envisioned the rocky ground she covered a few lengths ahead of fifty running horses.

He and Clay followed the band into the narrow canyon, Deacon and Cade close behind. By the time the horses reached the mouth of Echo Valley, they'd slowed considerably before fanning out across the grassy park.

Betsy waited, watching the horses settle, then she trotted around behind them and met up with Deacon and Cade.

Clay sat tall in the saddle, his smooth cheeks ruddy from the wind of their ride, blue eyes bright with pleasure at the challenge.

"You did good." Garrett gave the boy a direct look.

Satisfaction straightened his shoulders.

"You sure you haven't done this before?"

"No, sir. I've moved a few cows on the farm, but nothing this exciting."

Garrett could relate. Riding drag with a remuda on a cattle drive, or even point on a bunch of slow-moving beeves, was a sight less daring.

The men ground-tied their mounts, but Betsy took the sorrel a few paces beyond and stood apart, watching the mares graze.

Garrett singled out the white with a black foal at her side, then looked back at Betsy. Sure enough, she was watching the pair.

When she dropped her reins and joined the circle with her meal pack, she was quiet, content. Calmer than Garrett had ever seen her. She was almost a different woman, and he wished he'd known her before.

A maverick thought for sure. The trails they'd each ridden over the last half dozen years couldn't be any more unalike or farther apart. His driving herds north, before and after Abilene and George Booth. Hers in Denver doing he had no idea what.

She dropped down beside him and set to.

Why are you here, Betsy Beaumont? And what brought you home now?

It wasn't so much the sheriff side of him that wanted to know, but the lonesome side.

"They came in easy."

Her quiet comment broke through his ruminating.

No tension between them, just two people talking to each other, open and uncluttered as the sky. His curiosity was killing him, no decision ever harder than the one he faced at that moment—enjoy her company and their peaceful surroundings or take advantage of the situation and pry into her thoughts.

"It must feel good to be back," he said.

She broke her biscuit in two and took a bite, unlike the men who shoved them whole into their mouths, himself included.

"It does. Life is uncomplicated out here with just the parks and horses to think about."

No argument there.

She bit into the second half, regarding him as she chewed and then swallowed. "You ride like you know what you're doing."

He chuckled. "You could say that."

She watched him, waiting for more.

"I trailed a few herds up from Texas."

"You have family in Texas?"

"My grandfolks. They raised me."

"How'd you end up as the Olin Springs sheriff?"

"Long story." That he wasn't going into at the moment, since it was *her* story he wanted to hear.

"So there's more to you than a Colt .45 and a lawman's star."

"And there's more to you than a velvet handbag and a Remington type-writer."

She smiled and contemplated the stand of timber bordering the valley on the north. "There was a time in my life when I thought I'd never leave this ranch. That I'd spend the rest of my days either riding Blanca or working yearlings in the round pen."

"What changed your mind?"

A cloud scuttled across her face.

He read the signs, another maverick thought circling his good sense. This time he followed it.

169

"Forgiveness is hardest when it's ourselves that need forgiving."

She cut him a look through her lashes without raising her head, then packed up her meal and walked back to her horse.

The sun warmed Garrett's back as he sat watching the mares and foals graze their way across the valley. He mulled over what he could have—should have—said to Betsy that might have turned out better, but there was no point in it.

Truth often hurt. A fact he'd learned firsthand.

Cade rolled up his dinner remains and stuffed them in his saddle bags. "We'll walk 'em back easy," he said to no one in particular as he mounted. "But keep an eye on the bay in case she changes her mind."

Garrett swung to his seat and trotted around to flank the band on the south side. Clay stuck close. Like a flock of birds, the mares flowed as one body, moving easy down the park toward the ranch. When the border fence came into view, Betsy gave the sorrel its head and rode for the wide gate. She unlatched it without dismounting and swung it back against the fence, then casually walked her horse into the pasture. The band followed, parting around her like the Red Sea around Moses.

That woman had as much business sitting at a type-writer for Anthony Rochester as Garrett did slingin' hash at Bozeman's. But getting inside her head was harder than getting in the bank vault without the combination.

A couple hours at best, and they'd be heading back to town. He wanted to talk to her again while they were here on the ranch, where she seemed to spread her soul out over the land, not tuck it inside proper manners in Maggie's dining room.

There was more to Betsy Beaumont than he'd first figured, and he wanted to find out all he could before town life corralled her again.

CHAPTER 16

Elizabeth cut Blanca and her foal away from the herd and edged them toward the barn corral. The mare's soft eye and the easy way her ears followed Elizabeth made her think the horse might remember her. But when Blanca let her walk up to the foal with outstretched hand, she was certain of it. A nicker and nudge of the fine white head against her shoulder started tears behind her eyes.

"How I've missed you." The whisper squeezed out of a tight throat, and she was grateful that no one had followed her to the barn. Cade and Deacon understood, of course. But Garrett and his sidekick could nose their way into her privacy at any moment.

Just like Garrett had nosed his way into her hidden wound and poured in his salty truth.

She focused on the filly, black as type-writer ribbon, like Blanca had been as a foal. Slowly she ran her hands along the dark neck and withers, over the back, smiling as the filly's flesh quivered beneath her fingers. Ears swiveled back in nervous curiosity, but the eye was gentle. The filly was sound and strong, like its mother, and Elizabeth hoped Cade wouldn't sell it.

Better than that, she'd buy it from him. As soon as she had enough money set aside.

Under different circumstances, the foal would have been hers, but she'd left everything behind, essentially cutting ties to property as well as family. Finding Blanca still on the ranch was more than she'd hoped for.

But Cade never had been much like their father.

She turned the pair out with the others, then unsaddled Ginger and rubbed her down and brushed her. A ration of oats rewarded her for the day's work while the men took care of the others.

The barn was ripe with the smell of fresh hay, and Cade had it piled high, with more stacks fenced off in the pasture. The mares would fare well this winter, the cattle too, better than most ranchers' herds.

She slapped dust from her skirt and sleeves on her way to the house, then went inside to check with Sophie. Garrett would want to leave soon, but Elizabeth had a couple of things to do first.

"How was it bringing in the horses again?" Sophie came down the stairs, her face glowing with long-held affection. Not a miserly bone in her body, she knew what the horses had meant to Elizabeth growing up.

But Elizabeth had things she needed to say. "How is Mae Ann?"

"Resting." With a sigh, Sophie fell into one of the wing chairs. "She ate a good dinner—as good as I can convince her to eat. But she won't starve. I keep telling her she's feeding two people and needs to keep her strength for the baby." She glanced up with a wry smile. "Truth laced with a bit of bribery."

Elizabeth took the other chair, sitting on the edge, eager to share her heart and not wanting to linger and miss what might be her only opportunity during this rushed visit.

"Sophie, you're a true friend. And I want to apologize for how I treated you when—"

"You don't need to say a thing." Sophie reached for Elizabeth's hand. "I could see what was coming. Anyone could. We've been neighbors and friends all our lives, Betsy. I couldn't be mad at you if I tried."

Elizabeth let the pent-up tears fall, unashamed in the warmth of Sophie's faithfulness. "I live with such regret. Seeing you and your mother, and Deacon and Cade's welcome, means more to me than I can say."

Sophie smiled her sweet, crooked smile. "Regrets never did anybody any good. Don't waste your heart on them."

Elizabeth palmed her face. "I know. But I just don't very often remember that I know."

"From what I've managed to worm out of your brother, with Mae Ann's help, you're doing what matters, which is making a fresh start." She fiddled with the corners of her apron. "Edward just up and left you?"

Hearing someone else speak the truth robbed some of its sting.

"My regret pales only to my humiliation."

"Oh, Betsy, please don't." Sophie pressed her apron corners flat. "I'm not much for platitudes, and I know it sounds simple-minded, but it's true that everyone makes mistakes."

And hers were bigger than most.

"So will you and your friends be staying for supper?" She slid a sly glance at Elizabeth.

"It's not what you think."

"And how do you know what I think? Did you learn mind-reading in Denver?"

Elizabeth rose and pushed her loose hair behind her ears, realizing she'd lost her ribbon in the ride. "I hear it in your voice. Like you said, I've known you all my life."

Planting her hands on her hips, she turned on Sophie in mock severity. "While we're on the subject, I saw the way you looked at that Clay fellow Garrett brought along."

Sophie jumped up. "I do believe the beans I started this morning are cooking dry. Can't have them scorching now, can I."

Elizabeth went out the back door laughing and stopped on the covered porch. Mama's garden plot looked the same as always, but fuller for the time of year. The last of the tomatoes still hung round and red, waiting to be harvested.

A sharp wind swept off the mountains, whipping her hair across her face. She pulled it back with one hand and set out toward the hill north of the house, where the ponderosa stood like a sentinel. Cade had written to her about the graves, told her that he hadn't buried their parents in town but on the land they loved.

It was time she visited them as well.

Gray-bellied clouds churned over the mountains and rolled down into the valley, dampening the sun's warmth and light. She hurried up the gentle slope, racing against the storm to the great tree's shelter.

A small fence bordered two cedar crosses, and a pink rose flourished between them—all new additions since she had last climbed the hill. She stepped over the low pickets and knelt between the graves. Weathered and gray, each cross bore hand-carved names. Deacon's doing, no doubt.

"I miss you, Mama." Tears welled and she let them fall unchecked as she leaned to trace the letters of her mother's name. "I was foolish. I went against everything you taught me. I'm so sorry…"

Her voice blew away on the rising wind, and with a wrenching sob, she hugged her waist and doubled over the grave.

Garrett stood on the back porch, Betsy's oversized coat on his arm and her blue hair ribbon in hand. He'd found it lying on the ground near the corral and recognized it from the ride.

Atop a hill behind the ranch house, she knelt beneath a big ponderosa pine, near what looked to be two crosses. Her parents' grave markers, he'd wager. He hated to intrude on her grief, but they needed to get back to town before a full-fledged storm kept them from leaving at all.

He rolled the ribbon around his finger and slipped it in his vest pocket, then set out, slowing near the top to listen. No sound came from Betsy's bent form as she swayed over one of two graves, hair blowing like a curtain against her face.

He cleared his throat.

She lifted her head, calm and unstartled, as if she'd heard him coming. Her cheeks were wet, and her dark eyes pooled like bottomless wells.

Stepping over the low border, he draped the coat across her shoulders and helped her to her feet, instinctively wrapping his arms around her. She didn't resist, but leaned into him and rested her forehead on his chest. He held her, taking the rising wind with his back, determined to protect her from the coming storm but unable to shield her from the squall within.

He hadn't held a woman in a long time, and then it'd been only a boy's eagerness. Now it was different, and Betsy Beaumont was more woman than he'd ever encountered. Something about her drew him and made him ache to hold her as long as she'd let him.

The old tree sighed above them, mourning the dead, and she stepped back, gripping the edges of her coat and looking up at him like he knew her deepest secrets.

For the life of him, he wished he did.

They walked down the hill in silence, and when they reached the house, she stopped and shrugged into the coat. "I'm going to gather what's left of the tomatoes for Mae Ann."

"We need to leave as soon as possible with this storm blowing in."

"I'll be ready before you get the buggy hitched." Halting, she faced him. "Whose buggy is that, anyway?"

"Lolly wasn't up to another trip."

Her hands found her waist. "You rented a rig."

"Either that or bring you back on Rink. Behind me."

She snorted. "If you think I'd ride double with you all the way back to town, you are sadly mistaken."

Relieved to find her sorrow displaced, he squared off. "Well, if you couldn't handle it, it's just as well I brought a buggy."

"I can *handle* anything you throw at me, Sheriff Wilson, but I refuse—"

"Just bein' neighborly, Miss Betsy." He touched the brim of his hat. "It's a long walk back."

She snapped like dry twigs, and he nearly laughed, giving away his pleasure at seeing her high spirits return.

She marched through the garden gate and began ripping tomatoes from over-grown vines. Rather than wait around for her to take up target practice at his expense, he went inside.

Cade sat at the kitchen table, looking like the bank had just called in his loan.

"There's nothing to worry about, Cade," Sophie tried to reassure him. "She's just further along than anyone thought. She may have miscalculated." The girl blushed, and Garrett joined her, his ears heating up to what he figured must rival the tomatoes.

He beat a trail through the house and out the front door.

Deacon leaned on the corral, one foot planted on the bottom pole and Clay his mirror-double next to him. Now there was a pair to draw to. The old cowboy was probably just what the kid needed. Someone to teach him a trade and keep him out of trouble.

But Garrett didn't know enough about him to leave him out here on the ranch. He could be exactly what he'd boasted—a thief. And exactly what he'd tried to prove—a man who could hold his liquor.

Garrett's gut told him the boy was neither.

Maybe Erik could use a tack and stable boy at the livery. Let him sleep in the loft.

He harnessed the buggy horse, checked Rink's hooves, and tied him behind the rig. Then he joined Clay and Deacon.

"Get your horse ready to ride," he told the boy. "We're leavin'."

Clay nodded at Deacon, and the old man returned the gesture.

Watching him walk away, Deacon said, "Good kid. Make a fine cowboy someday."

They watched Clay with his old mount, his confident but gentle manner, and Garrett's hand ached to get ahold of whoever had horse whipped him.

"Says he's from La Junta. Sort of between outfits, if you take my meaning. Lookin' for something."

Deacon huffed. "Way I figure, he's lookin' to belong."

Aren't we all?

At sound of the ranch house door opening, the cow dog and Pearl's pup dashed out of the barn.

"What's Cade call that yellow dog I gave him?"

Deacon chuckled. "He don't call it nothin', but the missus calls it Cougar. Sort of a joke between the two of them, the best I can tell. Dangdest thing I ever seen. When she's out and about, it shadows her like the big cat it's named for. She can't pick eggs without that hound trailin' her every step."

He squared his stance and stretched his back as if working the kinks out. "Betsy goin' back with you and the boy?"

Icy blue peered through Garrett, reading his intentions like a tally book. Nothing much got past the old cowboy.

"Last she said, she was."

Deacon glanced at the sky. "No need to hurry off. That storm's not settlin'."

Garrett wouldn't bet on it, though the old timer'd been around this country a lot longer. "Gotta keep my day job. So does Betsy."

Deacon took in Garrett's vest front, clear of his badge. Garrett pulled it back, revealing the star pinned to his shirt.

The old man's sharp eyes said more than most sermons.

Betsy and Cade came outside. She was wearing her town clothes—trussed up, closed up, and ready for civilization. At the buggy, she embraced Cade. "Thank you." Her voice broke, and he kissed her cheek before handing her up.

Garrett shook Cade's hand, saddened by the loss of the woman he'd glimpsed in Echo Valley, then climbed in beside her.

"Don't be a stranger," Cade said, his attention lingering on his sister.

Garrett turned the buggy about, and they trotted out of the yard and along the ranch road. At the juncture to the rutted trail into town, Betsy looked back, holding her gaze until Garrett figured she'd worked a kink into her neck.

He had a nearly palatable urge to pull her close and tell her everything would work out just fine. And then a fat raindrop hit his brim and he decided he'd make a poor prophet. So would Deacon, from the looks of the low-bellied clouds skimming the horizon.

He snapped the horse into a fast trot. Clay stayed even with them. The wind kicked up and twisted the clouds until they soon lifted and blew away. He shook his head.

"What?" Betsy was looking right at him, trying to read his thoughts.

"Deacon said the storm wouldn't break. I figured he was wrong."

A sad smile pulled her mouth, and she settled against the seat back as if it were comfortable. "Deacon's rarely wrong about anything."

He was tempted to ask what the old cowboy thought of the mysteriously absent Mr. Beaumont, but decided he didn't need to know. Probably wasn't far off what Garrett thought of him.

The buggy cast a long shadow as they neared town, reaching out to join up with Clay and his sorry horse. Clear sky hung at the edge of evening, except for a long puff of dark cloud fingering up near Olin Springs.

Garrett squinted toward the gray tower, and a sick feeling gathered in his gut. Betsy saw it too, and looked at him with alarm.

"Clay!" he hollered. "Ride ahead and lend a hand."

At the boy's questioning stare, Garrett pointed toward the buildings huddled at the horizon's edge.

"Hang on." He slapped the reins. "Y'haw!"

The mare bolted. Clay's gelding kicked up dirt clods as it tore off from the road and across the fields.

Betsy gripped her end of the narrow seat with one hand, the front edge with the other. "It looks like it's just beyond town," she yelled above the rattling buggy, "near the depot."

Or Snowfield's, Garrett's heart shouted above pounding hooves.

CHAPTER 17

Elizabeth's pulse pounded as Garrett cut a two-wheeled turn at the edge of town and raced down the alley. Dark smoke belched up on Saddle Blossom Lane.

She capped a cry with her hand. *Oh, Lord, please.*

She hadn't prayed so earnestly since her prayers began going unanswered.

Townsfolk worked a bucket line from the pump and trough at the pasture fence to the carriage house where hungry flames chewed through its old, dried wood. Maggie held a barking, straining Pearl by a dishtowel knotted through her collar, an arm around the dog's neck as if they were blood kin.

The situation defied belief—that Maggie could keep that monster from dragging her off.

Garrett pulled up next to the house and hit the ground before the buggy came to a full stop.

Elizabeth jumped out and ran to Maggie.

"I'm so glad you're safe." Emotion choked off more that she wanted to say, and she pulled the dear woman close. "What happened?"

"This dog," Maggie yelled over the fire's roar. "This dog is what happened. Had it not been for Pearl raising a ruckus and drawing me out of the house, I never would have seen the smoke."

The dog strained at the towel, facing away from the disaster and barking in the opposite direction.

"What was Pearl doing here?"

"Garrett left her in a stall rather than at the jail today. I told him it was all right, and I'm so glad I did. Heaven only knows how far things would have gotten had I not had warning."

"Where's Lolly?" Elizabeth craned her neck to see past the smoke and men.

"She broke through the fence, poor thing. Nearly scared the life out of her, I imagine. Garrett will find her for me."

Maggie's undying confidence said she depended upon him more than anyone knew. What kind of man earned such faith from a woman who had seen most of what life had to offer?

This time, Elizabeth didn't join the bucket line. Instead she stood with an arm around her landlady's thin waist.

As day faded from the sky, the flames died down, and another blackened skeleton joined the landscape of Olin Springs.

In the seventeen years she had lived at the ranch, she'd heard of only a handful of fires in town. Now there'd been two in the three weeks since she'd returned.

A warning sparked, cautioning her about something she'd read recently. But she couldn't put a name to it, and in a moment the thought faded.

Clay went for Rink, took down Garrett's rope, and gathered his horse he'd loose-tied to an apple tree near the house. With a swing up, he loped off to the east.

Garrett stood apart from the others, talking to the blacksmith, who took a badge from his blackened apron and handed it over. If he was Garrett's deputy, ne'r-do-wells would have no chance against his brawn.

Soon they were joined by a little man in a bowler hat and sack suit, and Mr. Harrison from the bank. Other men drifted away, carrying their buckets, several in groups talking low and shaking their heads.

An uneasy feeling settled in her stomach, matching the wet-cinder stench in her nose as she looked around for her employer. He wasn't the sort she expected to join in an endeavor that would foul his fine suit and fingernails, but it had looked like every other man in town was there. Even the newspaper reporter had been there and taken a photograph from a distance.

Elizabeth suddenly noticed Pearl's silence. The dog no longer barked and tugged at Maggie's arm, but sat at her feet watching Garrett. When he headed their way, the dog's tail swept the dirt, and a gentle whine rose from its unbecoming head.

He reached for Maggie's end of the towel, then rubbed the dog's ears. "Good girl," he murmured, loosing the unusual tether.

"She certainly was," Maggie said. "I'm so grateful that you left her in that stall. She alerted me to the fire."

Urgency colored Garrett's voice as he handed Maggie the towel. "Alerted you?"

"She certainly did. And that's not all."

Maggie took a torn piece of dark cloth from her apron pocket, similar to what a man's suit would be made of, and gave it to Garrett. "This was on the ground when I went out to see what she was having such a fit over." She kept her voice low. "That's when I saw the smoke and let her out of the stall before ringing the old triangle on the back of the house."

Garrett turned the piece over in his hand, fingering a darker edge that looked damp. Blood stained his fingers.

Elizabeth shuddered.

"I think Pearl left her mark on someone poking around in the carriage house," Maggie said. "Someone who may have started the fire."

"This was in the stall where I left her?"

"No. It was on the floor near the buggy."

Garrett frowned and looked at Pearl, who flattened her ears and turned her head away.

"I believe she broke her promise." Maggie lowered her voice to a whisper, as if to keep the dog from hearing. "And I'm glad she did."

Promise? Elizabeth rubbed her temples, suddenly weary from the day's events. Pearl made a promise? Such a thing was absolutely not possible.

"You ladies go on inside. I want to sift through things, make sure no hot spots flare up."

At Garrett's managerial tone, Elizabeth wanted nothing more than to *not* go inside. She could sift as well as the next person.

Maggie latched on to her arm and addressed Garrett. "I told you I'd say a prayer for you both today. The good Lord heard it."

A prayer for Garrett and the promising Pearl? Or a prayer for Garrett and Elizabeth?

Her insides quivered. Garrett Wilson was the most infuriating and kindest man she'd ever known. Poking into her affairs one minute and rushing to someone's aid the next. But in spite of his tendency to always find her amusing in some way, she was tempted to trust him.

A frightening predicament. She'd trusted one man, and he'd let her down. Why was she inclined to trust another? Especially one intent on telling her what to do.

Turning for the house, she stepped closer to Maggie. "I desperately need a bath. Could I commandeer your bathing room?" If she didn't wash her hair, she'd smell like trail dust, horses, and cinders at work tomorrow.

"Oh my, yes." Maggie leaned heavily on her arm, less for emotional support, it seemed, than physical.

Elizabeth slowed her step, taking note of the woman's stooped shoulders and unsteady bearing. "Why don't you rest in the parlor with a book or some needlework, and I'll see to a bath and then fix dinner."

Maggie bristled half-heartedly. "I can't let my guests prepare their own meals."

"Yes, you can. I insist."

Clay rode into the yard leading Lolly, a lariat looped around the horse's muzzle and behind her ears in a loose figure-eight.

Maggie pulled away to greet them. "Oh, Lolly, you poor dear." She hugged the mare's neck and rubbed her shoulder, assuring herself as well as the horse that all was well.

All is well. There it was again—another phrase of reassurance, sweeping through Elizabeth's weary mind like a wheel in a familiar rut.

Clay stepped down, and Garrett took the lead from him. "Nice work."

"She was about half a mile from here." Clay rubbed her left shoulder and indicated a shallow gash above her knee. "She took out a chunk of the back fence. Got any more of that salve?"

"That I do. Take her to the livery and tell Erik I sent you. I'll lock Pearl in the jail, get the salve, and meet you there."

As Clay led the mare away, Maggie shrank even further, letting out a ragged sigh. "Lolly and the carriage house are all I have left of Daniel."

Elizabeth's heart squeezed with a kindred ache at the little woman's cherished memories of someone loved and lost. "Come on." She slipped an arm around Maggie. "Let the men take care of things out here."

Maggie stopped short. "Garrett, you can't take Pearl to jail. If it weren't for her, the fire might have spread. Bring her inside. I have something for her. And she can stay in your room tonight."

Elizabeth felt Garrett watching them, and peeked to find his encouraging regard supporting her as she supported Maggie.

Then it was gone, replaced by a scar-tugging quirk. "If I can stand her snoring."

In spite of his turning the moment with humor, the impression remained, and a shiver ran up Elizabeth's back the same way the filly's flesh had quivered beneath her fingers earlier. A man's support was as foreign to her as her touch was to the foal.

188

A truly strange sensation, but one she wouldn't mind feeling again.

~

Garrett walked the ashy perimeter of what was once the buggy shed, looking for clues. Looking for anything. A lamp, a kerosene can, an empty bottle. This was no accident.

The rancid odor of burned hay and smoldering wood pinched his nose.

Not one fire during his couple of years in Olin Springs, yet since Rochester arrived, there had been two.

His skin chilled as he realized he could say the same of Betsy, though she'd come upon both fires after the buildings were fully engulfed. In fact, she'd been with him when this fire started.

He crumpled the dark, torn cloth in his hand.

What if she had a conspirator? What if she and Rochester were in cahoots? And if so, why?

He jerked his hat off and scrubbed through his hair. Dad-blastit, he didn't like the direction his thoughts were headed. Rochester was the more likely suspect, not a beautiful, bull-headed woman. But like it or not, before the whole town burned down, Garrett had to suspect everyone.

And then he saw it.

Near the far corner where old hay had been piled, a dark spot stained the soil. He stepped over the remains of the buggy and stooped for a closer look. Smooth beneath his fingers, the substance had cooled and hardened.

Who would bring a candle to a barn?

Pearl bounded toward him.

He waylaid her before she plowed through the debris.

"Hold on there. You can't be runnin' over the evidence." He led her over to Rink, took a latigo strip from his saddle, and tied her to an iron garden bench at the back of the house.

Then he rode Rink to the jail and finally the livery. It hadn't been all that long since he'd ridden her *from* the livery.

Inside, Clay leaned over a stall gate, watching Lolly nose through clean bedding. She'd been rubbed down and groomed, and had already cleaned up most of the hay and oats in her feed tub.

Garrett held out the jar and a rag.

"Me?" The boy looked at the salve as if it were a rattler. "But I—"

"Know exactly what to do."

Blue eyes flicked between Garrett and the jar, and Clay finally took it.

He stepped through the stall door, talking easy to the old mare and moving slow.

"That'a girl," he murmured. "You're doing just fine." He worked around her to the left side.

Garrett lifted his rope coiled on a knob in the alleyway and stepped inside. He eased the loose end around the mare's neck and stood close against her opposite shoulder. If she reared, she'd have to lift his weight.

"Where'd you learn to work with horses?"

Clay dipped the rag in the jar, then smoothed his other hand down Lolly's shoulder and leg. His tone of voice never changed, but remained low, easy, and comforting as if the mare was his only audience. "Back home."

He carefully applied the salve.

Lolly jerked her head up, tugging on Garrett's firm grip.

"I preferred working with the animals over working the land. Pa and I saw things differently."

Garrett's earlier suspicions solidified.

After the mare was settled, he and Clay unsaddled their mounts, brushed and grained them, and turned them into the livery's corral. Erik was already gone, but Garrett would settle up with him in the morning. If he needed a night man, Clay might fill the bill.

Garrett took a dollar from his vest pocket and slapped it in Clay's hand. "Go get something to eat at the café, then take that bedroll I saw on your saddle and bunk in the loft."

Stunned, Clay turned the new Morgan coin over in his hand, then gave Garrett that sideways look, as if waiting for him to take back the money and the offer.

"If I hear you spent a nickel of that at the Pike, the deal's off and you're outta here."

Clay closed his fingers over the coin. When he looked up, he'd aged. Stood taller. "Yes, sir."

Garrett walked back to Maggie's, where the pinch of burned hay and charred wood filled the night air. But as soon as he opened the back door, the stench gave way to fried potatoes and onions and the subtle scent of lavender soap. The bathing room door was slightly ajar.

Betsy stood at the stove, her back to his quiet entry, for he'd not stomped his feet or rattled the door.

Didn't know why. He just knew he wanted to take in the sight of her there, apron strings tied in a bow at her waist, her skirt draping the gentle curve of her hips. A lonesome corner in the back of his heart opened up, that place he kept closed off and sealed up.

The crazy notion to pull her into that place sparked like kindling on banked coals, and he cleared his throat and shut the back door before he made a fool of himself.

Without any sign of surprise, she glanced over her shoulder, a pleasant look on her face. Almost a smile. "Maggie's resting. I told her I'd fix supper."

Foolhardy bravery pushed him toward her, close enough to smell that fancy soap in her loose damp hair.

She didn't move away, just kept stirring the big skillet as well as a feeling in his gut he'd avoided for too long. His hand twitched as he reached into his vest pocket for the ribbon.

Without saying a word, he laid one hand on her shoulder. She stilled and turned her head to the side. Gently, he gathered her hair in his hands, then tied it at her neck with the blue ribbon. Even managed a bow. Then he stepped back before he took her in his arms and kissed the breath right out of her.

She laid down her wooden spoon and reached up to the bow as she turned to face him. "Where was it?"

Her tone was hushed like the evening, warm like the kitchen, and full of wonder.

His hands found his pockets on their own, a good thing. "At the edge of the corral where you took Blanca and her foal."

Her look struck fire in his veins and he stepped back again, bumping into a chair at the small kitchen table. "I, uh, need to go wash up." He caught his boot in the chair leg as he turned, nearly breaking his neck trying to get away. But the sound of his name as he reached the door stopped him cold, and he braced himself for a cutting remark about his clumsiness.

"Thank you."

Not until cooler air hit his face did he remember that he didn't have to go outside to wash up. Maggie's indoor plumbing warred with his sense of habit. But what was done was done, and he trudged out to the trough beyond the ash heap that had been the buggy shed.

Emptiness met him across the pasture fence, the absence of animals an uneasy void. And in the stillness he stood listening, waiting for a sense of direction, a course to follow. A clue about the fires and life itself.

What was he going to do if there was an arsonist in town?

And what was he going to do about beautiful, unmarried Betsy Beaumont?

CHAPTER 18

What was she going to do about Garrett Wilson, and why did she think she needed to do anything?

Elizabeth set the skillet on the back of the stove, pulled the coffee pot to the front, and went to the parlor to check on Maggie. The poor woman was sound asleep, curled up on the settee like a kitten. Elizabeth found a shawl on the back of a chintz chair and draped it over her, then lit the wood already laid in the fireplace and set the screen in place.

She and Garrett would eat at the small table in the kitchen.

The suggestion of such intimacy fluttered through her insides, and she reached up to touch the ribbon. Again, he'd shown himself a kind and thoughtful man. If she wasn't careful, she'd stumble and fall once more.

As she set the table, the differences between Garrett and Edward paraded through her mind. She'd noted only their similarity of broad shoulders and gallant gestures. But they differed on many levels, and if she were honest with herself, they were nothing alike at all. Further honesty demanded she admit she was attracted to Garrett Wilson. Not on a shallow, social level, but deeply in her innermost being.

Frustration added weight to her placement of the silverware, and she pushed honesty aside. She'd come home to start fresh, not have her head turned by another man.

She thought of the Eisners, displaced from their hotel room so soon after their arrival. How they worked together to establish their business and life. How a sense of oneness emanated from them. She had never felt she was one with Edward, though they'd shared a sometime bed and a piece of paper that said they were married. Regret boiled over again, and she shoved it aside with the honesty, clamping a lid on the both of them.

Garrett returned, looking sheepish, probably over his forgetfulness of Maggie's running water in the kitchen or the washstand in his room. Yet he'd fairly run out the back door. Wet spots showed on his trousers where he'd dried his hands after washing at the trough pump. Without soap.

She resisted the urge to remind him, choosing instead to return kindness for his kindness. Again she touched the ribbon.

Keeping with the informal setting, she served their plates from the stove top and set them on the table along with the coffee pot. She then took her seat, carefully tucking her feet beneath her chair. They would share the small floor space with Garrett's boots.

He ate heartily, apparently satisfied with her meager cooking skills. But little could go wrong with a skillet of potatoes, onions, and shredded beef.

"Biscuits would have been nice." She hadn't intended to voice the thought. It simply fell out of her mouth when she opened it for a bite.

Garrett nodded, full of food rather than complaint. His gray glance didn't fail to make her heart skitter. "True, but this is good. Maggie's missing out."

Unaccustomed to compliments, Elizabeth hardly knew what to say. She deferred to their landlady. "She's sleeping in the parlor, but I'll save a plate for her in the warming oven."

"The fire took the starch out of her."

Observant.

"I think her loss was more than just the carriage house. The fire encroached upon memories that she holds dear. Memories of her life with Daniel." Elizabeth paused to sooth her ire with a sip of hot coffee. "That someone would do such a thing, and without cause, is simply malicious."

The muscle in Garrett's jaw flexed, and he threw her another look. "So you don't think it was an accident."

No, she did not think it was an accident. "If you ask me, I find it highly unlikely that the building would just ignite, especially considering Maggie's comment about Pearl and that bit of torn cloth she found."

"All right, I'll ask you." His penetrating look set her back. "Any ideas on who that malicious someone might be?"

Trying to write off his demeanor as the suspicious nature of a lawman, she squirmed in her chair. He was making her uncomfortable. Completely unlike what she'd felt only moments before.

"I hardly know everyone in town. What makes you think I could point a finger?"

He frowned, laid his fork on his plate, and seemed to be gathering his thoughts before speaking. A wise move on his part.

She held in her agitation, waiting quietly for once.

When he raised his head, his eyes were dark.

"Call it gut. Call it intuition. Sometimes a person just knows."

In spite of her innate tendency to not back down, she knew she never wanted to be on the suspect side of his questioning.

"Does Maggie have fire insurance through Rochester?" he asked.

So that was why he'd pinned her. Relief eased the tension building in her shoulders, and she relaxed her clenched hands. "I suspect she does not, but she hasn't said one way or the other. And since it's really none of my business, I never asked her."

Garrett pushed his plate back, picked up his coffee, and planted his elbows on the table. Maggie would have been horrified.

"If I asked for your help, would you give it?"

The man was completely capable of stealing her breath with his outlandish remarks.

She took a moment, reminding her lungs to admit enough air so she didn't tumble to the floor.

He considered her over the brim of his cup. She wouldn't be surprised if he knew absolutely every pathetic detail of her life, though she'd told him very little.

"That depends."

An inquisitor of the highest degree, he didn't flinch or reveal his thoughts in any way. What happened to the man who'd tied a ribbon in her hair and stumbled over a chair on his dash out the door?

His gaze held steady. "How much do you trust me?"

Again, her lungs locked in place. At this rate, she'd be out cold in a matter of minutes. But before she could find an answer for herself as well as for him, he asked another question.

"How much do you trust your employer?"

The content of two letters in particular sharpened into focus, a letter she wouldn't mind discussing with someone else. However… "What exactly are you asking me?"

"I'm asking you if you trust me more than him, and if you'll tell me—provided you know—what he's up to."

Garrett Wilson didn't beat around the bush.

~

Betsy's wide-eyed stare betrayed her surprise, but Garrett couldn't be sure what surprised her—his suspicion of Rochester or his request for her help. Unethical though it was.

He was asking her to divulge confidential information, an act—if she agreed to it—that would speak to her character. Just as Clay Ferguson was being measured by his actions, Betsy's character would be revealed by hers. Trouble was, he wanted her help. At the same time, he didn't want her to be the sort of person who would willingly cross ethical and possibly legal boundaries.

He should have kept his mouth shut.

"You're asking me to spy."

"Some people might look at it like that."

"To betray my employer's trust."

Her character was rising to the surface, contributing to his internal battle.

Her jaw tightened and she looked down her nose at her plate, still full of a meal she'd hardly touched. "I'll give it some thought."

A non-answer either way. She was stalling, measuring her options. Exactly what a co-conspirator would do.

Or in spite of her reluctance to reveal personal background, she could be an honest woman with scruples.

He wished he knew which.

A mournful howl seeped through the door and windows, and he scooted his chair back. "Thanks for supper. I need to see to my dog."

"Wait."

Again, a single word from her made him stop.

"Maggie said she had something for Pearl, and I'm guessing it was this." She handed him a small dish of bony raw meat. "I hope so. I'm not particularly fond of oxtail."

He took the dish, but she didn't let go.

Her eyes narrowed in warning.

"Not that I'm a fan, mind you. But the dog did alert Maggie. Just don't tell it I had anything to do with this."

"I'll be sure to put in a good word for you."

He closed the door on her fuming, enjoying their banter. It almost squashed the impulse to kiss her.

Cooler air cleared his mental muddle for the second time that evening, and he set the dish in front of Pearl and untied her. She wolfed a few meaty pieces, then bounded into the dark pasture, hopefully running off energy and tiring herself.

He needed to sleep.

Not that he would with a personal tug-o-war pulling him between desire and professional duty. His insides churned. Not a good sign for things to come.

As he sat on the bench to rehash the day, a faint glow fanned out low in the east. Apprehension peppered the pot that was his gut, and he whistled for Pearl. By the time she returned and plopped down near the bone dish, the upper lip of a full moon had risen off the horizon, silhouetting the pasture fence and a distant windmill. He let out a heavy sigh.

He'd deliberately mentioned intuition to Betsy, hoping to bait her with the word. His grandmother had insisted that a woman's intuition was never wrong, and he was hard pressed to recall a single time when hers had been.

Something told him Betsy's intuition was keenly developed. But until she gave him an answer about sharing information, he needed to look at the situation from the male perspective: logic.

Mom logic, George Booth called it, based a three-legged-stool approach. A deliberate breech of the law required motive, opportunity, and means—mom.

The hotel fire could have been an accident. Though Garrett doubted it, he couldn't prove it wasn't, so for now he'd allow the possibility. But a similar situation so soon after the first one, on the opposite end of town in a rarely used private building? That lessened the chances of a second accidental fire.

And what about the melted wax he'd found?

Who would profit from the two fires? Not Thatcher, unless he had a large insurance policy he was sure Rochester was good for. Means and opportunity the man certainly had. But his labor and concern over getting the place up and running again made Garrett doubt he had motive.

Who would profit from burning Maggie's carriage house? Or was malice the motive, as Betsy suggested? Did Maggie have enemies?

For the second leg, opportunities abounded for both fires. The hotel housed people, and people were always up to something, whether being malicious or just plain stupid. Knocking over oil lamps. Falling asleep with a lit cigar.

The carriage house, on the other hand, was tucked away behind Maggie's oversized house, out of sight and off the beaten path, yet easily accessed from any side without alerting the owner.

The third leg was the easiest to find. In both fires, fire itself was likely the means. An oil lamp and a candle. Both carried a flame. Both could be left behind with time to spare for escape.

Another phrase from his church-house upbringing chimed in: *See how great a matter a little fire kindleth.* For sure, it didn't take much.

He picked up the bone dish and went back inside, leading Pearl through the kitchen and into the porch. "You'll sleep in here tonight because Maggie likes you."

The dog looked up at him with her possum grin and banged her tail against the bed frame.

"And you'll sleep over there without making any noise. Clear?" He pointed to a braided rug in front of the door.

Dutifully, Pearl plopped down on it, eyeing his bedroll-covered tick.

"Don't even think about it."

She dropped her head to her paws and shot him a soulful look.

He stripped off his boots, trousers, and shirt and crawled between his soogans—minus the tarp and wishing he had it. He'd need it before winter.

In the light of day, he'd comb through the remains of the carriage house again and check with Thatcher about insurance on the hotel. If Rochester was trying to drum up business for fire insurance, Garrett intended to find out and find out fast.

And if Betsy Beaumont was part of Rochester's operation, the quicker Garrett found that out, the better. Because from where things stood now, buildings weren't all that was burning.

CHAPTER 19

B uilding up her courage for the new work week, Elizabeth walked into the dining room the next morning only to find the table bare. Concerned, she turned immediately down the hall to Maggie's room on the ground floor and knocked gently.

No answer.

Knocking harder, she gripped the knob and put her ear against the door. Nothing. She edged it open and peeked inside.

Her landlady nestled childlike in the center of a four-poster bed, blankets mounded around her like colorful clouds.

"Maggie?" Elizabeth tip-toed to the bedside and leaned in to hear if the woman was breathing. What would she do if—

"Good morning, dear."

She startled back at Maggie's voice, nearly the victim of her own imagination. "Are you all right?"

"Just a bit weak, but I'll be fine once I'm up and about. I'm afraid I overslept." Maggie threw off the covers and pushed herself up, but then fell back against her pile of pillows. "Oh, dear."

Elizabeth laid a hand against her forehead. "You're feverish. I'm sending for the doctor." But she had no clue whom to send other than herself.

"Oh, posh. I'm fit as a fiddle. Just a bit over-vexed by the fire, I suppose. I'll be right as rain in no time."

"But you'll be resting in the *mean*time. I'll get you some water and a cup of tea, and be right back. Promise me you'll stay right there."

Maggie waved a hand. "Don't make such a fuss, Bets—Elizabeth."

"You call me whatever you want, but promise me you won't try to get up by yourself."

A heavy sigh of resignation settled the little woman even deeper into her nested bedding.

In the kitchen, Elizabeth put on a kettle of water, set out teacups and saucers, and found a serving tray. Then she looked through the door glass into the porch where Garrett slept. He was gone and his bed smoothed over.

Rummaging through Maggie's stores, she found chamomile tea and some English wafers—*biscuits*, the tin said—which she arranged on a small plate. The water soon boiled, and she poured two cups, arranged everything on the tray, and carried it to Maggie's room.

According to the tall case clock in the hallway, she had two hours before Mr. Rochester expected her.

His office was not where she wanted to be this morning, especially now with Maggie ill and Garrett asking her to spy. The idea still rubbed her wrong, with the emphasis on *wrong*. But what if Anthony Rochester was somehow connected to the fires? Garrett seemed to think so.

"Betsy?"

Maggie had pushed herself up against her pillow mountain and was watching Elizabeth with a frown.

"Oh—yes." She shook off her worry and set the tray on the edge of the bed with plenty of room to spare next to Maggie's small frame.

"I see you're ready for a cup of tea and wafers. Or biscuits. I'm not much of a baker, but I found these in your pantry."

"How sweet of you, dear. But you mustn't worry about me. I'm fit as a fiddle."

Fit enough, Elizabeth noted, that her hand trembled as she lifted her tea cup.

"Have a cookie, Maggie. Or whatever they are. I'd be happy to fix something more substantial for you. Eggs perhaps?"

Maggie shook her head. "These ginger thins will do just fine." She snapped one in half and dunked it in her tea.

Elizabeth giggled.

"This is my bedroom, so I'm permitted to indulge. Join me."

Encouraged by Maggie's lightheartedness, Elizabeth did just that and dunked a thin cookie in her tea.

Since manners—and Maggie—were momentarily set aside, she grasped the opportunity. "I'm so sorry about your barn, and terribly grateful that Lolly was in the pasture. You're fortunate that the flames didn't spread to the house."

Maggie spooned a broken cookie out of her teacup. "Fortune had nothing to do with it. The good Lord was watching out for me like He always does. And this time, He used that ugly-as-sin dog of Garrett's."

Elizabeth choked back a snicker.

Maggie glanced up. "You don't believe me, do you?"

"Oh, but I do. That dog is as ugly as you say."

"Speaking of Pearl, did Garrett eat before he left this morning?" Maggie rubbed her forehead.

"He was gone when I checked. Pearl too. But I'm sure he won't starve."

Dunking a second cookie, she added, "I'm also sure that the insurance money should allow you to rebuild the carriage house or a small barn. Would you like me to check on it this morning when I see Mr. Rochester?"

"Humph."

Elizabeth slid a sidelong look at Maggie, who seemed much improved since the arrival of tea and cookies. Maybe she just needed rest and sustenance.

In the course of one informal meal at a kitchen table, Garrett Wilson had succeeded in turning Elizabeth into a nosy busy-body. "You do have insurance don't you?"

"I don't *need* insurance, dear."

So Maggie wasn't running a boarding house to make ends meet?

"I wouldn't give that Rochester fellow a red cent. You should see what he's asking the Library Committee for to insure that tired old house."

Yes, I should. "Do tell."

Maggie wasn't so sick that she didn't know a hook when she heard it.

She returned her cup and saucer to the tray and slid down into the covers. "I think I'll rest a while longer, if you don't mind. And you best be off to work.

We wouldn't want Mr. Rochester here looking for you."

Dismissed, Elizabeth picked up the tray. "Can I get you anything before I leave?"

"No, dear. And thank you for the tea. It was just what I needed."

While tidying the kitchen and herself, Elizabeth combed through her memory for the location of the sign she'd seen for the doctor's office. It wasn't where it used to be, but was upstairs, above either the drugstore or the hardware store, both on her way to the sheriff's office. If she hurried, she'd have time to tell Garrett about Maggie's health and lack of insurance, ask the doctor to stop by and check on her, and make it to Rochester's by nine.

If Garrett had stayed for breakfast, it would have saved her a stop. Why couldn't he be on hand when she needed him?

Irritated and surprised, she dashed the idea with a quick yank of the curtains in her room. She didn't *need* any man.

The window afforded a view of the waking town, already busy with wagons and buggies and riders. Smoke curled from every visible chimney, and scattered cottonwoods shone gold in the early light, their leaves not yet fallen like those in the mountains.

She looked toward the jail, imagining the potbelly stove ticking out warmth in Garrett's office the same way her emotions ticked through her breast at the mere thought of him.

Her gaze shifted north where the Eisner's store held a place in the next block, and she almost envied their good company with each other.

Straight ahead rose the high false front of the building that housed Mr. Rochester's law office and the feed store. From the back, the framed boards looked bleak and barren, presenting their more colorful side to Main Street. Did that mirror her employer? Was he a man with an artificial façade held in place by rough ways and sharp motives? Such a thing could be said about her previous employer, though they differed in other respects.

However, she knew instinctively that Rochester was not a man in whom to place her trust.

Her gaze wandered back to the alley behind the jail, and she tried to imagine what it would be like to depend on a man who *was* trustworthy.

Leaving the window and her wondering, she pinned on her hat and picked up her satchel, realizing with sudden clarity that she'd just answered one of Garrett Wilson's questions.

~

"Yes, Sheriff. I've got insurance. For all the good it'll do me now *after* the fire."

Garrett looked around the hotel's refurbished lobby. The floors had been sanded, furniture and rugs replaced. The wallpaper held steady, and the stairs had a new runner. "You afraid something like this might happen again?"

"If it does, I'm done." Clarence Thatcher's anger smoldered just below the surface. "The premium has already eaten into my profit before I even rent out the first room. But Harrison wouldn't lend me the money to rebuild without it."

"How long have you been in the hotel business?"

Thatcher gave him an angry once-over. "You insinuating that I don't know how to run a hotel?"

"What I want to know is how many fires have you had over the years?"

The man huffed. "One. And it nearly cleaned me out."

He shoved a hand through his hair and heaved a sigh, not as defensive as he had been. "I've been here ten years, and this is the first fire." He lifted weary eyes to Garrett. "And now the Snowfield barn? If you ask me, we've got a firebug on our hands, and I'd appreciate you finding him before he sets the whole town ablaze."

Garrett shut the hotel's new door behind him, wondering if the dry-goods drummer Thatcher mentioned earlier had been burning the midnight oil.

He headed for the livery. Thatcher was plumb scared, and Garrett couldn't rightly blame him.

As he neared Bozeman's café, the aroma of fresh donuts hooked him in the gut and slowed his progress, but a movement across the street caught his eye.

Betsy Beaumont charged around the corner and up the block like a school marm huntin' a truant. She trumped Bozeman any day of the week, and Garrett stepped into the street. Maybe she'd have a bite with him, seeing as how Maggie wasn't in the kitchen this morning when he left—

The hair on his neck rose. That explained Betsy's hurry.

"Hold up!"

She halted and looked his way, her initial ire giving way to relief.

He joined her on the boardwalk. "What's wrong?"

"Maggie's not well. Or at least weaker than she should be. I just stopped at Doc Weaver's and asked him to check on her, but I wanted to see you before I went to work."

She wanted to see him. He let that sink in deeper than he should, rather than counting it a common turn of phrase. How could he suspect her?

She lowered her voice and took a half-step closer. "I have something to tell you."

The news both worried and encouraged him. Maggie might be in trouble, but Betsy might be willing to work with him.

"I was about to stop in at Bozeman's for coffee and a couple doughnuts. Care to join me?"

She cocked a fine brow and tilted her pretty head. "Don't you mean *bear sign*?"

Surprised again by another side of Betsy Beaumont, he chuckled. "How do you know about bear sign?"

"Deacon makes the best."

Of course. The old cowboy had probably trailed his share of longhorns back in the day.

He turned toward the street, offered his elbow, and nearly bowled over when she took it. If he wasn't careful, he'd have the whole town jawing about the two of them before noon.

His usual table was available, but he chose one in a back corner, figuring Betsy wouldn't want to sit in the window, a spectacle for everyone who passed by.

He helped her with her chair, not that she needed help, but Grandma's schooling was hard to shake. Betsy should be treated like the lady she was, whether she was straddling a horse in a run for her money or dressed for town in her skirt and straw hat.

She rewarded him with a tight smile. Something was up.

Bozeman brought coffee and took their order. Garrett hung his hat on his knee, waiting for her to tell him whatever it was that was running through her eyes like a jack rabbit.

"Maggie does not have fire insurance."

That was one of the things he liked about this gal. She avoided small talk. "Is that so."

She glanced across the room, then leaned forward, her voice even quieter. "She told me she doesn't need it."

Not a revelation. "Few folks think they do. They see it as an unnecessary expense. Far as I know, there's no insurance on the jail." Another back trail he needed to check.

Exasperated, she gave him a reproachful look. "I know. But that's not what I mean. Maggie said it in a different tone—as if she had enough money to build ten barns."

"Well, her place isn't exactly a pauper's house."

Another scolding glare. He almost laughed, but managed to drown the impulse with a swig of Bozeman's charred brew.

"So if she doesn't need the money, why is she running a boarding house?" she asked.

The innocent look on her face made him feel guilty for pointing out what he thought was obvious. "She's not."

Betsy stared at him for a beat, then rolled her eyes. "Pardon me, Sheriff, but we're both living there, or hadn't you noticed."

He set his cup down. "Where's Rochester staying?"

"At his office."

"And the Eisners?"

"Their store." She picked up her coffee.

"What about the other folks burned out of their rooms at the hotel? Where are they staying?"

Her brows pulled together and her focus shifted to table's edge. "But I thought—"

Bozeman interrupted them with a plate of greasy, sugar-smothered doughnuts and two napkins. "Beggin' your pardon, ma'am, but might you be Betsy Parker?"

Unfaltering, she met his look. "Why do you ask?"

"Who wants to know?" Garrett's hackles rose.

Bozeman ignored him, addressed Betsy. "I've heard people sayin' what a fine shot you were. Years back, before I settled here. They say you could outshoot all the men around here."

She coughed discreetly, pressing a napkin at her lips before answering. "You can't believe everything you hear."

She hadn't given Bozeman an answer either way, and Garrett chuckled to himself. Elizabeth Beaumont at work.

"I need a half dozen of these in a sack when we leave."

Bozeman swelled up and grinned like a turkey in a hen pen.

"Don't bust your surcingle. I've got a kid who'd eat your boots if you put sugar on 'em."

With an admiring glance at Betsy, the cook turned on his heel and went back to work.

Garrett helped himself, reading confusion on her face. He'd known her only a few weeks, but this was the first time he'd seen her stumped.

She tried her coffee and grimaced.

He pushed the sugar bowl toward her. "Stout, isn't it?"

A load of sugar and a gentle sip, and she met his gaze again. "Horned and barefoot."

"Deacon?"

Nodding, she smiled thinly. Even though it was a sad, half-hearted smile, it warmed him more than Bozeman's swill ever could.

The smile faded. "But Maggie answered my letter of inquiry and said she had a room for me."

"Did you see a sign on her front fence when you got here?"

Betsy looked up at him, searching his face for something he wished he had.

"No. But she used to have one. Six years ago, when I...left." She lowered her gaze.

He wanted to pull her close and fix whatever it was that took the wind out of her. Or punch someone. Almost anyone of the male persuasion. "You're right. I heard she closed down a couple years ago after her husband passed on. Word was it got to be too much for her."

213

"How did you get a room with her?"

The memory brought wry a twist to his mouth. "She saw me in the mercantile buying canned peaches and beans, and flat out asked if I needed a place to stay other than one of my cells."

"Why not the hotel?"

He shook his head. "Doesn't work for a sheriff."

She accepted his answer without pressing him. "So Maggie put you in that porch off the kitchen."

He risked his own question. "Why did you write to her rather than going home to the ranch?"

She bristled, but not as stiff as usual, and seemed to resign herself. "I want to make my own way, not come running home after failing at my marriage."

The urge to punch someone rose again, and he wrapped one fisted hand in the other and hid them in his lap. "I don't see you failing at anything you put your mind to."

Color rose to her cheeks. "Surely I did, or my husband would not have gone to the Dakota gold fields and left me with a petition for divorce."

She cringed on the last word.

The woman kept throwing him off center. She wouldn't tell him anything when he asked, and then she up and spilled her story when he wasn't ready.

Trying her coffee again, she took a sip, then bit into her doughnut, and stared out the window. "Why do you suppose Maggie rented me a room? Habit? The kindness of her heart?"

"Both are probably true. But I think there's more to it."

He sensed the fissure in Betsy's wall fingering down into the foundation.

"I think she's lonely."

The notion played across her face with something akin to empathy.

"She's livened up quite a bit since you arrived." So had he.

"Well, she wasn't very lively this morning, and I'm worried about her. Maybe I should tell Mr. Rochester I won't be staying today."

As much as he didn't want her working for that scoundrel, he *did* want her to find out what she could. "I'll check with Doc first, then stop by and let you know."

She gave him a doubtful look.

He ignored it. Time was against them where fire and Maggie were concerned. "You said there was more."

Choosing a second doughnut, the smallest that remained, she took a tiny bite. Powdered sugar dusted her lip, and he clenched his hands so he wouldn't reach across the table like a fool.

She dabbed her mouth with the napkin. "All this sugar is going to spoil me."

"I doubt it."

A shy smile tilted her mouth. "Maggie and I ate cookies for breakfast."

"Is that the *more* you wanted to tell me?"

She grew serious again, wiped her fingers off, and looked him square in the eye. "Maggie insinuated that the fire insurance premium for the library is outlandish, but she wouldn't tell me how much. And she said she wouldn't give Anthony Rochester one red cent."

"Does that surprise you?"

"I'm surprised that her opinion of him has changed so drastically."

"How so?"

"When I first considered working for him, she thought it was a grand idea."

Strange. "What changed her mind?"

Betsy picked up her coffee cup and peered at him over the cup's edge. "I believe you did."

CHAPTER 20

Elizabeth felt her insides teetering, as if she were riding toward rimrock at a dead run, about to plunge over the edge.

Garrett's lawman's mask slid into place and he fixed her with a steely gaze. "You willing to help me?"

Apparently, telling him about Maggie's lack of insurance and her opinion of the attorney wasn't enough. "I just did."

His mouth slid up on the scar side. Not exactly a smile, more of a twitch. She was drawn to that crescent dent in his cheek, still curious about how he got it.

"I need more. I need to know what Rochester is working on. Specifically, if he's involved in the fires."

"I doubt he started them. He'd be hard pressed to dirty his hands and shoes in such an endeavor."

The scar deepened, as did the color of his eyes.

She shifted in her chair, uncomfortable with her instinctive response to his—what, charm?

"We read him the same on that level."

His casual use of *we* didn't help her at all. "Well, what level are you looking for?"

Garrett leaned forward. "You type-write for him. I want to know who those letters are addressed to and what he's saying in them."

Her heart dropped like a stone to her stomach. Again he asked for the ultimate breech of confidence—beyond spying, to her way of thinking. How could he do that? And how could she comply?

He held her gaze, reading her, until his jaw locked and he leaned back against his chair. By the way the fingers of his right hand rubbed the handle of his coffee mug, he'd decided she wouldn't help him.

But what if Rochester was behind the fires? Was her silence worth putting the public's safety and welfare at risk? Maggie's welfare?

Specific portions of several letters had baffled her from the moment she'd copied them. Should she share the puzzling text without revealing the recipient?

"I cannot betray a confidence, even for the greater good."

Garrett's expression did not change.

"But I did question some of the correspondence because it seemed to make no sense."

He hooked his thumbs in his belt and waited. She much preferred the gentler, soft-eyed Garrett, the one who had held her at her mother's grave and held her chair here in the café. Instead, she faced an unpredictable predator. One who would get his prey at all cost.

She'd not sell her soul for his approval, for *any* man's approval, but she saw nothing wrong with voicing her own questions.

She glanced at her lapel watch, surprised by the time that had already passed. Only minutes remained before she must leave for Mr. Rochester's office.

"What would you think of letters from an attorney that mentioned flowers, quite out of context with the rest of the letter?"

Curiosity flicked across Garrett's hardened features.

"Red bud. Geraniums. And another I didn't recognize—*hanabi*."

He leaned in. "What are you getting at?"

"I'm not getting at anything. I'm asking you a question."

She folded her rumpled napkin and tucked it under her plate. "Thank you for the coffee and doughnuts."

As she stood, he did the same, capturing his hat and clapping it on. He picked up his paper sack, paid the café owner, then held the door for her as she exited.

Together they headed toward the north end of town.

At the corner, she paused before crossing the street. "Are those doughnuts for Clay?"

Garrett fisted the sack. "From the way he put away food at the ranch, I figure he hasn't seen many good days lately."

"You arrested him, didn't you?"

The paper crackled in his fingers. "For his own good."

The man clearly had a penchant for strays. She glanced across the street and then regarded him once more. "You'll let me know what the doctor says about Maggie?"

He nodded, watching her with that piercing, knowing look.

"I'm sorry, but I can't give you more than what I've said already. It's unethical."

He dipped his head the slightest bit and ran two fingers along the brim of his hat as if caressing her cheek. "I anticipated nothing less from you."

Stunned into silence, she stood at the corner watching Garrett Wilson stride down the boardwalk. He never looked back, nor did she expect him to.

Frankly, she didn't know what she expected from that man.

Shaking off her reaction, she checked for oncoming wagons and horses, then crossed to the east side of the street.

Mr. Rochester, seated at his desk when she entered his office, glanced up briefly. "Good morning, Mrs. Beaumont."

A chill swept around his words, as if he were chiding her for being late, though the wall clock said she was two minutes early.

Fresh from her admission to Garrett, perhaps she should also tell her employer that she was divorced. But not now.

"Good morning." She removed her hat and situated herself at her desk.

He rose from his and came to stand in front of her, one hand thumbed in his vest pocket and the other fingering his thin mustache.

"You look different today."

She kept her eyes down, busying herself with her type-writer ribbon.

"More color, I'd say. Did you visit your brother at the ranch?"

Unable to keep her head from snapping up, she managed to squash what she wanted to say and reply courteously. "A pleasant weekend."

"Aside from the fire at the Snowfield mansion." He tsked. "Unfortunate loss, indeed. You are staying there, aren't you?"

Only so much fiddling with her type-writer would keep her hands, mind, and mouth in line. She looked up, considering how best to quit his employ.

His lip curled in more sneer than smile, and he went back to his desk where he gathered a stack of papers.

"I have some legal documents for you this morning. I need them by noon." He laid them on the narrow corner of her table, then handed her the box of stationery.

"That should be no problem." Unless Garrett showed up with troublesome news from the doctor. She looked at her hands, ruing the time she'd spent in the round pen rather than at the piano. If she'd paid more attention to her mother's coaxing, she could be teaching music or playing Sunday mornings for Pastor Bittman and social events rather than type-writing for Anthony Rochester.

She rolled a crisp, clean sheet behind the platen, straightened it, and forced herself to focus on the job at hand.

After thirty minutes of redundant and, to her way of thinking, purposefully confusing legal jargon, the front door opened and Garrett strode in without comment.

She suppressed the impulse to run to him.

He walked straight to her desk, doffed his hat, and said in a low voice, "All is well."

"Indeed." Mr. Rochester rose imperiously. "Good news is always welcome, Sheriff. I take it you are referring to the hotel fire, which you have had under *investigation*. And now we have the unfortunate conflagration at the Snowfield mansion." He shook his head as if mourning the loss of a dear pet.

A muscle in Garrett's jaw flexed and the vein in his neck throbbed. Given his dislike of her employer, Elizabeth feared he might go to blows right there in the office.

"I'll make my report at the next meeting." He tugged his hat on and left.

Mr. Rochester followed him out the door, which he held open. "Thank you for stopping by, Sheriff. Always a pleasure visiting with you."

He spoke loudly enough for half the town to hear. Elizabeth typed the last three words that he said. With a furtive glance his way, she removed the paper and started a fresh sheet.

~

Not much was left of the doughnuts by the time Garrett reached the livery. He'd nearly crushed the paper sack into a brown wad. Anthony Rochester's arrogance festered inside him without relief, and he was itching to lance it.

At the livery, he stopped just inside the open doors, adjusting to the dim light. A scraping sound rose from a stall farther back, and the familiar tap-*ping* of Erik's hammer sang above it.

In the third stall, he found Clay raking soiled hay and loading it in a wheel barrow. "Mornin'."

Clay grinned. "Mornin', Sheriff." He leaned on the pitch fork. "Need me to catch up Rink?"

"You sound like you work here."

The grin grew. "Yes, sir. Thanks to you." He shoved his hair out of his eyes and glanced up at the loft. "Slept good, too."

"You eat last night?"

"Yes, sir." He pulled a few coins from his pocket, and held them out as if to hand them over.

Garrett turned his hand upright and set the paper sack on top of the coins." Save 'em for dinner. Here's breakfast. What's left of it."

Clay sobered. "I appreciate it, Sheriff, but I can't keep takin' your charity. I—"

"No charity to it." More like penance. Garrett adjusted his hat. "Can't have you weakening on the job. You're here on my word."

He moved on before the boy said more.

The air warmed considerably as he approached Erik's anvil and furnace, even though the back doors were open wide to the morning.

"Thanks for puttin' Clay to work."

The big man's hammer bounced to a standstill and he looked up. "He is *gut* worker and welcome here as long as he stays that way."

Garrett continued his rounds, pausing at the newspaper office window. Fischer was waving his arms over his head and yelling, though Garrett couldn't make out what he said. The pressman stood with his hands on his hips and near-death in his eyes, and the young reporter was inching away from the rant.

Next stop, the bank.

Harrison rose from his desk and motioned Garrett back. "Good timing, Sheriff. Have a seat."

He took a puff on his cigar stub and laid it in a small brass dish.

A cigar could start a fire if the tinder was dry enough. Garrett rubbed his hand across his face, hoping to clear the thought from his mind as well.

"The fire at Snowfield's roused so much interest in a hose crew, that we now have enough money for a hose, reel, and Howe hand pumper. I put the order in Rochester's hands first thing this morning, and he assured me that the equipment should arrive in two weeks."

Rochester hadn't mentioned the order.

Harrison was obviously quite proud of himself, but blind as a liquored-up judge where the attorney was concerned. Garrett wasn't so sure he wanted Rochester knowing what he'd found at the two burn sites, but if they did have a firebug, it was best that someone else know about it too. He trusted Harrison more than the others, but not by much.

He thumbed his hat up. "I believe the Snowfield fire was set intentionally, and maybe the hotel."

Harrison looked like he'd just been sucker-punched. After a beat, he picked up his stogie and drew hard on it.

"If you don't mind, I'd appreciate you keeping that bit of information to yourself for a time."

The banker choked and coughed like a locomotive, apologizing as he wiped his mouth on a handkerchief. "Why? Shouldn't we alert everyone?"

"If we do, we could be alerting the arsonist. I'd rather not show my hand right off."

Harrison's eyes darted around the room as if looking for the culprit, but he showed no sign of nervous guilt. "Whatever you say, Sheriff."

He snuffed out his cigar, and the acrid smoke curled up toward the high ceiling. Smelled like somebody'd set a cat on fire.

"You call a meeting yet?"

"Friday at five."

"I'll be here."

Garrett saw himself to the door, grateful for the somewhat fresher air outside. He thought back to the freshest air he'd breathed in a while. Up in Echo Valley along the river where he and Betsy had eaten dinner on Sunday. He'd give his badge for more of the same, but then he'd be out of work and back on the trail.

Somehow, Betsy Beaumont made that option unappealing. He was going soft.

He spent the rest of the day reading through warrants, taking down outdated wanted posters, and catching up on paperwork—generally wasting as much time as possible before heading to Maggie's for supper.

The doctor hadn't seemed concerned over her condition and told Garrett that he cautioned her to rest and let someone else take care of the household chores and cooking. No misunderstanding on Doc's part that Maggie Snowfield was not running a boarding house.

Garrett smiled to himself as he slipped the latigo through Pearl's collar and headed down the alley. Betsy seemed to be the only one under the impression that the Snowfield home was still in the boarding business. But he had to admit that he was glad about the misunderstanding.

Going home every night and sharing a table with the opinionated but lovely Betsy Beaumont was something he could sit still for.

Aside from her last name.

Now that he knew the truth, future possibilities ran wild through his thoughts. Almost as wild as the woman herself, headed straight for him with her skirts hiked over her shoe tops and her hair flying like a horse's mane.

CHAPTER 21

E lizabeth flew down the porch steps and out the front gate—straight to the only person she was certain could help.

"Whoa-whoa-whoa." Garrett stopped her with a hand on each arm, dropping Pearl's tether in the process.

The dog jumped up, whining and sniffing around her chin, but Elizabeth didn't care.

"Someone...has been...in the house." She gripped Garrett's wrists, draping her weight against his strong arms as she caught her breath. "My room—someone's been in my room."

An odd look crossed his face, then he yanked Pearl down. "When?"

"Now. Today. I don't know. But since I left this morning." She stepped back and reached for a more ladylike bearing. "Maggie's been home all day alone, and *someone* uninvited was there as well."

Garrett quickly turned her toward the house, his pace barely slow enough for her to keep up. "The doctor was there."

"I know that." Honestly, did he think she was an imbecile? "Did you not hear what I said? Someone was in *my room.*"

"How do you know?"

"How did you get to be sheriff?" So much for ladylike.

He jarred to a glare-flashing stop in front of the house, and his jaw clinched back words she was certain she did not want to hear.

Tempering her temper, she drew a deep breath. Anxiety had deteriorated into frustration, and that would get them nowhere. "The drawers of my bureau were not closed flush, and my wardrobe had been riffled through. Even my trunk. And the drawer to the writing desk."

He sobered at her calmer explanation, then held the gate as she walked through. At the porch, he tethered Pearl to a post, then opened the front door. Maggie stood at the entrance to her room, holding onto the doorframe.

"Just in time," she said with less color in her usually spry voice. "I can use your help in the kitchen, dear, if you don't mind."

Elizabeth hurried forward. "Oh, but I do." She linked her arm through Maggie's at the elbow, then eased her across the hallway and into the parlor. "I think you should sit down with a cup of tea while I get supper on the table. Garrett will lay a fire, and we'll all be as cozy as a bug in a rug in no time."

"It's *snug* as a bug, dear. I thought you'd know that."

She did, but it sounded too intimate to include Garrett in such a phrase. She flashed him a cautious but pleading look, and he strode through the house and out the back door, for firewood, she hoped. Maggie accompanied her to the parlor settee without disagreement.

By the time Elizabeth returned with the tea tray and a plate of cookies, Garrett had come through with an armload of wood and had a fire roaring from the hearth, warming the room with heat and light as well as his protective presence. The setting was one she'd dreamed of with Edward that had never come to pass, and an odd hope blossomed like the flames growing around the split logs.

He pulled a chair closer to the settee where Maggie rested, her feet elevated to the burgundy velvet. "How are you feeling?"

"Never better." Maggie was a pitiful liar, much to Elizabeth's shame. She had perfected the sin.

Garrett palmed his mouth, presumably squelching what he really wanted to say. She offered him a cup of tea, and he politely took the china cup and saucer, dwarfing them with his large hands. He gave her a brief nod in thanks, and if she hadn't been so rattled about someone rummaging through her possessions, his look alone would have rattled her.

"Did anyone stop by today, other than the doctor?" he said.

"I blame the two of you for that visit. I don't need a doctor." Maggie sipped her tea and reached for a cookie. "But no one else came. Other than Elizabeth."

She froze, her cup halfway to her lips.

"I called out, but you didn't answer." Maggie gave her a scolding glance. "I assumed you were dashing in for something, hurrying to get back to Mr. Rochester's, and didn't want to visit."

"But I—"

"What time was that, do you know?" Garrett interrupted with a nearly imperceptible shake of his head. "Dinner time?"

"Oh no. Mid-afternoon. The clock chimed three as light footsteps ran upstairs. That's how I knew it was Betsy. I mean Elizabeth."

Stunned into silence again, she regretted her earlier insistence on her given name. It sounded more and more foreign all the time. She stood and refilled Maggie's cup. "I'm going to fix us some supper. You stay here, please, and rest. We can all eat in here by the fire."

Maggie fussed and sat upright. "But that's just not done."

Garrett gently lifted her feet back to the settee. "Think of it as being on the trail. You always eat near the fire when you're out under the stars. Where's your sense of adventure?"

Maggie waved him off, muttering under her breath.

Elizabeth fled the room before she completely melted at Garrett's tenderness, but waited at the foot of the stairs.

He joined her without comment and followed her to her room.

She'd left everything as she found it, and in a most professional manner, he looked in every spot she indicated. The desk drawer, the wardrobe, even her trunk, where he delicately moved her things aside as if they were priceless and fragile.

Edward had never shown such deference, and the sight of Garrett doing so struck her as remarkable.

Yet someone else had handled her most private things—uninvited. She shivered.

"Is anything missing?" He took in the room with a careful eye, from floor to ceiling and beneath every piece of furniture, including the bed.

"I don't think so." She'd checked for her journal and found it safely concealed in the bottom of her trunk. Even Garrett had not noticed the incongruity in the bottom.

"Why would someone come up here and go through things? And *who* would do it." He murmured more to himself than to her. Finally, he captured her with sober eyes. "What do you think they were looking for?"

She swallowed, longing to be straightforward and truthful, but not willing to give up her journal. It held every sordid detail of her miserable life in Denver, from her disastrous marriage and divorce, to Braxton Hatchett and his bold advances. Little good it had done her.

"Was Rochester in his office all day?"

His question saved her from either extreme— disclosure or deceit. "Yes. He was there the entire time I was. At one point he went into his back room and closed the door, but he frequently does that."

Garrett's right eye twitched. "Do you know for sure he was *in* the back room the whole time he was not in the front office?"

She did not.

～

Troubled by Garrett's final question and embarrassed by her lack of culinary skill, Elizabeth splashed cold water on her face at the kitchen sink, then lit the pull-down gas light above the small table. A warm glow spread across the room and into the once-dark corners, banishing some of her discomfort. She filled a bowl with potatoes and onions from the pantry, assuaging herself with Garrett's mention of eating on the trail. Fried potatoes, onions, and salt pork would be the fare, she knew. And coffee. She set a pot on to cook while she peeled potatoes.

Memories spread through her like the gas light, complete with the sweet tinge of sage and pine. Of riding the high parks with Cade and their pa and ending the day with whatever Deacon could fit in a skillet.

Sadly, she realized it was the first time she'd had good memories of her father since she'd returned.

The echo of Garrett's boots in the hall did little to prepare her for his arrival. She was quivering on the inside long before he stopped behind her and closed his strong hands lightly around her arms. He ran them up and down the sleeves of her dress, and she feared her legs would give way if he didn't stop.

"Is there a back door to Rochester's office?"

His question grounded her enough to focus, and she stirred the skillet supper and shook her head. "I don't know. I've not been back there, but surely there is more than one door."

She stilled. "You know I wasn't the one who ran upstairs at three, don't you?"

"Yes." His fingers gently pressed. "But didn't you come back earlier for dinner?"

"After all those doughnuts?"

Another squeeze. "All two?"

She breathed a small laugh. His hands slid up to her shoulders, and his thumbs grazed her neck. No more laughing. No more breath.

"Smells good." He moved closer still, trapping her between his warmth and the heat of the stove. He nuzzled her hair. "But not as good as you."

Lord, help her. If he didn't let go and step back, she'd burn their supper and have to start all over again.

As if sensing her distress, he pecked the top of her head with a chaste kiss and went to the sink where he rolled up his sleeves and washed his hands.

A kiss? That was completely unacceptable. He was becoming entirely too familiar, a dangerous situation, indeed.

And she ached for more.

~

Cold water brought Garrett sharply back to reality and to the truth of what he'd just done. He was lucky Betsy hadn't slapped him with her spoon.

But that was part of the problem. She could spit horseshoe nails at him with a look, but then ease into his touch. Turned him in-side-out trying to predict her reactions. And the smell of her, in spite of the fried onions and pork, was enough to make him loco.

He wanted more.

"Do you mind carrying this tray to the parlor for Maggie? I'll bring our plates."

Loose hair stuck to her face, shiny with perspiration.

His fingers itched to smooth that hair out of her eyes. Just the slightest touch. Instead, he took the tray and kicked himself all the way down the hall to the parlor.

Maggie was sleeping when he set the tray on a small table beside the settee. Rather than wake her, he laid another log on the fire and stood with his back to it, watching her. She was deathly pale in her dark dress, almost as white as her hair. He didn't know much about older women, aside from his grandmother who was boot tough and soft as a kitten. But she would have made three Maggie Snowfields. Why was the doctor not concerned?

"Here we are, all ready—"

Betsy stopped just inside the room, a plate in each hand and color draining from her face as well. Her eyes deepened with alarm, and she handed him one plate, then knelt next to Maggie, still holding the other.

"Is that for me, dear?"

Startled back, Betsy nearly dropped the dish. He caught her from behind and took the plate while she scrambled to her feet. Just like she had the first time he met her.

"I swear—"

"I hope not, dear. Help me sit up, please."

"Maggie, you'll be the death of me if you keep surprising me like that."

"No surprise. Just a hungry old woman. If it weren't for those cookies this morning, I'd have had nothing to keep body and soul together."

Agitated and no doubt wanting to give Maggie a piece of her mind, Betsy gave her the tray instead, then sat down in a chair across the room. Garrett joined her in another chair just like it, separated by a small table between them. He counted five tables in the gussied-up room, none of them any bigger than the top of his potbelly stove at the jail.

Maggie must have been telling the truth, for in no time she cleaned up everything on her plate. Betsy helped her to her room while Garrett took the dishes to the kitchen.

If it were just him, he'd pile them in the sink and wash them tomorrow, but it wasn't just him, and if he played his cards right, he could wrangle some more time up close to Elizabeth Betsy Parker Beaumont.

That last name set his blood to boiling quicker than the water in the kettle on the stove. What kind of weasel exchanged a pretty young wife for a miner's life in Dakota Territory? *After* the rush had petered out.

"She's exhausted." Betsy marched into the kitchen, pushing up her sleeves, and stopped dead in her tracks.

Then she clapped a hand across her mouth.

He frowned. "It's hard to get my clothes warmed up in the morning if they're wet."

She rolled her pretty lips, a sparkle in her eye. "Turn around. If you're going to wear Maggie's apron, you need a bow in the back."

He might as well let her tie a bow. She'd already tied his insides in knots.

She went to one of the many drawers in the kitchen and pulled out a long towel. "You wash, I'll dry." Then she filled a pan in the sink next to his dishpan with a mix of cold and boiling water. "Set the dishes in there after you wash them. And start with the cups and silverware. Then the plates, then the skillet. Doesn't hurt to wash it once in a while."

He never washed his skillet. Just wiped it out or took a knife to what stuck. Stepping back, he spread his stance. "Next, you'll be tellin' me how to run my jail."

Her lips puckered, fighting a smile, and he fought to keep from kissing her.

They worked side by side in amiable silence, Betsy stashing the dishes in their proper places until a thoughtful expression worked its way off her face and out of her mouth.

"I've been thinking about what you said regarding Maggie not running a boarding house. And being lonely." She dried a flower-flecked plate until he thought she'd wipe the flowers right off. "What if there's more to it than loneliness?"

He dunked the skillet and went to scrubbing. "She doesn't need the money."

"True. But what if she needs something else?"

He stopped and looked at the beautiful woman beside him, light glinting off her dark hair. "Like what?"

"Help."

He dried his hands on the apron. "What do you need?"

She shot him a side-long look that questioned his intelligence, and he bristled.

"Not me. Her."

Oh. Confounded woman had him where he couldn't think straight. He picked up the scrub brush. "Doc said he wasn't worried. She just needed to rest and not do so much."

"Exactly. Look at this place." Betsy spun around, sweeping her hand through the air as if clearing the fog. "She does everything. Cooks, cleans. Does up the linens and runs this sprawling home without a housekeeper. And she's not getting younger."

None of 'em were.

"What if having us here is for her sake as well as ours?"

He liked the sound of *us* and *ours* and wanted to chew on that for a minute.

Betsy's voice dropped to a hush. "What if she's afraid of growing old alone?"

A thought he'd had a time or two himself.

He propped the skillet upside down in the sink, drained the dishpan, then laid the apron over the back of a chair and poured two cups of coffee.

Betsy joined him at the table and studied him over the brim of her cup.

The look was a warning—not a threat, but an honest, open query, and he prepared for whatever unwanted question she was about to spurt.

"What brought you to Olin Springs?"

Like that one.

"Tired of trailing cattle north."

She just kept watching him. Maybe he could hire her as an interrogator.

"My former employer, Marshall Booth in Abilene, said it was a good fit—me and this town. I thought I'd give it a try."

He knew what was coming, and also knew he wasn't about to spill his guts right there all over Maggie's white tablecloth.

"So cattle took you to Abilene. And you became a deputy there."

He nodded once, drew in a mouthful of coffee as cover.

"Why'd you leave?"

"Why'd you?"

Her eyes snapped, but she held steady. "I asked first."

The fingers of his right hand twitched, and he set down his cup and rubbed his hand on his trousers. "Trouble. You?"

She sniffed, unhappy with his brief answer, but she let it lie.

"I blamed my father for getting himself and Mama killed in a buggy accident. I was young, headstrong, and looking for…" She blinked. "I'm sure you've heard the story elsewhere by now."

He held her attention, wanting to hold her.

"People have been very kind to me since I returned, more so than I imagined possible." She set down her coffee cup and tucked her hands in her lap. "Though I believe Cade is still quietly angry with my *independent streak* as he would call it. In that way, I am much like our father."

She frowned at mention of her pa.

"Forgiveness is healing medicine. For both sides."

She cut a glance across the table, taking in the words his grandparents had lived by.

"A couple of people have shown their disapproval, but it seems most have forgiven me. I didn't expect that."

He could change the subject. Talk about the arsonist. Maggie. The weather. "Someone hasn't."

The idea sent her on a frantic mental search, as clear on her face as if she were lining people up, hunting for that one person until realization hit. "My parents can't forgive me. They're gone."

He shook his head, testing the waters.

"Who?"

"You ran off the last time I mentioned it."

"I did not." She drew up. "When?"

"Echo Valley."

"I did not run off."

"Well, what do you call getting up and riding away?"

"I call it work. We had things to do." Another pointed look. "What are you suggesting?"

"I'm suggesting that you haven't forgiven yourself because you don't believe you deserve it." He let the words settle, then lowered his voice. "None of us deserve it, Betsy. It's a gift."

From the fire in her eye, he fully expected her to ignite.

"You don't know what I believe or don't believe. In fact, you don't know me as well as you think you do, Sheriff Wilson."

He leaned in. "Last names and titles, is it now?"

She stood, and the chair legs barked across the wooden floor. "You don't know what you're talking about."

He joined her—slowly, so his chair didn't scrape. So she wouldn't run away again. "Yes, I do."

Her neck could have snapped with the force of her chin lifting. "That is completely impossible. What gives you the right to tell me I need to forgive myself?"

"Hauling guilt around, that's what. It's the same as lugging a dead body."

She recoiled at the image. "Who says I'm carrying guilt?"

"You."

The word fell between them, blocking his view of her heart through her eyes.

He turned and walked out the back door.

CHAPTER 22

E lizabeth's stomach turned like a grist mill wheel. She pressed one hand against her middle, the other over her mouth, and ran upstairs to the narrow door at the end of the landing. Twisting the glass knob, she yanked. The door stuck, sealed by time and disuse. She tugged harder and it gave way, expelling a chilly cough. Five steps into the narrow black throat, her toe kicked against the first stair. Fourteen more, and she burst out into the night.

From the shelter of the cupola, she could see the whole of Olin Springs. The railroad twisted away into the foothills, a silvery ribbon in the moon's thin light, and to the north, the Big Dipper stood on its handle, spilling countless stars across the sky.

Tears spilled across her cheeks.

She hated Garrett Wilson. She hated him for stealing her heart when she wasn't looking, for making her want to love again. For making her wonder what life could be like with a man like him.

But she hated him most for being right.

Her fingers curled around the railing. How could he have guessed her secret when she didn't even know it herself until he pointed it out? How could he so calmly strip away her carefully layered veneer and make her see the truth?

She wrapped her arms around herself to keep from breaking apart and tipped her head back, standing soul-naked in the night.

"Oh, God." Her voice squeezed up and floated out to the countless stars. "Oh, God, help me. I've deceived others and myself as well."

A light breeze brushed against her, and with it came the aroma of someone's supper—evidence of home and family and togetherness. All the things she longed for that seemed as far from her reach as the sparkling Dipper.

Slowly, another essence whispered through the cupola. Nearly unnoticeable at first, it grew with soothing warmth, washing over her bare soul, her past mistakes.

Come, Thou fount...

Not her mother's voice this time, but her own—small and thin and bleeding. "Oh, to grace how great a debtor, daily I'm constrained to be."

The words came with new meaning, not just words to a song, but words for her life. Unexpected and full of peace.

"Praise the mount! I'm fixed upon it. Mount of Thy redeeming love."

~

Pearl whined, but Garrett strode off without her. He needed to be alone. Completely alone. And she'd be better off tied to the porch. Unless she pulled out the

242

post and brought the whole thing crashing down on her. It'd be just his luck if she did.

No such thing as luck, son. Life is what you and God make it. If you let Him.

His grandfather's advice bounced off the insides of his skull, and not for the first time.

So why couldn't he *make* Betsy see what he saw— that her misery was self-inflicted?

He'd seen the way everyone had welcomed her, Cade included. Yet, still she believed she didn't measure up. Hadn't paid enough recompense. Didn't deserve to be happy.

The same song he'd danced to for a half dozen years until George Booth got ahold of him.

Maybe she'd have listened if he'd told her the whole story.

The livery was shut up, but a lantern flickered low in the alleyway. Using the muzzle of his gun between the doors, he lifted the bar, saddled Rink, and rode out. Some night man Clay turned out to be. Probably snoring like a bear in January.

But it suited Garrett. He didn't want to explain anything to anybody. He just wanted…he didn't know what. Other than Betsy Parker. Beautiful, irritatingly stubborn Betsy Parker.

She was no more Elizabeth Beaumont than he was.

The moon threw long shadows from the building fronts along Main Street, and Rink's hooves clopped a lonesome beat as they rode north out of town.

Garrett's nose twitched.

He drew rein, and Rink's ears swiveled back to ask why. Leaning down, he patted the gelding's neck. "You smell that, boy? That's no campfire."

Alerted to a new danger other than his racing emotions, he followed his nose and cut between buildings to the west side of the street. He rode the length of the alley, past the church, and on toward the library house.

As he approached, a shadow lurched out from the fenced yard and cut in front of Rink.

"Hold up!"

The figure ran with an awkward limp and disappeared between two buildings. Intent on chasing him down, Garrett gave Rink his head, but the horse backstepped.

He smelled it again.

Whirling round, he saw yellow tongues licking up the back of the old clapboard house. As much as a hose and reel crew, they needed some kind of bell. He drew his Colt, took aim at the base of an old cottonwood twenty yards away, and fired three shots.

He counted ten heartbeats, each one thudding in his ears, and fired three more. Then he rode around to the front of the house and bailed off at the nearest water trough, praying that folks would smell the smoke.

Three gunshots shattered the stillness. Betsy turned in their direction and waited. Again, three more—the universal call for help.

Garrett.

She dashed down the narrow stairway, counting the steps so she didn't tumble off at the bottom, and ran into her room, where she threw open her trunk. After tossing clothing onto the floor, she opened the secret compartment, loaded her Remington derringer, and slipped it into her skirt pocket.

It was no Winchester rifle, nor would it hold a candle to Garrett's Colt, but in a tight spot, the double-barreled derringer could be the difference between dead or alive.

She ran downstairs and paused at Maggie's door. The little woman lay curled like a child amidst her pillows and quilts, undisturbed by the gunfire, thank the Lord.

Yes, thank You, Lord. Please, watch over Maggie. And Garrett.

Elizabeth's heart raced as fast as her feet to Main Street, where running men shouted, some in nightshirts, others with suspenders flapping. Two blocks away, flames leaped up the backside of what she thought was the library. The church stood in her line of vision, and she couldn't be sure. Hiking her skirts, she ran across the street, on to the next block, and into the livery for a bucket.

A sputtering lantern gave little light from a post in the alleyway, but she took it down and headed toward the back. The few horses stalled inside were quiet, yet alert, but a shuffling sound from the dark interior stopped her cold. She raised the lantern, fully aware she was revealing herself and not much else.

"Who's there?" Her voice sounded less forceful than she'd hoped.

More scuffling, and a shadowy figure half-ran, half-limped into the alleyway, straight for her.

"Stop right there!" She shifted the lantern to her left hand and slid her right into her skirt pocket.

He didn't stop.

With a grunt, he lunged at her. She fell against a wheel barrow and dropped the lantern onto the load of soiled straw. With a life of its own, it flared high, lighting up the livery and her assailant.

"You! What are you doing here?"

He pulled back his fist.

She ducked, feeling for her derringer, and raised it still concealed by her skirt. "Get back, or I'll shoot."

His sharp laugh hit her before he did. They both fell to the ground while he groped for the gun. Fighting her tangled skirts as much as her attacker, she kicked and shoved him off, then rolled across the alleyway.

Above them, a man stood at the edge of the loft, illuminated in the split second before he jumped. *Clay.*

He landed with a yell, and the two men wrestled near the blazing wheelbarrow, oblivious to its deadly threat. Clay quickly got the upper hand and pinned her attacker down.

Regaining her feet, she grabbed the handles and turned the burning load to the door. The movement blew flames toward her. Cinders dotted her bodice, stinging into her flesh. Again she turned, and this time ran backward, praying she wouldn't fall and spill the burning straw inside the old wooden livery.

As she cleared the front door, the express agent came up beside her. "I'll take that!"

She relinquished her hold and ran toward the bigger fire. Most of the men ran with buckets, a few had dishpans. She assured herself that the derringer was secure, and worked her way through the growing crowd of onlookers and volunteers, searching for Garrett.

She needed to find him. She needed to know that he was safe so she could tell him that he was right.

CHAPTER 23

G arrett needed answers, but first he had to douse the anger rising like a storm inside him. He'd trusted that kid. Given him money and gotten him a place to stay. A second chance. And the boy had bitten not only the hand that fed him, but others' as well.

Who else would have limped away from the fire flaring up the backside of the library? He certainly hadn't been there to read books. Just torch them.

Betsy's lovely form filled his mind's eye as the old guilty corpse crawled up and perched on his shoulder. How could he have suspected her?

But wasn't that his job? To suspect everyone?

He jumped off Rink at the livery and dropped the reins, puzzled by the pile of scorched straw in the street. Was the kid trying to burn down the whole town?

Angling up to the open door, he laid a hand on his holstered gun. Not that he wanted a bloody repeat of Abilene, but he was no fool, either.

There were certainly two sides to this sheriffing coin, and the way he saw it, he was just about bankrupt.

"Get off me!"

Garrett crouched against the shadows and slipped inside.

"Not until you tell me who you are and what you're doing here."

Clay. Had someone caught him doing the deed?

Garrett eased toward the voices at the end of the box stalls. Two figures struggled on the ground, but the uppermost kept his seat. Garrett straightened, pulled his gun, and held it low.

"Stand up, both of you."

"Sheriff." Clay glanced at the gun and raised his hands.

"Boy, am I glad to see you," the other fella said. The photographer for the newspaper. He struggled to his feet and hopped over to a stall.

What were the odds of finding two men who limped, fighting each other in a barn on the night of a deliberately set fire?

"Prentiss, what are you doing in here?"

The reporter jerked his chin toward Clay. "He jumped me as I was cutting through the livery."

"He's lyin'." Clay took a step forward.

Garrett nosed the gun barrel up a notch.

The boy stopped.

"He had Miss Betsy on the ground, Sheriff. I swear it. I jumped down from the loft and she took off."

"What was she doing here?"

"I don't know, but I heard her threaten to shoot him."

Things were just getting worse, not clearer.

Prentiss started inching back.

"Hold on." Garrett pointed with his gun. "Your leg. What's wrong with it?"

"Uh…I hurt it running through the livery, on my way to get my camera. When he jum—"

"Show me."

The reporter, photographer, whatever he was, glanced between Clay, Garrett, and the door.

"In case you haven't figured it out yet, I can shoot you in the other leg quicker than you can hobble by me and out the door. Now, get on with it."

Watching Garrett, Prentiss bent slowly and started tugging on his trouser leg.

Garrett gritted his teeth. "The other one."

"Garrett!"

Betsy's voice swung him around. She stared at the gun he held on her, then glanced over his shoulder. A thump behind him, and he turned as Clay hit the dirt, out cold.

Prentiss was gone.

Garrett's gun hand was sweating, his heart stampeding. *Not again.*

As he took off down the alleyway toward Erik's furnace, a shaggy blur shot past him.

"Pearl!"

He wouldn't look back a second time, but it sounded like Maggie calling his dog. What were either one of them doing here? What was Betsy doing here?

"Pearl, you come back right this minute!"

It was Maggie, all right.

What was this, a parade?

Out the back door, the too-familiar stench of water-soaked ash and charred wood hit Garrett in the face. Instinct told him Prentiss didn't go toward the fire. He swung left.

The moon had climbed high enough to light up the yard, and just past the corner of the livery barn, Pearl stood over someone sprawled on the ground. One of them was whimpering.

It wasn't Pearl.

"Call him off!"

Betsy ran around from the front and climbed over the corral fence as if she wasn't wearing a skirt and fancy underthings.

"I think he started the carriage house fire," she puffed out. "Check his leg."

"Now there's an idea." Garrett holstered another snide remark as well as his gun and pulled Pearl off the sniveling man.

"Show me your leg, or I'll let my dog rip your pants off right here in front of God and everybody."

Complying, Prentiss pulled his left pant leg up. Three puncture wounds in his calf were festered and swollen, and a bloody bandage above them wasn't exactly fresh.

Garrett looked at Pearl and then at the punctures. It wasn't her nature to bite a person, but he figured she'd gotten ahold of the fella at Maggie's place. Unless the reporter had a more plausible story.

"How'd you get that bite?"

A furtive glance at his dog was answer enough.

"Don't you mean *when* did you get that bite?" Betsy walked up close enough to get a good look and horn in on his questioning.

Garrett grabbed Prentiss by the arm and hauled him up. "You're coming with me."

"You can't take me to jail. I didn't do anything. You can't prove I started those fires."

Betsy planted her hands on her hips. "Maybe not, but you just did."

Prentiss swore under his breath.

"Watch your language around the lady." Garrett caught her surprised look, even in the moonlight. "You're goin' to Doc Weaver's and *then* you're goin' to jail."

Maggie tottered around from the front of the livery and up to the corral. "Come here, Pearl," she cooed.

The dog lowered its head and wagged its tail, whipping up a wind.

"You good girl. Come to Aunt Maggie."

The diminutive woman patted her knees, coaxing Pearl to step through the corral poles. From beneath Maggie's ministrations, the dog lifted soulful eyes to Garrett.

"Go on, you two-timer."

Pearl licked Maggie in the face, then dropped into step beside her as if the woman had fed her every day of her pitiful life. Maggie rested her arm along Pearl's bony back, a perfect four-legged crutch.

Betsy pushed the corral gate open and waited beside it.

Garrett hoisted Prentiss up, helped him hobble out to the street, then stopped.

"Will you check on Clay for me?" he asked her.

"Of course." She stepped back inside the corral and slid the board latch, then waited as if she had something to say.

He wanted to ask her what she was doing here, but not with Prentiss in earshot. "I don't know how long I'll be."

She gave a quick nod and then turned for the livery barn.

Garrett would have preferred to see to Clay himself, but he couldn't let this no-account take off again. And if he knew Betsy as well as he thought he did, Clay wouldn't be the only one on the receiving end of her attentions. She'd have Rink rubbed down and fed as well. He almost envied the gelding for the gentle touch and sweet talk sure to come along with a can of grain.

On second thought, he *did* envy his horse.

~

Doc had his place open and a lamp lit, anticipating a crowd, Garrett figured. But it looked like Prentiss would be his only customer.

While Prentiss was laid out on the table half naked, Garrett took advantage of the situation and probed along with the good doctor.

"Did you set the hotel fire?"

A huff, followed by a curse at Doc's timely snipping of the makeshift bandage.

"Might as well tell me. You're gonna be a guest of the Olin Springs Iron Bar Inn until you're fit to ride to Cedar City and introduce yourself to Judge Murphy.

"No."

"No, what?"

"No, I didn't start the hotel fire."

"I saw you there, taking pictures for the newspaper. How do I know you weren't there before the fire started?"

"I wasn't. You can ask Fischer. But I caught the results with my camera. Best photograph I ever made for the paper. Had people in the picture and everything. Good enough to get me out of this two-bit town and up to the *Denver Tribune*."

So that was it. "You set the fire at the Snowfield place?"

Doc applied a cleansing agent with impeccable timing, and Prentiss jerked upright only to be shoved back down by the good doctor.

He sucked air between his teeth. "That ol' rickety barn was falling down anyway. A real hazard. I just saved Old Lady Snowfield the trouble."

Garrett's hands clenched, and Doc threw him a warning glare. A fairer man than Garrett wanted to be at the photographer's disrespect.

"More photographs?"

He grunted.

Red streaks fed out from a deep tear in his leg. Not a good sign, Garrett knew, but he was fresh out of sympathy.

Doc prepared to stitch the wound and gave Prentiss a whiff of chloroform.

Garrett snugged his hat down. He'd question him about Rochester's involvement in private. "I'll take him off your hands after he comes to, but I've got another fella to look after right now."

"No hurry, Sheriff. He won't be running off anywhere soon, plus I'd like to keep an eye on that blood poisoning. Worse comes to worse, we might have to take his leg to save his life."

Garrett left and trotted down the stairs, determined not to be the other half of Doc's *we.* He much preferred sharing that position with Betsy, but he had to check on Clay first. He'd held a gun on the kid. Unjustly. And then left him behind. That could tip the bucket the wrong way.

Men ambled by, wet, grimy, and tired, but Rochester wasn't in the mix. No surprise there. Probably pounding on doors trying to sell his fire insurance, using this latest scare to his advantage.

He still wasn't exonerated in Garrett's mind. He could have egged Prentiss on by building up his dreams of writing for a big newspaper. But that matter would have to wait until he cleared things with Clay.

Erik met him coming out of the livery. "Another fire, *ach.* When will this stop?" He slammed the two heavy doors together as if they weighed nothing. "The boy is gone but not his horse. Is he in some kind of trouble?"

"No, I think he'll be all right."

Erik gave him a puzzled look. "I am going home. You should too."

What Garrett wouldn't give for one to go to. The closest thing to home he'd had in a long time was Maggie's, and that was exactly where he hoped to find Betsy and Clay.

But first he had to check out Pike's Saloon. Clay better not be there either.

―

Elizabeth poured coffee for Clay, then stepped over Pearl's tail on her way back to the stove. The dog had stretched out beneath Maggie's kitchen table with a soup bone between its paws. Elizabeth feared that all the excitement had addled the poor woman into allowing the smelly creature into her home.

Clay held a piece of raw meat against his swollen lip—as if that would help. But Elizabeth had learned that arguing with Maggie Snowfield was useless.

Maggie brought another cookie tin from the pantry, arranged the thin ginger wafers on a rose-edged china plate, and set it before Clay. "Keep your strength up, dear," she said with a pat of his shoulder.

He blushed around the slab of meat, and followed Maggie with a grateful eye.

Elizabeth joined her at the stove. "Please, sit down. You don't need to be serving everyone. I'll make you a cup of tea."

"I slept all day, dear. Don't you remember?" The half-hearted resistance lasted until Maggie sank into the chair across from Clay.

Elizabeth had already taken her derringer upstairs and tucked it into the desk drawer, uncomfortable with it loose in her skirt pocket, but too concerned about Maggie to take the time to return it to its hiding place.

She joined the table group, grateful that the ordeal was over and everyone was safe. "I never thanked you for coming to my rescue, Clay. That was very gallant of you."

The poor boy blushed to the color of the meat he held. "You were in danger, ma'am."

"Please, call me Bets—" She caught Maggie smiling against the edge of her tea cup. Pleased as a peafowl, the woman was, but correct in her own way.

Something broke loose inside and ran like a long-tethered horse set free. "Betsy. You may call me Betsy."

The kitchen door closed. "It suits you."

She twisted in her seat, mostly irritated at how Garrett could open a door without being heard. And mostly glad to see his haggard self at home and safe.

Their eyes locked and held for too many heartbeats, but Betsy couldn't look away as she stood.

Pearl yelped.

Betsy stumbled, breaking the spell. She wouldn't broken her neck too, had Garrett not moved in and steadied her with a hand on each arm.

Heat flooded her face and neck, and she likely rivaled Clay with his red meat. "I'll get you some coffee."

Garrett joined them.

Maggie beamed. "Now this is more like it. A full house." Looking at Clay, she continued, "Where are you staying, young man?"

Clay shot Garrett a silent question.

Garrett cleared his throat and shifted in his chair. "He's staying at the livery where he works."

Tension drained from Clay's shoulders, but Maggie was having none of it.

"Not tonight he isn't. Not with an injury. I have plenty of rooms in this drafty old house, and I'm sure one of them will work just fine."

"You can have mine," Garrett told him, jerking a thumb over his shoulder toward the shuttered porch. "I'll be at the jail with the photographer."

Betsy's heart sank at the pending separation, which was absolutely childish and uncalled for. Not to mention inappropriate.

"Is that necessary?" Maggie's dark brows drew together in a motherly fashion.

Garrett nodded. "It is. I'm convinced that fella is our firebug, and I'm not about to let him get away before I can prove it."

Clay relaxed even further, and Betsy feared he might fall out of his chair and do more damage to his face than what Prentiss had done.

"Well, I suppose that will be acceptable." Maggie gave Garrett a scolding scowl. "Are you taking Pearl with you?"

His mouth worked sideways as he fought against laughter. Betsy covered her own with a napkin as the conversation continued.

"She could stay on the porch with Clay, I guess." He stood and pushed his chair in. "Do you happen to keep your old newspapers?"

"As a matter of fact, I do. They work quite well starting a fire in the parlor. Right there in the pantry. Help yourself."

In a moment he came out with one tucked beneath his arm and tipped his hat to Maggie. "I'll check in tomorrow."

He turned to Betsy. "You too tired to walk me out?"

Grabbing her heart by the throat and shoving it back inside her ribcage, she stood and excused herself. "I'll just get my wrap."

Garrett held the door for Betsy, then followed her down the steps and around the side of the house, where she stopped and tugged her cloak tighter. Her hair shone beneath the full moon, straight above them now on its dash before dawn.

He pulled a piece of straw from a strand, twirled it in his fingers, and smiled down at her nervousness. She hadn't looked him in the eye since coming outside. "You tumble in the hay with someone this evening?"

With the desired spark and a huff, she gave him a scathing look. "And what if I did? It's entirely none of your affair."

He moved closer. "It is if you were with anyone other than me."

The tilt of her head told him she was blushing, though it didn't show in the moon's wash.

"What were you doing at the livery, anyway?"

"If it is any of your business—which it isn't—I was looking for a bucket. The library was on fire, if you hadn't noticed."

He chuckled and thumbed his hat up. "A bucket, is it. That's not what I heard."

A daring glance. "Then why did you ask?"

"I heard you were armed and dangerous."

She sniffed and turned her pretty face away defensively.

With his thumb and forefinger, he gently turned that face toward him, then leaned down and did what he'd wanted to do since he saw her wrestling with Pearl.

She stiffened at first, but then leaned into his kiss like she'd leaned into his hands the few times he'd touched her. Her mouth was soft, as he knew it would be. Warm. Sweet, in spite of the coffee on her breath. Pulling back just enough to breathe, he whispered, "What were you going to do, save me?"

He felt her lips tilt in a smile. "If need be."

Enclosing her in his arms, he kissed her more deeply, praying he wasn't dreaming. Her hands slid up and around his back, and she clung to him like she meant it.

He refused to let her go and rested his chin atop her head as she turned her own and laid it against his galloping heart. "There's a need all right, Elizabeth Betsy Parker Beaumont."

"And what might that be, Sheriff Garrett Wilson?"

Her breath warmed a spot on his chest and fired through him like sheet lightning through a summer's night. "I need you to let me court you."

CHAPTER 24

C live Prentiss's court date was set for a week out.
Garrett folded the telegram, slipped it inside his
vest with a nod at Holsom, and returned to the jail.

He had taken the photographer's confession and
statements from Maggie, Doc Weaver, and the Widow
Fairfax and sent them all to Judge Murphy in Cedar
City. Should be an open-and-shut case, but the man
was entitled to a trial if he wanted one.

Garrett slid the telegram into his desk drawer, right
on top of a month-old newspaper with a picture of the
hotel fire on the front page. Watching from the
boardwalk, behind a group of onlookers, was Mr. Fire
Insurance himself, Anthony Rochester.

The photograph could be Prentiss's insurance
against Rochester if he'd been paid to start the fire. But
until Garrett knew for certain, he had a house guest and
would be spending the better part of his nights in his
desk chair by the stove dreaming about Betsy.

He wanted to just haul her down to the church and
marry her on the spot like Cade had Mae Ann. But he
sensed that things needed to be different for Betsy this
time around. Not a big wedding, but a big lead-up to it.

She'd teared up last week when he'd asked to court
her. Not what he'd expected. She wasn't the crying,

swooning type, which was one of the things about her that appealed to him. She had more fight in her than frivol, but she was still full of surprises. Predictability was not one of them, however, though she had been right about Maggie, who finally came right out and asked her if she'd stay on permanently.

They'd all gone back to eating dinner in the dining room—Clay included—and Maggie had approached the subject in her typical fashion.

"I'd like you to give Mr. Rochester notice and come work for me."

Betsy stared. Clay kept shoveling in pot pie, as if he was afraid he'd be kicked outside with the dog.

She set her fork down and dabbed her perfectly clean mouth. "Do you need a type-writer?"

Maggie clicked her tongue. "No, of course I don't. I need someone to run this place. It's become too much for me, and I think you are just the person for the job."

Betsy had exchanged a quick glance with Garrett, edgy as usual, as if to say, "I told you so."

He'd kept a chuckle inside, but he didn't have to now, and Pearl raised her head and looked at him from her mat by the potbellied stove.

"What's so funny?" Prentiss limped to the near end of the cell and gripped the bars.

"Not you, that's for sure."

Garrett got to his feet and pointed Pearl to the cell. "Guard the prisoner till I get back."

Blamed dog walked over and curled her lip with a rumble. He ought to take up side bets on her savvy of the English language.

Fall had rolled off the mountains and settled in town, stripping all the leaves from the trees and blowing its crisp breath down Main Street and the neck of anyone who wasn't prepared. Garrett raised the collar on his coat.

No more fires since the library, but Rochester was doing a healthy business in premiums, from the looks of things. Batwing doors wouldn't be out of place with the traffic going in and out of his office.

Not to be taken advantage of, Widow Fairfax had hounded the man until he'd coughed up the money to tear down and rebuild the back of the library, replacing the old clapboard with brick. Garrett admired her tenacity.

He crossed the street for the livery, and gave the sky one more glance—so blue and clear it almost hurt his eyes. He figured he owed George Booth a heap of thanks. In fact, he owed George a telegram about the recent goin's on in town.

Erik was busy at his anvil, and Clay was cleaning stalls, whistling an unfamiliar tune against the ping of the hammer. At Garrett's approach, the boy stopped and stood straight as the pitchfork handle he was holding.

Garrett reset his hat. "I've been meaning to apologize for the other night."

Clay dropped his gaze and shoulders and fiddled with the fork. "It's all right."

"No, it's not. I jumped to conclusions that could have been costly. I'm asking you to forgive me."

The boy looked so shocked, Garrett was afraid he'd quit breathing.

He put a hand on top of the stall's half door. "You all right?"

"Uh, yeah. I mean yes, sir. It's just that no one's ever asked me that before."

Black thoughts rolled through Garrett's skull over what he knew Clay wore beneath his shirt. "Well, they should have. And I am."

Clay looked at him with such strong emotion, Garrett nearly second-guessed himself. But his grandfather had been right about a lot of things, and this was one Garrett would hold to as long as he had air in his lungs.

"Yes sir."

"Yes sir, what?"

The boy swiped the back of his hand across his eyes before standing straight and tall. "I forgive you."

Garrett jerked a quick nod. "Obliged." He slapped the stall door. "Don't be late for supper. Maggie won't let you off the hook. You'll be washin' dishes or pickin' chickens or some such."

Clay grinned near like Pearl. "I'll be there."

"Can you run a hammer?"

The boy glanced back at Erik.

"Not that kind. Hammer, nails, wood planks, and levels."

"I've done repairs, and I'm willing to learn."

"Good. When Erik hasn't got you working on something for him, we've got a barn to build for Maggie Snowfield. You up to it?"

The boy nearly grew a foot. "Yes, sir."

"See you at supper."

Betsy had *given notice*, as Maggie put it, and today was her last day with Rochester. Garrett crossed the street, flipped his collar down, and stepped inside the attorney's office.

"Good afternoon, Sheriff." Seated behind a stack of papers, Rochester didn't bother to get up. "I thought you might be by this afternoon."

He thought right.

Betsy blushed most becomingly from her small table across the room and gave Garrett a shy smile. "I'm almost finished with this last correspondence."

"Take your time. I've got all day."

Rochester leaned back in his chair and fingered his thin mustache. He may not have been behind the fires, but Garrett still didn't trust him. Just because he walked upright didn't mean he wasn't a varmint just waitin' to grab hold of an unsuspecting passerby.

If George Booth said he was a gold-fanged snake, then snake he was.

Betsy rolled the paper out of her type-writing machine and took it to Rochester for his approval.

He read through it as slowly as possible, then looked up at her.

"I hate to lose you, Mrs. Beaumont."

Garrett crossed his arms, hiding the fists he'd like to bury in Rochester's gut.

"But I understand that life is full of twists and turns. It's been my pleasure to have you in my service."

He pulled a large book of checks from the top desk drawer, filled out one, and handed it to her.

Surprised by what he'd written, she started to speak but stalled at Rochester's pale hand raised in protest.

"Remember me kindly. You may meet another young woman who is skilled at type-writing, and I would appreciate you sending her my way. Though I will be surprised if anyone's skills surpass yours."

Garrett thought he'd be sick.

"Thank you."

With that simple parting, she returned to her desk and picked up the crate that was under her table.

Garrett loaded the machine, and they left the narrow, airless office of Anthony Rochester, Esquire.

Once they rounded the corner, he leaned toward her. "Will you miss working for him?"

She snorted.

~

Betsy felt free. As free as the mares in late spring when Cade and their pa turned the band out on the high parks. She wanted to hike her skirts and run all the way home—her new home, the Snowfield mansion.

But it wasn't really a mansion, just the biggest, grandest house in Olin Springs. She'd seen true mansions in Denver, at least from the outside. Besides, Garrett was walking her. *Courting* her, she supposed. She'd never been courted, truly. She'd thought she had, until she realized too late that she'd merely been duped in the midst of her sorrow.

A heavy sigh rolled out ahead of her, and her steps slowed. She'd not told Garrett he'd been right. In all the excitement of the library fire, fighting off the photographer at the livery, and Maggie asking her to take over the boarding house that wasn't a boarding house, she'd forgotten about what sent her searching for him that night.

How grateful she was that he had pressed past her façade. Today was a perfect example, when he showed up to carry her type-writer back to Maggie's. Rochester still made her skin crawl, in spite of his spotless manners. Something about the man wasn't quite right, and she was grateful that she had not been alone with him when she took her leave.

"What is it?"

Gentle concern edged Garrett's dear voice.

She looked up with trust she'd never expected to feel again. "Just thinking how glad I am that you came to help me with my type-writer today."

"You'd have done fine without me. You hauled it once from the depot all by your sweet lonesome."

She stopped cold and turned to face his brash honesty. "Are you admitting that you watched me hobble away with that crate on my sore hip, and never said a thing?"

Those laughing eyes shone like silver coins. "Not so, Betsy Parker. I offered to carry it for you, but you flatly refused."

He was right again, of course, and that was just too many rights for one afternoon.

"Humph." She picked up her skirt and her pace and outdistanced him to the front gate. He chuckled behind her all the way into the house and up the stairs.

At the door to her room, she felt a sweep of modesty even though he'd already been in it. Soon they would be sharing this room, or the one that had once been Maggie's and her husband's, complete with a small parlor and a bay window overlooking the orchard. She and Garrett must discuss it, but not now, not here.

"You want to set that on the floor for me?"

Lost in self-conscious thoughts of the future, she'd not noticed him waiting while he held the Remington, the crescent dimple in play. She snatched the crate out of the way, and he set her type-writer in place, for what reason, she didn't really know. Perhaps she would find time to practice and keep her skills in top condition.

Garrett turned toward her, still in no hurry. She held the empty crate, and with the other hand tentatively brushed her fingers across the scar on his cheek. He took her hand and pressed her fingers to his lips, his eyes dark and hungry.

Her breathe fled, her heartbeat close behind. "How did you get it?" She'd wondered since she first met him.

His jaw tightened, his eyes shaded, and he released her hand. Taking the crate from her, he set it against the wall, then looked out the window.

"A mistake I made a long time ago."

She waited for him to go on, but he did not. Instead, he walked out to the landing.

Justice raised its prideful head, and she marched after him, stopping him before he descended the stairs. "So it's perfectly fine for me to relinquish my past to self-forgiveness, but not you?"

He didn't face her, but spoke harshly to the open air above the hallway that ran the length of Maggie's house. "It's not the same thing."

She wanted to know *him*, the real person, even the hidden parts, and she longed for him to share all of himself with her. To hold nothing back.

"Garrett," she whispered and lightly touched his sleeve.

He flinched.

"I don't want anything between us."

His left hand came up and covered hers on his arm, reassuring her with its rough warmth and strength. "I have to get back to the jail."

And then he was gone. Down the stairs and out the door in the time it took her to draw a deep breath. She gripped the banister and stared at the ornate oak door that had closed soundlessly behind him, as solid and impenetrable as his parting look.

She'd been warned to back off, and she wasn't so sure she liked that.

What was the point of marrying—if that was Garrett's intention when he used the word *court*— when one closed himself off to the other?

Cold and lonely nights in a Denver rooming house rushed back with brittle clarity, and she rubbed her arms against the memories. In spite of Maggie's warm house, she shivered. Was she making the same mistake all over again?

"There you are." Maggie looked up from the hallway, her white topknot disheveled and her apron askew. "Could you help me in the pantry, please?"

Betsy hurried downstairs, shelving her worries in the face of Maggie's need. "Of course. What can I do for you?"

"I have a mouse cornered behind the flour barrel, and I'm having a difficult time catching him."

Betsy shook her head in amazement. "I'm surprised you reacted this way."

"Oh, it's not reaction, dear. It's response, and that's altogether different. We get to choose our responses—anger, trust, kindness, et cetera. More often than not, we just don't think about it."

"And you chose mercy over a stiff broom?"

"Heavens, yes. I don't want to kill the mouse, just relocate it."

If Mama'd had that sentiment, Betsy and Cade would have been permanently employed relocating field rodents. "All right. Have you a bowl you wouldn't mind using to capture it?"

Maggie reached for a cookie tin and removed the lid. "Use this. I've been saving it for some reason, and this one sounds as good as any."

"Perfect. Now a dust pan and a broom—not for spearing, just for herding."

From behind the pantry door, Maggie retrieved both items and handed Betsy the pan. "I will herd. You corral."

Betsy squatted in the narrow space and held the tin's open edge against the floor, facing the flour barrel. "Ready when you are."

Maggie slid the broom between the wall and barrel, and out came the mouse, straight into the cookie tin. Betsy clapped it down flat on the floor.

"You did it!" Maggie clapped.

"Now to get it outside." Lifting the tin just enough to fit the dust pan beneath it, Betsy scooped up her prisoner. Maggie hurried to open the back door, and Betsy rushed out. Set free in its new orchard home, the creature scurried around a tree.

"We make quite a team." Maggie dusted her hands together. "Life is full of choices, as is running this house, which you'll soon learn." She twisted her apron into place and went back inside.

Betsy resented the lesson. She'd been making choices since her mother asked her if she wanted syrup or jam on her hotcakes. Or what dress she wanted to wear. One pigtail or two.

She walked over to the blackened earth where stacks of fresh-cut lumber waited to be raised into a barn, and her gaze traveled beyond to the pasture fence and trough. It was there that she and Garrett had first begun to open their hearts to each other. She hadn't realized it at the time, but that was the beginning of something new and hopeful. Would it all come to an end so soon?

The question weighed her down as she went back to the house and returned the dust pan to the pantry.

"Let's keep that tin, dear. We may need it again."

Betsy washed her hands along with the cookie tin, then set it against the sink to dry. "What do you plan for supper?"

"I've a soup bone simmering, and we'll add a few vegetables. If you'll mix up a batch of corn bread, that should stick to everyone's ribs tonight."

Betsy tied on an apron, found a paring knife, and started in on carrots and turnips, onions and squash.

"I've been thinking, dear. About the wedding. I'd love to host a reception for you and Garrett here at the house, and invite your family, the library ladies, and anyone else you'd like to have come celebrate with you. I haven't held a party here in I don't know how long, and I think it would be grand. What do you say?"

Tears marshalled in Betsy's throat and rose to press against the back of her eyes. One blink sent the first traitor down her cheeks, followed by its fellows.

"Why, whatever is the matter?"

Maggie's small hand on Betsy's shoulder drew a sob from her aching chest. "What if Garrett doesn't come back from Cedar City? He hasn't exactly asked me to marry him." Like a weak-witted school girl, she pressed her apron against her face.

"Posh. Of course he will ask you."

The confident tone raised Betsy's head. "How can you be so sure?"

Maggie looked at her as if she'd asked how to peel a potato. "Because he's in love with you, dear. Can't you see that?"

"But he's keeping secrets from me. If he loved me, wouldn't he share everything with me?"

Maggie salted the broth on the stove and added pepper and spices. "Do you need to know everything in order to love him?"

Whose side was the woman on, anyway? "But we shouldn't have secrets between us."

"True, secrets should be few and far between. Such as a pending gift, a surprise outing, a woman's personal matters—such things as that. But why must he tell you every detail of his life before you entered it? Unless he was a scoundrel, ruffian, or mean-spirited soul, and I highly doubt it, or running from the law, of course, and I highly doubt that too, since he *is* the law in our fair city."

Betsy had not yet applied the word *love* to how she felt about Garrett. Frankly, it frightened her. She'd thought she loved Edward and that she knew him. That had not turned out well.

But Maggie's question bore deeper, down into her core. If she truly loved Garrett, would she love him less if he told her everything from his past? Had she told him everything?

"You know what the Lord has to say about a person's past."

Maggie's stirring paused, as if waiting for someone to fill in the empty space.

Betsy had nothing. Instead, she picked up a turnip and pared away the pink rim around the top.

"'Behold, I make all things new.'"

She looked at the woman standing before the stove, painfully aware that Maggie was not the subject of that sentence. She'd heard it before in church.

Maggie set the wooden spoon aside and faced her, pressing her veined hands down the front of her apron. "Maybe we should let Him do just that."

CHAPTER 25

A vein in Garrett's neck throbbed like a hoof beat. Why'd Betsy have to ask him to dig up the one thing he didn't want to exhume?

He'd told her about growing up in his grandparents' Texas home, about driving herds north. Even about settling in as a deputy for George Booth in Abilene for a spell. In spite of all that, she'd pinpointed the one thing he couldn't shake, the one thing that faced him every time he shaved.

The air in his lungs cinched off, and he stopped at the back of the jail, bent over with his hands on his knees, and tried to ease the band around his ribs.

What if she wouldn't marry a killer?

Pearl whined at the door and scratched.

Garrett lifted the latch and she bounded out. Ran in a wide circle, relieved herself, then loped back to him with her silly grin. She didn't care that he'd gunned down the wrong man.

"I'm starving in here, and it's cold as a well."

Neither did Clive Prentiss.

Garrett signaled the dog in ahead of him and shut the door. Then he dug through his desk drawer for the sack of jerked beef and held a piece through the bars. "This'll tide you over 'til I get supper from the café."

"What about the boarding house?"

"It's not a boarding house and you're in jail, not a hotel."

Garrett wouldn't be joining everyone at the dining table tonight, and he realized he'd miss his makeshift family. An odd bunch they were, but they'd taken up residence in his thoughts and feelings. Maybe too much so.

He could light out after the hearing in Cedar City. Find a herd headed to Wyoming and cut a new trail.

And leave Betsy behind—exactly like that low-down, lily-livered husband of hers.

Former husband.

He slammed the coffee pot down on the stove, mad at himself for being a coward. If he couldn't tell Betsy Parker what pained him more than anything ever had, then he wasn't man enough to marry her.

And marry her was exactly what he intended to do. As soon as possible after he returned from the hearing.

The next six days dragged by, his stomach missing Maggie's cooking and the rest of him missing Betsy. He checked on them both from time to time, making pleasant conversation with them—as pleasant as possible if Betsy didn't run upstairs and hide in her room, which was completely unlike her.

Why didn't she brace him? Challenge him to a duel. Yell at him and call him every name in the book that he deserved. Fire and brimstone were easier handled than tears and distance.

It was clear he'd hurt her, and he didn't know the first thing about making it up to her. Not with a prisoner in his jail and a pending trip to Cedar City.

Monday morning, he cuffed Prentiss to the saddle horn of the horse Erik rented him, stepped up on Rink, and headed out.

Clay and the other men hammering behind the house every afternoon drove Betsy to near distraction. Her nerves were as tight as a corset, and all that pounding gave her a headache. Maggie, however, was thrilled with their progress and spoke of nothing but how fine the new barn would be and how she hoped it would be completed before the wedding and reception.

How could the woman be so optimistic when there hadn't even been a proposal?

Betsy needed escape. She needed to ride free, fast, and immediately.

From the Eisners' store, she bought a youth-sized pair of dungarees and a shirt. Bless the couple, they needed the business and didn't know her well enough to question her purchases. Willa and Fred Reynolds would have whispered their concern to every other customer who darkened their door.

Lolly's scrape had healed nicely, and with Maggie's approval to take the mare, Betsy rented a saddle at the livery and readied for a ride to the ranch. Apparently concerned by her attire, Erik tried to persuade her to take a buggy instead. A tarnished deputy's badge hung incongruently from his leather apron, and to turn his argument, she asked how long he thought Garrett would be gone.

"No long," he said, his face brightening. "Do not worry. *Er ist verliebt.*"

She didn't know enough German to understand what the man meant, but the twinkle in his eye gave her a good idea.

At the edge of town, she squeezed her heels into Lolly, and the old mare perked her ears and took off in a dead trot.

It would be a long ride to the ranch.

Painfully long. By the halfway point, Betsy regretted not taking Erik up on his buggy offer. She slowed Lolly to a less-jarring walk and tried to enjoy the scenery—the familiar roll of the countryside, scattered junipers on the high spots, and farms or grazing cattle in the low.

The land had faded from green to brown, and hay fields lay bare. A few meadowlarks called to each other from the edges. Lolly's slow pace provided not the sense of escape that Betsy craved, but plenty of time to consider all that Maggie had said and Garrett hadn't.

Like the day's ride, just the opposite of what she longed for.

Of course, Maggie was right about a person's past. One didn't divulge every former occurrence or acquaintance, as if giving a detailed account of years gone by. But Garrett had closed off so completely from her question. By doing so, he had not doused her curiosity but left it in a pile of smoldering doubt.

Maggie would say Betsy faced a choice. Rather than reacting to Garrett's reticence, she could choose to respond with—what?

The dogs announced her arrival at the ranch, but their yapping failed to rouse the Price's nag which stood hitched to a farm wagon, head drooping and a back leg cocked at the knee.

Betsy's skin prickled in warning. She left Lolly at the hitch rail and walked through the front door without knocking.

Cade paced before the long hearth but stopped and looked up at her entry. "Betsy."

"What's wrong?"

He raked both hands through his hair and pulled in a ragged breath. "It's Mae Ann's time and the baby's coming."

She went to him and laid her hand on his arm, with no idea of what to say. She knew nothing about childbirth, but she knew a little about God's ability to watch over His children. "Don't worry, Cade. The Lord's with them both."

His near-black eyes, so like their father's, shone with banking tears, and she gave him a quick hug before running upstairs. Sophie's earlier warning rang in her ears.

Mae Ann lay in the middle of the four-poster bed, looking like she'd just come from the river. Knees bent and slack, she was soaked to the skin, her hair clinging to her neck and shoulders.

Sophie leaned over her on one side, pressing a cloth against her face and neck. Travine sat on the other, holding her hand.

Suddenly, Mae Ann lurched up, her face red and contorted, and she squeezed Travine's hand until the woman muffled a cry.

Just as quickly, and completely spent, Mae Ann collapsed back on the pillows, panting and sweating.

Dear God, help her.

"Betsy!" Sophie's strangled whisper sounded like Betsy felt.

"Keep the damp cloths coming, Sophie. I'll be right back." Travine stood and touched Betsy' elbow, inclining her head toward the door.

In the hallway, she swiped her sleeve across her forehead, then gripped Betsy's arm with startling strength. "Something's wrong, but I'm no midwife. I need you to ride to town and bring Doc Weaver back. *Now*."

At the landing, Betsy saw that Cade was gone— probably to the privy. She scuttled down and out the front door, then ran for the barn. She'd take whatever horse she came to first, but Deacon had beaten her to the draw. As if he'd known.

Blanca was saddled and ready to go, her foal whinnying from a box stall.

"Don't worry 'bout the filly," Deacon said. "I'll get hold of her and settle her down. You just punch a hole in the wind and get Doc back here 'fore nightfall."

Betsy swung up and dug her heels in again. This time, her horse flew from the barn and took the ranch road at a dead run. Blanca couldn't gallop the whole way, but they'd get a good start, then Betsy would pace her between an easy lope and a trot.

Leaning low over Blanca's neck, she pressed into the run, invigorated. "Lord, since I started talking to You again, it seems I've done nothing but ask." The wind of her ride snatched her voice away, but still she spoke as if God was right there with her. "Please, keep Mae Ann and the baby safe, and give Blanca speed and stamina. And help me find Doc Weaver, preferably at his office in town."

Whether her mind was distracted by prayer and urgency or they had cut the usual travel time in half, Betsy soon loped into town. She slid off Blanca before they reached Doc's hitch rail, then dropped the reins and ran up the back stairs to his office and through the door.

Gasping, she clutched her waist and said the first thing that came to mind. "Do you have a fast horse?"

Doc rose from his desk and pulled his eye glasses off for a better look "What's wrong, Betsy?"

"Not me. Mae Ann. At the ranch. She's in labor, but the baby's not coming and we need you to be there before now."

"My horse is at the livery. You run and tell Erik to saddle him. I'll get my bag and meet you there."

~

Cade sat with his head in his hands, and Betsy shifted in her seat across from him. Deacon straddled a kitchen chair, and the coffee pot perched on the hearth with two untouched cups long since grown cold. Deacon was nursing his.

Her hair tangled and face still stinging, Betsy felt as if she'd run all the way from town rather than ridden. Hours ago, it seemed, but Doc hadn't slowed them down. He could horseback. Country doctoring required it, she supposed.

A faint wail broke out above them, and as one they stood, looking expectantly toward the landing.

In a moment, Doc Weaver stepped out of the bedroom, his sleeves rolled up and a pleased expression on his face.

"You're a papa, Cade. It's a boy."

Betsy covered her mouth with both hands. Deacon whooped and spilled his coffee, and Cade just stood there, stunned, weak, and speechless.

"Go see him," she managed.

Gingerly, he walked toward the stairs, his sheepskin moccasins making not a sound, as if he were sneaking up on a newborn calf.

"Go on, or he'll be weaned 'fore ya get there." Deacon coughed and swiped at his face, struggling against such uncommon emotion.

Betsy let go a long, weary sigh. Thank God for His perfect timing.

CHAPTER 26

G arrett's timing could have been better.

According to Erik, the Howe hand pumper, hose, and reel had arrived in Garrett's absence, and a volunteer brigade was practicing under the mayor's direction. Betsy and Clay had just taken Lolly back to Snowfield's pasture and left behind a sorrel mare. The barn was completed, and the Parkers' baby had arrived—a boy. That might explain why the sorrel was in town.

Erik pulled the badge from his farrier's apron and handed it to Garrett. "*Ya,*" he said with mock concern. "She asked about you."

Hope shot up in Garrett's chest like a Yellowstone geyser, and he slapped Erik on his broad shoulder. The man didn't need a badge to quell a fight. His brute strength was enough.

"Thank you, friend, for watchin' after things."

"All was *gut.*"

Garrett prayed it'd be *gut* between him and Betsy. Better than *gut.* He had to tell her what she wanted to know and more. He had to tell her that he loved her.

Better yet, he had to show her. His grandmother had pointed out the difference one wintry night after Grandpa brought in an armload of wood and kissed her soundly on the mouth, right there in front of Garrett. Too old to blush like a girl, she did anyway, and glanced at him with a wink.

Don't just tell her you love her, show her, she'd said. *No matter how old you get to be.*

At twelve, Garrett squirmed and wiggled away from the embarrassing topic. Today, he thought he knew what his grandmother was trying to tell him, and again he felt for the small box tucked inside his vest.

He turned Rink down Saddle Blossom Lane, skirted the apple orchard south of the house, and drew rein in front of the new barn. Clay and the others had done a fine job. Ponderosa pine filled the evening air— no cedar-pole barn for Maggie Snowfield.

Pearl yelped and came at him on the run. He stepped off Rink and caught her front legs as she jumped up. Scrubbing her head, he calmed her, assuring her and himself that he was home where he belonged, though Pearl wasn't the one he wanted to see.

Of course, now that he smelled like dog as well as horse sweat and a long day in the saddle, he doubted if Betsy Parker'd have anything to do with him.

But there she was, standing by the back steps watching him, her apron bunched up in both hands.

He should take a bath before taking her in his arms, but his heart set his feet in motion, and nothing could stop him now, not even his brain.

And then she came running.

He caught her against him, lifting her off the ground in a furious hold. Maybe she didn't hate him after all.

"I love you." His voice cracked and he squeezed her tighter, trying to keep his heart from galloping away. "Marry me. I've got nothing but the jail house, a dog, and a horse, but I swear someday we'll have a place of our own."

Laughing, crying, choking for breath, she pushed against his chest until he set her down. "We have a home for now."

He frowned. "But is it enough? Living here at Maggie's and running what really isn't a boarding house?"

She raised both hands to his unshaven cheeks, and her whole soul seemed to float in her shining eyes. "If you're here with me, it's all I need."

He kissed her until he couldn't breathe, and she didn't pull away. Never resisted. Lord, help him, he was drowning in the arms of sweet Betsy Parker.

Clay nearly earned himself a night in jail when he called them in for supper.

Garrett looked up with enough force that the boy ducked back inside the house and slammed the door.

Betsy laughed. "You've scared him off, Garrett, and we need him. He's been a wonderful help around here since you've been gone. And what about Erik—"

With his lips, he stilled her, cutting off her words and worry until she melted against him. Finally he stepped back. "Maybe so, but his timing stinks."

Garrett laid a hand over the small bulge in his vest and took one of Betsy's hands with the other.

"Elizabeth *Betsy* Parker, will you be my wife? As soon as possible?"

She pursed her pretty lips and he knew he'd said something wrong. Maybe *soon* was pushing it.

"You left out one of my names."

Hang it all, he'd be hog-tied before he labeled her with that no-account's name of Beau—

"Madeline. Elizabeth Madeline Parker, after my mother."

Tension drained with a rush, and he took a deep breath and tried again. "Elizabeth Madeline Parker, will you marry me?"

She smiled to rival any dawn he'd ever seen. "As soon as possible."

~

Which couldn't be soon enough, as far as Betsy was concerned. With Cade and Mae Ann's baby born, nothing prevented the wedding, aside from planning Maggie's reception and finding a suitable dress.

The Eisners were thrilled with that request, and Betsy had left the ultimate design up to Abigail. Frankly, what she wore to her wedding didn't matter nearly as much as *who* she was wedding.

With hot pads in hand, she pulled a roasted chicken from the oven, acutely aware of Garrett watching her from a chair at the kitchen table. He wanted to take time off and go to Denver after the ceremony, until she convinced him that Denver wasn't a place she wanted to be.

"But I want to take you someplace fancy."

He looked like such a little boy when he said it, that she left the chicken on the counter, walked over, and kissed him on the nose.

"Take me on a long ride up in the mountains. Or maybe to Cedar Springs. There is a lovely hotel there with a splendid restaurant that my family used to visit on occasion. And Mae Ann told me the chairs in the parlor are quite comfortable."

Garrett stared. "Parlor chairs."

"Yes. Cade spent the night in one when he and Mae Ann stayed there."

His obvious horror burst Betsy's ruse, and she laughed outright.

He pulled her down onto his lap with a smoky look. "Not what I have in mind for *our* honeymoon."

She laughed and shivered and moved out of his reach, busying herself with dinner.

And to think, she'd been afraid he wouldn't return from taking Clive Prentiss to court.

She'd been afraid of too many things recently. Afraid of coming home to Olin Springs. Afraid of not being able to support herself. Afraid of loving another man. What a waste of emotional energy.

While Garrett washed at the sink, she hurried upstairs to tidy her hair and found her desk drawer ajar. She stopped short with another rush of fear before remembering that she'd been looking for her Lincoln pen earlier to show Maggie.

With her pulse thumping in her temples from sudden relief, she felt for the derringer shoved against the back, then set the drawer squarely before pushing it in.

At the mirror, she twisted another pin into her updo, recalling the night she'd discovered her things riffled through. The incident had paled in light of Maggie falling ill and needing help. That evening seemed like forever ago.

Maggie retired early, as was becoming her custom, Clay went back to his job at the livery as Erik's night man, and Betsy gave him an extra quilt to take with him.

"It's not that bad sleeping in the loft," Garrett assured her. "The warmth from the animals rises, and insulation from the hay helps hold it in if there aren't any holes in the roof."

"And you know this how?" She snuggled next to him on the porch swing, beneath the quilt she'd brought out for them.

He smiled, and the scar pulled into place. "I've spent my share of nights in a livery."

"Do tell."

He cut her a side glance. "You first. You said there was something you wanted to tell me. Isn't that why we're out here in early November, and it fixin' to snow?"

Right again, she admitted. It smelled like snow, and that was always a reliable indicator. She tucked her feet up beside her and leaned against Garrett's shoulder. "I did a lot of thinking the night we fought. Before the library fire."

He huffed. "I didn't fight with you."

At her raised eyebrow, he acquiesced. "I left before we went to blows, remember?"

She giggled. "I do."

"Save that line for this weekend." He lifted his arm and pulled her close, exactly where she wanted to be.

This weekend she would become Mrs. Garrett Wilson, and it seemed almost impossible. So much had changed since her less-than-ladylike arrival in town last summer, and she would be forever grateful.

"You were right about me not forgiving myself."

He tensed, as if she was about to give him bad news.

"It took your words to remind me of God's grace, something I hadn't thought about for quite some time."

He nodded slowly, watching, as it were, memories that only he could see. His arm squeezed tighter. "About my scar."

Quickly she laid her fingers against his mouth. "You don't have to tell me. Really. It's all right. I shouldn't have pried into a painful subject."

Taking her hand, he kissed her fingers. "When you asked, I was afraid you wouldn't marry me if you knew the truth."

She pressed through a smothering sensation. "If this is about forgiving yourself, I'm surprised you have a problem with that."

"It's not. Forgiving and forgetting aren't the same thing. And I couldn't bear it if every time you looked at me, you remembered what I'd done."

What could such a brave and caring man as Garrett Wilson have done that had him quivering in dread?

She turned as much as she could on the swing, and drew his hand into both of hers. "You don't have to tell me, Garrett." She didn't *want* him to tell her.

His jaw set with granite determination.

"A piece of splintered wood hit me during a shootout in Abilene."

"That's explains it." She was nearly weak with relief.

His eyes changed color, like a forest at night. "No, it doesn't." He swallowed hard." I killed a man. A boy, really."

Her hands jerked without her bidding. But she wouldn't let go when he tried to pull away. "You must have had cause. You were a deputy."

She wasn't sure who she was trying to convince. Garrett or herself.

~

The way Betsy was holding on, she wasn't going anywhere. But it grieved Garrett to tell her of his worst failing.

"It would have been easier to live with if I'd gone to prison for it, but the judge ruled it an accidental shooting."

Her grip tightened. "That's why you know what it feels like to carry guilt."

He looked out into the night where occasional snowflakes swirled past, sparkling when they got close to the porch lantern. "George Booth was marshal after the Hickock years. Things had quieted down considerably by then, but every so often someone got full of himself. One night, George called out a drunk who was shootin' up the bar. The man stumbled through the batwings, firing at us with two six-guns. A boy ran out behind him, right into our fire."

He rolled his lips in, considered telling her more, but something stopped him.

"I'm so sorry," she whispered. Her eyes glimmered with acceptance and what he thought might be love. "That's why you took to Clay, isn't it."

A knot formed in his throat and he pulled her closer. The feel of her against him was more than he deserved, much less her agreeing to be his wife.

She laid her head on his chest and let out a sigh that sounded like contentment, the last thing he expected from her.

"A wise little woman reminded me of something not long ago that I'd heard as a girl but had forgotten over the years. If God can make everything new again, in spite of the hard, painful parts, then we should let Him."

CHAPTER 27

B etsy had let him inside her heart, and there was no turning back. Garrett was a part of her in a way that Edward never had been. No one had been, and the thought of living without him left her feeling less than whole.

But thank God, she didn't have to. What she did have to do was decide which of two beautiful gowns she would wear at her wedding.

Hiram and Abigail Eisner had made two lovely dresses, one a rich chocolate silk with cream-colored lace ruffling at the wrists and neck and trailing down the center front, and the other a fashionable lavender silk taffeta with vertical pleats and four rows of ruffles at the hem.

Betsy chose the warm brown.

The Eisners refused to reveal who had paid for such extravagance. They also refused to take any money from her. Even Garrett's dog could have figured out who had so generously stepped into the bride's mother's position.

She thanked the couple and invited them to the reception on Friday evening, as well as to the ceremony Saturday morning. As she collected the dress along with a few new unmentionables and a new wrapper, Abigail presented her with another package, tied up in brown paper with a green satin ribbon.

"For the reception," she said, a heavy accent flavoring her newly learned language. "Something extra."

Betsy had to peek. The *something extra* was a stunning pale green gown appropriate for Friday evening, and the ribbon tying the package was long enough to work her hair into a fashionable style.

"It's beautiful. Thank you so much." Her gratitude outweighed all her wasted regrets from the last six years. There were not words or tears enough with which to thank the God of grace, and she silently prayed that He would hear the unspoken language of her overwhelmed heart.

With her arms and emotions full, she turned for the door and found it open and awaiting her exit. Anthony Rochester held it ajar and, with his signature aplomb, swept an arm toward the doorway, indicating she precede him.

The chill that encircled her did not come from the open door.

"May I assist you with your packages, *Mrs.* Beaumont?" One thin brow pulled like an archer's bow, unburdened by smile or mirth.

She glanced at the Eisners standing close to each other behind the counter, then stepped out. "Thank you, but no. I can manage quite well."

He closed the door behind them and followed her to the corner. "And so you have."

She stopped abruptly, emboldened by the barrier between them that she clutched so tightly. "Speak plainly, Mr. Rochester. If you have something to say, then do so."

He drew himself up, looking down upon her as if she were a distasteful morsel. He had exactly five seconds to speak before she crossed the street.

"You managed quite well to misrepresent yourself to me and others in this town, and apparently, Sheriff Wilson is the biggest dupe of all."

She would beg his pardon, but she didn't want it, so she refrained from the conversational cliché and merely held his eye, waiting.

"You wanted us all to think you were married, when in fact, you were not. And now that you've convinced the sheriff that you were unjustly abandoned by a fortune-seeking husband, I find that is not the case either."

She slid one foot slightly behind the other to keep from toppling backward at his hateful barrage. "You find?"

Seemingly aware of the effect of his words, he curled his lip with satisfaction. "Indeed. While that fool of a sheriff was investigating the fires, I did a little investigating of my own. A personal letter from one Mr. Braxton Hatchett was quite illuminating. It appears that you were let go from the Denver law firm due to indiscrete behavior on your part, in spite of your so-called *notes* to the contrary. Your friend, Miss Clarke, has since been let go as well."

The last bit of news nearly drove Betsy to the ground.

He smirked. "So you don't deny it."

Spitting was entirely unacceptable for a woman in any and all situations, but she was about to make an exception. To prevent it, she turned on her heel and stepped into the street.

"I'm sure Sheriff Wilson would like to see the letter I received from Mr. Hatchett."

Do not run.

Do not look back.

Do not stoop for a rock to lob at him.

She made it to Saddle Blossom Lane before her vision began to darken. Realizing she hadn't breathed in the last sixty seconds, if not longer, she stopped at the edge of the road and drank in a precious lung-full. Tiny darts of pain shot through her temples.

Had the lies followed her home? And if she tried to argue against them, would her partial truths upon arriving brand *her* as the liar?

Now Erma couldn't even vouch for her, and she probably rued the day of their meeting, since Betsy had cost the dear woman her job.

The weight of her blessings turned to stone and she bowed beneath them.

Would Garrett believe her if she told him the truth? Would Maggie? Would anyone?

It was said hell had no fury like a woman scorned. But if she were to hold the pen, the line would read, *A proud man spurned seeks a demon's revenge.*

Who would take her word against that of a renowned Denver attorney?

Ironically, a refrain pressed upon her as she trudged along the road, losing a tearful battle in full view of any and all that might pass:

Hither by Thy help I'm come; And I hope, by Thy good pleasure, safely to arrive at home.

Fresh tears fell, for that had been her hope all along.

~

Maggie busied herself over the next few days washing china and glassware that Betsy had never seen, and she refused to let Betsy do a thing in preparation for the big event. She also refused to let Mr. Rochester's threat dampen her excitement.

"Some people are sore losers, dear, and it seems to me that Mr. Rochester is one of them."

Desperate for something to do, Betsy brought the broom and dust pan from the pantry. She failed to see what Anthony Rochester had lost, but Maggie was more than happy to explain.

"You, dear. He lost you."

Betsy shuddered at the suggestion.

"Think about it. If you haven't realized it yet, you are the only type-writer in this town. Perhaps not for very much longer, but you were the first and you worked for Mr. Rochester. You were a feather in his cap, so to speak. And you are an attractive feather, at that. To add insult to injury, as they say, he lost you to an uneducated cowboy who wears a badge and carries a gun."

Betsy quickly looked through the windows and down the hall to be certain Garrett wasn't within hearing distance.

"How can you say that?" She found it hard to believe that Maggie could be so classically prejudiced.

"Say what? That he lost you to a cowboy or that the cowboy is uneducated?"

Out of respect for the elder woman, Betsy held her tongue and attacked a dusty corner of the kitchen. "Both. Garrett is one of the most—"

"I know, and I couldn't agree more. He's smarter, kinder, and more generous than most men I've met, but his schooling came from life experience, not come from the halls of education in which Mr. Rochester spent too many years with too little success in what really matters."

Though still stinging, Betsy began to see Maggie's point.

"You are the prize." A tender smile underscored the endearment. "And all the law books and halls of justice in the world cannot outshine the love I see in Garrett Wilson when he looks at you."

Betsy leaned the broom in the corner and sank into a chair, weary of the emotional teeter-totter she'd been riding. "But what if he doesn't believe me when I tell him what really happened? What if he thinks I'm lying again, like I did at first by not admitting I was single?"

Maggie dried her hands on her apron and poured them each a cup of tea before taking the other chair. "In all my years, I've learned several important lessons through repetition—as if the good Lord knew I'd not catch on the first time. Or the second or third."

Betsy huffed into her teacup, rippling the surface of the amber chamomile. "I certainly understand that approach. Like training a green-broke colt in a round pen."

"Well, I don't know about any of that, but I do know that the great majority of the *what-ifs* I worried about never happened."

Betsy met her landlady's steady gaze across the table.

The woman had unflappable faith.

~

From the way the dining room had been rearranged, Garrett figured Maggie had invited half the town to her party. *Reception*, she'd called it. And her fancy dishes and hardware and doodads beat anything he'd ever seen.

A new suit of clothes was in order.

Of course, he'd planned on that anyway, but a man's wedding is an invisible event hard to imagine, and he wasn't about to send a telegram to George asking him what he suggested. Erik was no help, Clay was half grown, and that left Hiram Eisner to do right by him.

"Don't give me anything like Rochester wears," he told the tailor. "I'm a simple man with few needs, and I intend to stay that way."

Hiram and his wife shared a look that Garrett interpreted as withholding information from an officer of the law.

"What?"

"He was here the day Miss Betsy picked up her wedding dress. Waiting at the door for her."

Garrett's right hand slid to his holster, the left balled into a fist. Mrs. Eisner caught his reaction and blanched. Garrett flexed his fingers. He didn't need her fainting dead away from fright.

Why hadn't Betsy told him? "What happened?"

Hiram cleared his throat and lowered his head, his eyes darting sideways as if he regretted mentioning it. "He offered to carry her packages and she refused."

Good girl. "Anything else?"

"She's not happy to see him," Abigail offered in her broken English.

Garrett set his hat, paid for his new clothes, and thanked the couple. Then he headed for Snowfield's, fighting the urge to relocate Rochester's mustache. First, he had to get the facts straight from the filly's mouth.

He stashed his duds in his room, then nosed around the stove to see what smelled so good, hoping Betsy would show up.

"I suppose you're hungry since you missed dinner."

Maggie sure enough had a soft-footed Ute's silent approach.

He backed away from the stove and removed his hat. "Yes, ma'am. I got tied up in town. Plus, with things all laid out in the dining room, I figured you might have other plans."

"Humph." She poured him a cup of coffee and set it on the small table. In her book, that meant sit a spell.

He sat. "Thank you, but I don't want to put you to any trouble."

She gave him a look that could put the whoa in a runaway, then set a slice of rhubarb pie and a fork in front of him. "No trouble yet, young man."

That stopped the first bite in midair.

"If you want more pie, it's under the towel there on the counter. Help yourself." And she left him there with his mouth open.

Confounded females. He didn't have problems like this trailing cows to the railheads. But he didn't have rhubarb pie like this either. Or the sweet, warm kisses of Betsy Parker, which was the reason he was sitting in a kitchen in the middle of the day and not at the jail.

He eased into the first bite and sat up at the sound of her footsteps.

At the look on Betsy's face, he set the fork down and stood.

She didn't walk into his arms, but took the chair across from him and folded her hands in her lap. Nervous. Guarded. *Afraid.* His heart hitched. Betsy Parker wasn't afraid of anything.

Anthony Rochester's days were numbered.

"What's wrong?"

She avoided his eyes, so he sat down in her line of vision. He offered his hand across the small table, but she didn't take it. The first bite of pie turned to lead in his belly.

"I have something I must tell you, and frankly, I don't want to."

He'd known dread and he'd known fear. He'd known the smoking end of a gun barrel, but none of it had twisted his gut like those words. "Whatever it is you've got to say, I can take it."

"Something happened in Denver."

The tension in his neck and shoulders eased. She hadn't backed out of the wedding.

Silently, she studied the tablecloth, and he let her, knowing if he didn't fill the empty space, she would.

"As you know, I worked as a type-writer there. I was employed by the Gladstone, Hatchett and Son law firm." She clinched her jaw, the muscle bulging below her ear.

"Braxton Hatchett made advances toward me." She flicked a glance Garrett's way, testing his reaction, then she took up the tablecloth again.

Fighting to slow the stampede in his chest, he opened and closed his hands, keeping them under the table, his boots flat on the floor, and his eyes on the woman he loved and would die to protect.

She sat a little straighter, bracing her shoulders in that way she had. "I rebuffed him."

Garrett let out an old breath and checked his voice to a steady walk. "Did he hurt you?"

With a dead-eye look, she answered plainly. "He tried to. He even told me it was my fault that he couldn't restrain himself. I told him I was an expert shot, and if he ever touched me again, I would shoot him. Not dead, but his wife would never again have to worry about his wandering ways."

Garrett bit back what he wanted to say about this Hatchett fella, rested his arms against the table, and leaned in. "Why didn't you want to tell me that?"

"I was afraid you wouldn't believe me."

He believed her, all right. He also believed that if Rochester had tried a similar move, the local sheriff would have beat Betsy to the draw.

He started to rise, but she stopped him with a raised hand and a warning look.

"There's more. Most didn't believe my side of the story, other than my friend and mentor from Denver, Erma Clarke, who has since been fired." At that, Betsy wilted and teared up, and he didn't think he could stand not touching her.

"Mr. Hatchett's wounded pride preceded him. He sullied my reputation, spreading vile rumors about me as a divorcee. He, a highly respected attorney, was believed. I was not."

So far she hadn't mentioned Rochester, so there had to be still more. "Why was your friend fired?"

She regrouped at his question and pressed the heels of her hands against her eyes before continuing. "Erma offered to write letters of reference for me if I needed them. She was Mr. Gladstone's personal secretary, and often wrote letters on his behalf. Of course, he knew of his partner's indiscretions, but he would never take my side over Hatchett's. The chances of receiving a favorable report were nil, so Erma offered to help me in any way."

"And she wrote a reference letter to Anthony Rochester."

Betsy nodded. "My deception has robbed her of her livelihood. For whatever reason, Mr. Rochester wrote to Mr. Gladstone and heard the other side of the story. The side he chooses to believe, like everyone else. He intends to show you the letter he received from Gladstone."

The chair scraped back beneath Garrett's rising, and one stride took him to her. She came to him willingly, releasing her tight-fisted hold on her emotions. Hot tears soaked through the front of his shirt, and he prayed for a level head when he faced that no-good viper who called himself an attorney.

His voice was a ball of barbed wire, but he forced it out, breathing the words into her hair. "I love you, Betsy. And I believe you. And I'll kill the man that spreads lies about you."

She pushed back, her eyes pleading. "No, Garrett. Please don't do anything so foolish. It doesn't matter what others think of me, just so you know the truth." She tipped her forehead against his chest. "If I'd not misled everyone from the beginning, when I first arrived in town, people might be more inclined to believe me. My deception paved the way for them to think I'm lying."

He pulled her closer, fully encircling her, determined to shield her from the cynics in the world and anyone else who threatened to hurt her.

CHAPTER 28

B etsy pulled a sheet of paper from her portfolio, retrieved her cherished Lincoln pen from the desk drawer, then settled against the pillows atop her bed. Erma Clarke deserved a handwritten letter, not one from the type-writer.

Discretion was called for, since Betsy had no specific address and anyone might read the missive. But urgency pressed upon her, as well as the need to present things honest in the sight of all, and she prayed the letter would reach Erma via General Delivery at the Denver post office.

My dearest friend,

I hope this letter finds you well.

> *Please know I grieve to hear that you have lost your employment on account of me, but I pray the Lord will reward your faithfulness and provide for all your needs. If you can forgive me, please write care of the woman and town we discussed earlier.*

Ever,
EP (EB)

P.S. I can never thank you enough for your advice to return and wait.

Betsy felt lighter of heart after posting the letter at Reynolds' Mercantile, and even enjoyed visiting with Willa while there, again inviting her and her husband to attend the reception.

Willa didn't take issue with the reception occurring the evening prior to the ceremony rather than the following afternoon.

In fact, no one seemed to care when the party was held. They were simply glad that there would be one.

Betsy stopped at the jail on her way home, but Garrett was gone. Tending to a typical sheriff duty, she hoped, and not going to blows with Anthony Rochester. She'd managed to draw a solemn vow from him yesterday in the kitchen, which made her love him even more.

The thought stuttered her steps at the corner. Yes, she loved Garrett Wilson. With all her heart. And she had no doubt that the attorney would somehow tie his own noose, given time.

Rather than continue on to Saddle Blossom Lane, she crossed to the west side of Main Street. An hour remained before she must be home to help Maggie with dinner, just enough time to confer with Mrs. Fairfax. The librarian might be able to answer a lingering question.

~

Friday evening, Betsy stood before the mirror, her hair done up with the green ribbon. She turned to see as much of the matching evening gown as possible, marveling at Abigail Eisner's, or her husband's, giftedness as a dressmaker and attention to detail, right down to the white lace edging the neckline. Betsy had never felt so…pretty.

After she and Edward arrived in Denver and were married, he never again told her she was pretty. He never again said any of the things with which he had wooed her childish heart.

With a flounce of her silky skirt, she brushed the past aside. Tomorrow she would be Mrs. Garrett Wilson, the wife of a man who, with his laughing eyes, said over and over again that he loved her, whether she was dressed in her Sunday best, sweeping the kitchen in an apron, or riding horseback across Echo Valley. Yes, even then she'd known he loved her.

Voices in the hallway below drew her back to the moment, and she trimmed her lamp and slipped out to the landing.

Garrett waited at the bottom of the stairs in a new white shirt and dark vest. He stood hatless, his hair recently cut, but the look on his face when she rounded the railing to the first step made her heart stand still. He was either shocked speechless at her appearance or he'd eaten something that didn't agree with him. She considered fleeing to her room until her name floated up the staircase.

"Betsy…you're beautiful."

She could kiss him. In fact, that sounded like a wonderful idea.

The doorbell buzzed, and Maggie welcomed Mae Ann and Cade, who were followed by Sophie, Travine, and Deacon. All of them stopped and stared up at her, and she prayed she hadn't left something untied, unfastened, or uncinched.

The baby whimpered in Mae Ann's arms, drawing everyone's attention except Deacon's. He just kept watching her, his bushy mustache spreading across his face.

If Betsy didn't know better, she'd say he was the proud papa of the bride. Exactly the reason she'd asked him to walk her down the aisle tomorrow morning.

She descended the stairs as gracefully as she knew how, and accepted Garrett's outstretched hand. He lifted hers and brushed his lips across her fingers, thrilling her into a fever right there in front of her family and dearest friends.

The door opened again, and several people entered, but she was too taken by Garrett's attentions to see much farther than his handsome face. Grasping the moment she'd waited for, she leaned toward him and whispered, "I love you."

His hand tightened on hers and his eyes shone like polished silver.

Besides kissing him, she wanted to take him aside and tell him what she'd learned from Widow Fairfax, but this was not the time or place. Her news would have to wait, and it might be prudent to delay it until after the wedding, when they arrived in Cedar City and he couldn't immediately act upon the information.

"Betsy." Sophie approached, hands reaching, and Garrett stepped back with a gentle squeeze.

"Thank you for coming all this way, Sophie. And your mother too. I so appreciate it."

"I wouldn't miss it." Sophie's sincerity warmed her smile as well as her embrace.

"I'm sorry you missed the first wedding, though in reality, you didn't miss much at all."

"Stop apologizing, Betsy. The past is gone. Look at all these people who have come to wish you well."

Sophie glanced over her shoulder toward the door and then looked beyond Betsy into the dining room.

"He's in the kitchen, helping Maggie."

Sophie blinked rapidly, aghast. "Whoever are you talking about?"

"Clay Ferguson, of course. Who else?"

Sophie fussed with her hair and cast a few side glances. "Is it that obvious?"

Betsy snickered, which set them both to giggling like school girls.

"Maggie told me she has rooms for both our families, so later, after everyone else is gone, I'll show you how to get to the cupola. It's as romantic as we used to imagine."

"You've been up there?"

"Yes, though I must admit, it wasn't for romantic reasons. But you can see forever."

Recently arrived guests were admiring young William Cade Parker, and Betsy noticed Deacon laid a roughened hand against Travine's waist as they all gathered around the baby. Perhaps Travine was the one to see the cupola.

When Cade and Mae Ann worked their way toward the dining room, Betsy joined them, reaching for her nephew. "May I?"

"By all means." Mae Ann beamed with motherhood, and Betsy squelched a small jealous impulse as she snuggled the warm little bundle. By God's grace, at twenty-three she still had time for a child of her own.

Lively conversation, sincere well-wishes, and delectable aromas filled the Snowfield house and Betsy's heart as she watched Maggie reveling in her hostess duties. The woman should always have a home so full, and Betsy was glad she would have a part in making it a welcoming place for guests and visitors alike.

Welcomed visitors. With a shiver she recalled one unknown person who had crept upstairs and ransacked her belongings, and she worked her way through the guests to the hall, where she had a clear view of the landing. Hadn't she left her door ajar?

Across the dining room, Garrett, Deacon, and Cade stood locked in conversation. The perfect opportunity. Gathering her full skirts in hand, she stole out of the room and up the stairs.

~

One minute Betsy was there, the next she was gone. Garrett's neck chilled. He told himself he was letting his sheriff side get in the way of enjoying the evening. She was a grown woman, surrounded by people who cared about her, and she had every right to go powder her nose or fuss with her hair or do whatever it was that women did.

But the sheriff didn't shut down on command, and he took another headcount. No one had gone with her. The Price women were standing near the punch, Clay falling all over himself trying to talk to Sophie with her mother standing there.

Betsy had five minutes, then he'd go find her.

Deacon's throat-clearing drew Garrett's attention, and the old cowboy shot him clear through with a blue-eyed threat made to sound like well wishes. "Take care that you take care of my girl."

Garrett gripped Deacon's hand, sealing a solemn agreement between two men who loved the same woman in different ways. "I promise you, I will."

The mantle clock's ticking drowned out his future brother-in-law's voice as Garrett planned a discreet exit. But a thud from upstairs and breaking glass sent him running from the room.

Lamp oil fumes met him on the landing.

He kicked in Betsy's door. With a hungry rush, flames followed the path of spilled oil and leaped up the window curtains. Garrett jerked them off the wall, yanked the quilt from the bed, and smothered the fire. Water from the basin and pitcher soaked the smoking mound, and he stomped it into submission. Only then did he sense he was not alone.

Betsy stood in the corner near the door, eyes wide, hands gripping a man's arm clamped across her throat.

Garrett slapped his right hip—and found nothing. His gun and holster were in his room.

A double-barrel derringer pressed into Betsy's right temple, held steady by the hand of Anthony Rochester. He laughed. "Unprepared, are you, cowboy?"

Garrett's hands balled into fists and he took a step forward.

"I wouldn't do that if I were you. Elizabeth's Remington is closer to her pretty curls than you are to me."

Never taking his eyes from Garrett, the slimy rat dipped his head forward and kissed her hair. "And pretty she is. Don't you agree?"

His left arm squeezed against her throat.

She shot up on her toes, gasping for air.

"What do you want, Rochester?" *Lord, calm me. Don't let me get Betsy killed.*

"I hadn't intended for things to work out this way, Sheriff. A simple entry, a more detailed search, a quiet exit. But Elizabeth's brash interference called for a change of plans." His tone darkened. "She is quite the journal-keeper, I've learned, and I suspect that she may have found some of my correspondence fascinating enough to record."

From the corner of his eye, Garrett saw Cade and Deacon crouching at Betsy's door, ready to charge in. Without looking at them, he opened his left hand, fingers stretched flat, praying they'd heard enough to know the situation and read his message. Any sudden move could startle Rochester into pulling the trigger—whether he intended to or not.

Garrett met Betsy's strangled glare. Her face was as white as the lace on her bodice, but she flicked her eyes toward her trunk. Once, twice.

"Put the gun down, Rochester, and let Betsy get the journal."

"Really, Sheriff. Do you think me a simpleton?" His arm pressed harder and Betsy's eyes grew rounder. "Betsy. Such an innocent endearment for a less-than-decorous divorcee."

He sneered at Garrett's effort to contain himself. "Easy, there, cowboy. Do you even know what *decorous* means?"

Garrett lifted both hands waist high, palms flat, pulse pounding. "Okay, Rochester. I'll look. Just relax your hold. Let her breathe."

"Oh, she's breathing just fine. I can feel every inch of her quivering body."

If not for the derringer at Betsy's head, Garrett would have shoved the man's words down his throat one bloody blow at a time.

Again she looked toward her left.

"I'm going to check the trunk."

Rochester's sneer vanished and he stepped sideways toward the door, distancing himself from the camelback trunk. "Slowly, Sheriff. No sudden moves."

The eerie quiet in the house assured Garrett that Cade and Deacon were keeping the guests calm, a miracle in itself. But most likely, everyone smelled the burned curtains by now.

Garrett took a knee and lifted the trunk's lid as a triangle clanged outside.

Rochester flinched and looked toward the door. Garrett coughed, trying to cover the sound, and started throwing petticoats and stockings onto the floor—any distraction to keep Rochester focused on the search.

When the trunk was empty, Garrett looked up at Betsy. Her head had lolled to the side.

"Betsy, I don't see a journal."

Slowly she revived, as if fighting for consciousness, and threw a frown toward the trunk before sagging again.

"She's passing out. Let up. She can't tell you anything if she's unconscious."

Betsy's hands dropped from Rochester's arm, and she slumped against him. Alarmed, he lowered the gun to catch her as she fell.

Garrett lunged.

The front door of the house crashed open, and men ran into the hall, yelling, "Everybody out!"

Betsy rolled and kicked the gun from Rochester's hand. Garrett grabbed him by the shirt front and drew his fist back. One blow opened the man's nose and blood splattered against Garrett's face and shirt. The second punch knocked him cold.

Garrett let him lay where he fell and stooped to retrieve the gun. Betsy flung herself into his arms, grasping the back of his vest as if she'd never let go.

Straightening, he lifted her with him and just held her, thanking God she was safe.

Downstairs, Cade and Deacon out-shouted what must have been the hose team before they doused the inside of Maggie's home.

Pearl started barking, and the Parker baby wailed.

"But the call," Mayor Overholt yelled. "We heard the triangle call."

"And I'm glad you did," Maggie said. "That was the whole point."

Garrett tightened his hold on Betsy, kissing the top of her head over and over, smothering the spot that Rochester had fouled until she lifted her face to his and met his lips with her own. He would never stop kissing her. A lifetime would not be enough.

A light knock at the door to her room turned their heads but failed to draw them apart.

"Excuse me, Sheriff, but would you like my help getting him to the jailhouse?" Clay blushed pinker than a beet top and indicated Rochester's crumpled form.

"Sure thing, Clay. I'll drag him downstairs for you."

"But don't you want to carry—"

"No, son, I do not."

Clay grinned and made no comment about Garrett's use of the word *son*. "Yes, sir."

"Tack up Rink for me, and I'll meet you outside. You can help me throw him over the saddle."

Alone again, Garrett focused on Betsy. He brushed her fallen hair from her face and pulled the ribbon free. "Mind if I use this to bind his hands?"

She rubbed her temples. "Please do. It smacks of poetic justice."

Reluctantly releasing his bride, he rolled Rochester face down and tied the man's hands with a couple of loops and a hard knot. The ribbon wouldn't chafe his wrists, but he wouldn't be breaking its hold anytime soon either.

There was something to be said for the combination, soft yet strong—similar to a certain woman he was in love with.

He dragged Rochester out to the landing and pointed him feet-first down the stairs. Betsy followed, hands propped on her hips, eyebrow cocked and loaded.

"You're serious, aren't you?" he said.

"As a banker."

He swung Rochester around, grabbed him by the back of his coat collar, and dragged him down, not nearly as pleased with the bounce of the man's shiny shoes off each stair as he would have been with the alternative.

His horse and Clay waited in the front yard, and they made light work of throwing Rochester across the saddle.

"Walk him down, and I'll catch up with you."

Clay led Rink through the front gate, and Garrett pulled Betsy close against his side as they watched the attorney jostle down Saddle Blossom Lane, hinder side to the stars.

"Can I ask you something?" He grazed her hair with a kiss.

"Anything."

"Why'd you act like the journal was in your trunk when it wasn't?" Even without looking at her, he could feel her make that little huffing noise.

"What makes you think it's not in the trunk?"

"You're going to keep me guessing the rest of my life, aren't you, Elizabeth Madeline Parker?"

"You left off Wilson."

"You'll have to wait until tomorrow for that."

She cuffed him on the shoulder and tried to wiggle away, but he held her tight.

"If you're as accurate with a gun as you are with your foot, you could be dangerous."

She leaned into him and slid her arm around his waist. "Maggie told you that I hit what I aim at. I'll match you any day of the week, but not with my derringer."

He chuckled, grateful to have her living and standing close beside him. One more day, and she'd be there forever. "Mighty sure of yourself."

She moved in front of him, and slid her left foot between his boots. Lifting daring eyes, she lowered her voice to a level that made his blood hot. "I got you, didn't I?"

CHAPTER 29

B etsy's blood boiled when she read the letter Mr. Gladstone had written to Anthony Rochester. Lies and nothing but.

Sliding it back beneath the desk blotter, she closed her eyes and took a deep breath. She'd have to forgive Gladstone too.

For the moment, she preferred to think about the few days she and Garrett would spend at the ranch—after the U.S. Marshall took Rochester off Garrett's hands.

Evidently, the man was wanted in Kansas for the same insurance premium scam he'd run in Olin Springs. He may have not been the actual arsonist, but he consumed people's hard-earned money just as quickly as a fire.

She pushed away from his mahogany desk and walked into the back room. Precious little there, aside from a cot, boxes of books, and a lock box. Garrett and Mr. Harrison would be in to open it and count the money before Harrison deposited it in the bank.

She wanted to take a shot at it herself. Literally. Garrett's Colt would easily disable the lock, but a well-aimed Winchester rifle would blow it off.

Until then, Garrett had entrusted her with going through her former employer's records for names of people who must be reimbursed for exorbitant fire insurance premiums and others who had entrusted important legal matters to the scoundrel. A reputable attorney was expected any day from Denver to take over matters for the residents of Olin Springs.

She returned to the desk chair and waited for Garrett and Mr. Harrison, reminiscing over Saturday's perfect wedding and her first day as the sheriff's wife.

Inevitably, she and Garrett had their first argument as a married couple that very same day. He wanted them to go to Cedar City as planned. She argued that he couldn't afford to leave Rochester without a decent guard, in spite of Erik sleeping at the jail each night. Besides, she didn't need to go *someplace fancy*, as he called it, and much preferred a few days riding at the ranch before heavy snow flew.

They eventually made up, and warmth flooded her neck and cheeks as she recalled how well they did so that night in their suite of rooms beneath the cupola.

The office door opened, and the object of her reminiscing walked in carrying a Winchester.

She stood. "Where's Mr. Harrison?"

Garrett stopped and frowned. "That's a fine welcome for your husband."

Laughing, she hurried around the desk and into his embrace for a breath-stealing kiss. "I've missed you," she whispered. "What's the rifle for?"

"Not one for small talk, are you?"

She laughed again, something she'd done more in the last few weeks than she had in years.

He handed her the rifle and a box of .44-40 rounds. "Follow me. I'm going to take that strong box out back and see if you're as good as everybody says you are."

The man had completely stolen her heart, and he continued to do so over and over.

Just to be on the safe side, she turned the key in the lock on the front door, then followed Garrett out the back.

The feed store was the last building on the east side of Main Street. He marked off fifty paces, set the box in the middle of the alley with the lock facing east, then stepped back several yards and waved his hat.

She slid in two rounds, set her left foot forward, chambered the first round, aimed, and fired. After chambering the second, she aimed and fired again. Both shots hit the lock clean, and the second kicked it into the air.

Garrett whistled.

Lowering the rifle barrel, she followed him to the box.

He flipped over the padlock with the toe of his boot. "Nice work. A clean shot through the shank. Which one do you think hit it?"

"They both did."

He gave her a challenging look, and the scar tucked into place before his focus shifted over her shoulder.

She turned to see Mr. Harrison running toward them, red-faced and out of breath.

"I heard gunfire and thought Rochester had broken out of jail." He stopped and leaned on his knees to catch his wind, all the while eyeing Betsy and the rifle.

"Betsy shot the lock off for us. Clean as a whistle."

"I'm not surprised," Harrison said as he straightened. "She used to shame the boys in town during the annual rifle match."

"That's what I hear." Garrett picked up the lock and box, looped an arm around her waist, and gave her a quick squeeze. "She hits what she aims at."

"I'll see you at supper," she said and turned toward Maggie's, rifle in hand. Garrett either hadn't noticed that she'd walked off with his Winchester or he hadn't cared.

Perhaps it was a wedding gift.

~

That evening, Maggie shooed them away from the table and convinced Clay to help her with the supper dishes. Betsy took Garrett by the hand, then led him upstairs and along the landing to the door with the glass knob.

"Where are you taking me?"

"You'll see."

She'd soaped the edges of the door so it opened smoothly, and it gave easily beneath her hand. Lifting her skirt, she trotted up the fourteen steps with Garrett close behind.

At the top, night spread out around them, lights flickering from homes in town and nearby. But the stars outshone them all.

Garrett stepped close against her back, encircling her in his arms.

"I found out something before the reception," she said as he nuzzled her neck, clouding her thinking and making her giggle. She hunched her shoulders. "Wait. Let me tell you first."

"I'm listening," he said, ignoring her request.

She turned to face him, bracing against his warm chest. "I wasn't going to tell you until we left, but it doesn't matter now that Rochester is in jail and we're not leaving."

Garrett sobered instantly and his eyes darkened to match the night.

"I visited Mrs. Fairfax at the library and she helped me discover what *hanabi* means."

His brows drew together impatiently. "What?"

"It's Japanese for *fire flower.* As in fireworks. It was Rochester's code word for fire insurance. And all those other flower names I told you, they're all red or orange—like fire. Now those strange letters he wrote to the Kansas address make sense."

"The judge will be glad to hear that, and I'll be sure to put it in my report. But is that the only thing you brought me all the way up here to tell me, Mrs. Wilson?"

She laughed, lifting her face to the stars.

Gently he pulled the pins from her hair, and it tumbled around her shoulders.

She framed his dear face with her hands, and ran her thumb over the crescent scar.

"There is one more thing, Sheriff Wilson."

"And that is?" He whispered the words against her neck and pressed her closer.

"I love you. I even love your animals with their ridiculous names."

He chuckled. "About that."

She leaned back to better see his expression. "What?"

He looked into her eyes as if drinking her in, and she could think of nothing for which she'd rather be spent. He was the least expected of all she'd found upon coming home, and she wanted to stay like this forever, on top of the world, far removed from the interference of life and circumstance.

Yet she was not so naïve as to think that was possible. "What are you thinking?"

With a smoky smile, he brushed his lips across hers and whispered, "I'm thinking you should name the babies."

～ ～ ～

Thank you for being an Inspirational Western Romance reader.

I hope you enjoyed Betsy and Garrett's story as much as I enjoyed discovering it. Be sure to check out Book 1 in the Front Range Brides series, *An Improper Proposal.*

If you'd like to leave a brief review on your favorite book websites and other social media, it would bless my boots off!

Acknowledgements

Thank you to all who aided and supported me in telling Betsy and Garrett's story, particularly my early readers Jill Maple, Judy Ackerman, and Nancy Huber; editor Christy Distler; cowgirl and horse trainer Lynne Schricker; Cañon City Fire Chief Dan Brixey, (Retired); and 1800s fashion expert Kim Aulerich Mahone.

About the author

Bestselling author and winner of the **Will Rogers Gold Medallion** for Inspirational Western Fiction, Davalynn Spencer writes heart-tugging romance with a Western flair. Learn more about Davalynn and her books at www.davalynnspencer.

Connect with Davalynn

Stay in touch via her quarterly newsletter:
http://eepurl.com/xa81D

Website: www.davalynnspencer.com

Facebook: Author Davalynn Spencer

Twitter: @davalynnspencer

Pinterest.com/davalynnspencer

Amazon Author page:
www.amazon.com/author/davalynnspencer

~ May all that you read be uplifting. ~

Made in the USA
Middletown, DE
12 July 2020